Lois Waisbrooker

Alice Vale

A Story for the Times (Edition 4)

Lois Waisbrooker

Alice Vale
A Story for the Times (Edition 4)

ISBN/EAN: 9783744743235

Printed in Europe, USA, Canada, Australia, Japan

Cover: Foto ©Andreas Hilbeck / pixelio.de

More available books at **www.hansebooks.com**

A Story for the Times.

BY

LOIS WAISBROOKER.

FOURTH EDITION.

BOSTON:
WILLIAM WHITE AND COMPANY,
BANNER OF LIGHT OFFICE,
158 WASHINGTON STREET.
NEW-YORK AGENTS—THE AMERICAN NEWS COMPANY,
119 NASSAU STREET.

1871.

.

William White & Co., Stereotypers and Printers.

DEDICATION.

TO my well-beloved sister, Mrs. SARAH M. BEARDSLEY, who went with the angels, from Crittenden, Erie Co., N.Y., Oct. 8, 1867.

Dear, patient, gentle, loving sister, though gone from mortal sight, thou art still with me, art still one of the brightest stars in love's firmament.

By the memories of our childhood, when thou wert ever by my side; by thy loving sympathy and appreciation in the trials of after years; and by our hopes of future companionship in the world of spirits,—I dedicate this book to THEE.

THY SISTER LOIS

TO THE READER.

KIND reader, in presenting to you the following combination of facts and fancies, — facts from the field of my own experience and that of others, and fancies wherewith to connect and clothe them, — I have tried to be true to nature.

How well I have succeeded, is left for you to judge.

THE AUTHORESS.

CONTENTS.

ALICE VALE.

CHAPTER I.

CHILDHOOD.

Leave not the vine to stand erect,
Nor train the oak to crawl.

 HAT a strange child!"

"Who?"

"Who? why Alice Vale, to be sure: I never saw another like her."

"What made you think of her now?"

"Why, don't you see her over the way there, talking with Crazy Pete? Other children, large and small, are afraid of him: even my Helen, though two years older than Alice, will cross the street to avoid meeting him."

"Is he dangerous, or troublesome?"

"Not as I have ever heard; but, somehow, he has a way of making the younger portion of the community avoid him, — all except Alice; and she seems to understand him as well as though she had had charge of an insane asylum for a score of years."

"Better, perhaps."

"Better! why do you say that?"

9

" Because some persons know instinctively what it takes others a lifetime to learn."

" I thought that instinct belonged to the animal kingdom only."

" Intuitively would have been a better word."

" Well, I can't see the difference; and this acting without thought never ends in any good : if she was a child of mine, I'd teach her better than to be wandering around with a crazy vagabond like Pete Stiverton. It can do her no good, if it does not result in positive injury : people are more or less affected by the company they keep ; and I shouldn't wonder if Alice went crazy herself yet."

" What makes you think so ? "

"Oh! a great many things. She is always doing or saying some out-of-the-way, unheard-of thing. Crazy people, you know, are remarkable for sharp, cunning speeches ; and I never saw her equal at that. What do you suppose she said about Uncle Edward the other day ? "

" I am sure I can not imagine."

" Uncle, as you know, lives with us, and has from the time he lost his wife. He has had trouble in the past, it is true, but nothing that need to affect him particularly now : still, at times, he becomes very despondent, so much so that it makes it really unpleasant for all about him. I was speaking of this at Mrs. Vale's one day last week, when Alice looked up and said, ' All he needs, Mrs. Roland, is a good tonic.'

" ' A tonic ? ' I asked in surprise ; ' what do you mean ? he is not sick.'

" ' N t in body,' she replied ; ' but life is moving too

easy with him: he has so much of the sweet that it sickens him, and he has to look back to the old times for something bitter; now, if he had some real present trouble, it would so stir him up that he would forget all about the blues.'

"I looked at the girl in perfect astonishment, while she continued, 'I know that it is so; for there is old Mrs. Frost, who has been mourning and complaining all summer: one could not be in her company ten minutes but she would commence talking about the loss of her husband and property, and of her hard lot in life; but she is happy enough now. I saw her this morning, and she looked so cheerful that it was like sunshine; and all because her Mary, who has been sick, is getting better.'

"'And is not that enough to make her glad?' I asked.

"'Ought she not to have been just as glad that Mary was well before she was sick at all?' was her quick response. 'No, no: she needed the bitter, she needed the tonic, that's all.'

"Now, what do you think of a child of fifteen making such a speech as that?"

"I think she has heard some older person make the remark, or something like it, and, treasuring the idea, has expressed it in her own language."

"No: her mother says that she is always making just such speeches."

"Yes; and mothers are very apt to think their children especially smart."

"But not so Mrs. Vale: she looks upon it as a fault, and chides Alice severely for being so 'forward and saucy,' to use her own words."

" Do you say that Alice is fifteen ? "

" Yes: she is two months older than my Fieddy; but she acts so much like a child, notwithstanding her smart speeches, that one would never suppose her to be that old: and such a romp!   Only last week, as I was passing there, Mrs. Vale came to the door and called for Alice; and where do you think she was ? up in the very top of the largest cherry-tree, sitting there as contentedly as if she were a bird, and her home a tree.

" ' Why, Alice ! ' exclaimed Mrs. Vale, ' how came you up there ? '

" ' O mother! the cherries are getting ripe. I found half a dozen, up here, where they have a fair chance to the sun, that were real good: then I got to watching a bird in the next tree, looking at the clouds, and listening to the bees, till I forgot all about my work; but I will come right down now, and do whatever you wish me to.'

" ' I wish more than any thing else,' replied her mother, ' that you would quit acting so much like a boy, and learn to be a woman.'

" ' But I am not a woman yet, mother: when I am, I will act like one.'

" ' Neither are you a boy,' said Mrs. Vale; ' but you certainly act like one, romping and climbing half the time.'

" ' Mother,' said Alice, ' did God make the sunshine, birds, nuts, bees, squirrels, and all the wonderful things that I find in the fields and woods, only for the boys ? '

" ' Certainly not: what a question ! '

" ' I should think he did by the way people talk when girls try to enjoy them in their own way.'

"'O Alice, Alice! what will ever become of you? You are such a strange child!' said Mrs. Vale, as she disappeared within the house; and I thought as much. I tell you, Mrs. Manning, I'd break her of some of her hoydenish ways if I had her to deal with."

Such, in substance, was the conversation held between two neighbors of the little village of Ellsville, in the old Empire State, one pleasant summer morning some twenty years ago. Mrs. Roland was a leader among the fashionables; and Mrs. Manning the wife of the wealthiest man in the place, and, though making no pretensions, was rather looked up to on that account. And now of Alice Vale and "Crazy Pete," or Peter Stiverton: who and what were they?

Of Alice and her disposition we have already learned something. Her parents, like thousands of others, had once figured in the mercantile world of a great city, failed, and, having removed to this little village, were trying life on a more humble scale. Mrs. Vale, a quiet, dreamy sort of a woman, had never been a favorite in the world of fashion, in which she might have moved when wealth was theirs, had she so chosen; but here she had the good sense to perceive, that, if she retired into herself the same as formerly, it would be mistaken by those among whom her lot was now cast as *city pride.* She therefore strove to make herself as agreeable as possible, and so far succeeded as to be well liked by the villagers.

The family, when they came to the place, consisted of Mr. and Mrs. Vale and three children, — Alice and two sons, — one older and the other younger than she was. The youngest one was drowned in a neighboring pond soon after they came there; and the elder one had left home in a fit of anger, some eighteen months previous, and had not been heard of since; that is, not directly, though the ship in which he was supposed to have sailed had been reported lost, and he was mourned by his friends as dead. Thus at the time our story commences there was only Alice left: consequently the affections of her parents naturally centered in her, making them very anxious that she should do and be all that their fond hearts could desire.

Alice, wild, wayward, thoughtless, — so the mother believed; but, could she have read the thoughts that welled up in her child's heart, she would have formed quite a different opinion. As she could not do this, she judged from the external, and from the opinions of those about her, and grieved in her soul lest this, her only remaining one, should not be all that she could wish.

" Was she a bad child ? " you ask.

No: not *bad;* but she cared for none of those things that interested other girls of her age. It mattered not to her whether her clothes were in fashion, or no. If she was invited to parties, picnics, and the like, all right: still, she seldom attended them ; and, if not invited, she never noticed the omission.

She would make the strangest, wisest speeches, and then romp with her kitten, or play with her doll, with as much earnestness and zest of enjoyment as though she had been but six instead of fifteen years of age ; and no amount of persuasion, argument, or ridicule, could tempt her to throw aside her childish pleasures.

" She didn't feel like a y ung lady," she said, " and

she didn't want to be one : if she tried, she would only make a fool of herself; and she just wished they would let her alone." The only one whose company she really seemed to care for was " Crazy Pete," as he was called ; and, when rallied upon her preference, she would stoutly maintain that he was not crazy, — that he knew more than others, and that was why they called him so.

She would wander with him through the fields, woods, and by the creek-side for hours, when permitted to do so, and never seemed happier than when by his side, listening to his quaint remarks about the shells, pebbles, and flowers that were found in their path. Once her parents forbade her going where he was, or having any thing to say to him if she chanced to meet him ; but she cried herself sick, and they were obliged to remove the prohibition. And now who was Crazy Pete ?

Pause, kind reader, and, as you hear the reply, wonder not that Alice Vale was a grief to her parents, ignored by her companions, and treated to a general shake of the head by the community at large. Crazy Pete was a pauper, and the son of a poor woman who had come into the neighborhood about the time of his birth, and of whom nothing was known further than " *it was supposed* that she had never been married."

This of itself was enough to condemn him to infamy : but, when you added to this the fact that he was counted insane, surely a girl of fifteen who could prefer his society to that of all others gave her parents cause for sorrow ; and a watchful community did well to shake the head, and wonder what would be the result.

O vainly wise world ! how little thou knowest of the

secret springs of action, of the wisdom that prepares its instruments for the accomplishment of the progressive changes that must come to the race in answer to its own prayers and aspirations!

O foolishly judging world! noting effects instead of causes. One in ancient times truly said, that "the wisdom of this world is foolishness with God;" and it is equally true that the wisdom of God is foolishness with the world.

But let us look into the nature of Peter Stiverton's insanity, if, indeed, it was such; let us trace some of its causes: but, to do this, we must go back somewhere near another score of years, — must go back to the mother who bore him, to the father whose villainy broke her heart, checked its warm life-currents, and sent her to the angel world for consolation, for sympathetic healing from earth's cruel wrongs.

CHAPTER II.

THE WOLF AND THE LAMB.

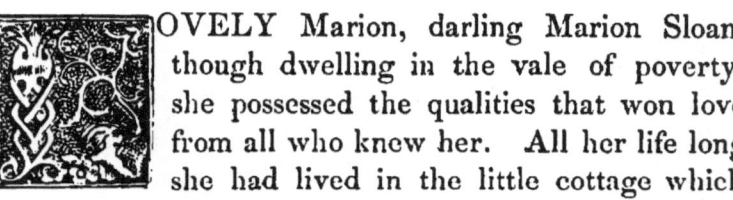OVELY Marion, darling Marion Sloan, though dwelling in the vale of poverty, she possessed the qualities that won love from all who knew her. All her life long she had lived in the little cottage which stood at the foot of one of the grandest of the Green Mountains; all her life had she been familiar with its rugged paths, its deep gorges, and its sunny nooks; had watched the birds from year to year as they built their nests in the little grove at the right of their humble dwelling; had listened summer after summer to the music of the rippling brook, and had long since learned where the choicest grapes were to be found. But, most of all, she loved to sit at evening in the cottage-door, and, looking across the corner of a ledge of rock, catch a glimpse of the church-spire in the village beyond, just as the sun was flinging his last backward glance upon the valley. In such an hour as this, she fancied that she could almost see the angels of God ascending and descending thereon, even as they did upon Jacob's ladder in olden time.

She was the child of many prayers, and the last of seven, the others sleeping in the quiet resting-place for the dead that lay just behind their humble place of worship; and for two years the mother had lain beside them.

2

Yes: she was a child of many prayers, and a prayerful child, or woman, as we must now call her; for eighteen summers had shed their light upon her brown hair, and given the hue of health to her rounded cheek.

Earnestly — oh, how earnestly! — had her parents plead with Father God that he would spare them this, their last remaining one, and make her a blessing to their old age, — would spare her, and make her his own by a life that should manifest his glory, instead of taking her to himself in childhood, as he had the others.

She was spared; and the aroma of piety surrounded her as naturally as fragrance emanates from the rose: while each rock, bird, and bee, and indeed all with which she came in contact, awoke emotions of reverence, and sent the incense of devotion upward from the pure altar of her heart. The mother died blessing God for this, to her, visible answer to her prayers; and the father continued the pæan of praise as he watched the outgoings and incomings of his child from day to day.

> "Morn amid the mountains,
>   Lovely solitude,
> Gushing streams and fountains,
>   Murmur, God is good."

And the heart of the aged man echoed, " God is good; " but could he have truly realized that, —

> Every thrill of anguish,
>   Could we see the why,
> Utters the same language
>   To the earth and sky;
> Every pang of sorrow
>   Rightly understood,
> Every bitter trial,
>   Murmurs, "God is good."

he would not have died broken hearted in the dark days that followed.

Marion Sloan was not only beloved by all, but she was looked upon as peculiarly favored of the Lord; for at the time she had united with the church, some six months before her mother's death, she had fallen into a sort of trance, and lay for hours in a state that many supposed to be death. Even her father had given her up, and, but for his wife, would have permitted preparations for her funeral to have been made; but the mother still insisted that Marion was not dead. Just at this juncture, she came back to consciousness, and said that she had been to heaven, — had seen her brothers and sisters there, and others that she had known when they were here.

" How do you know that they were your brothers and sisters, as you never knew them while here ? " asked the minister.

" They told me they were," she quietly replied; " and, if they had not, I should have known it, for I could read their very thoughts." Those who stood around looked at one another in silence, while Deacon Smith murmured,

"The very intents and purposes of the heart shall be made known."

" But did you see Jesus ? " asked her mother.

" That is right, sister," said the deacon: " it shows that your heart is in the right place, for there can be no heaven without Jesus." But Marion only smiled, and said, " I must not, or, rather, I can not, tell all I saw; for I have not the language to express it, and, beside, they told me that I must not try."

From this time forth, she used frequently to speak of

seeing different ones who were dead, as the wo·ld calls dead. A few shook their heads, and touched their foreheads; but by most of the people she was looked upon as one peculiarly favored of Heaven. It was not to be wondered at, they asserted; for, like Samuel of old, she had been devoted to God from her birth, and her whole life had been but a fulfillment of the vows made for her at the baptismal font.

After her mother's death, Marion would sometimes tell of seeing her; but latterly she had not seen her mother nor any one else, or else had become very reticent upon the subject, for she had spoken of nothing of the kind for some months. Mrs. Sloan had been an invalid for some time previous to her death; and her sickness had involved them in considerable expense, while the old gentleman's rheumatism rendered him unable to earn very much. This, with other things, had made them poor, and kept them so; but they retained their cow, had their garden, and, with Marion's help, raised a few potatoes, and corn enough to fatten a pig. This, with odd jobs that Marion did for a neighbor's wife, and a little cobbling by her father for the neighbors' boys, served to keep them quite comfortable.

But crops sometimes fail, as we all know; and this was the case in the summer of ——, in the region of country where the Sloans dwelt. Late frosts had destroyed much of the promise of spring; the summer months had been so unusually wet that things could not grow; while autumn set in dry and cold, so that altogether the prospect for the coming winter was any thing but inviting, even to the better class of farmers, to say nothing of the poor. It was just at this juncture that a stranger called at the Sloan cottage one pleasant afternoon, and asked for a glass of water, and the privilege of resting for a few moments.

"Certainly, certainly," said the old gentleman. "Marion, go and bring some fresh from the spring; or, sir, would you not prefer a glass of milk?"

"That would indeed be a treat," was the reply; and accordingly the milk was brought, while the gentleman cast upon the fair girl a look of such undisguised admiration, that she shrank away, and left her father to entertain him. And, more than this, she felt an aversion toward him at first sight, that surprised even herself, the emotion was so new and strange. Hitherto the feelings of her heart had flowed out toward all in love and kindness; and why should she thus shrink from this stranger?

"Surely, it was wrong, — a temptation from the evil one; for did not God command us to be kind to the stranger within the gate? yes, it was wrong, and she would banish it from her heart."

It was thus that she reasoned; but, instead of returning to the house, she went still farther away to a secluded spot among the rocks, where, humbly kneeling, she strove to plead with the good Father in heaven for assistance. Alas for short-sighted mortals! refusing to accept nature's true method, the warning voice within, and at the same time calling to something without and beyond them for aid. God no more certainly spake to Moses in the burning-bush than he did to the heart of this poor maiden, had she only heard and heeded; but she mistook it for the voice of an enemy, and so turned away from listening.

" Why should she feel thus toward this stranger ? "
thus she still questioned,—questioned instead of praying;
for when she had reached her chosen place of retire-
ment, and, kneeling, strove to pray, she could find no
words in which to prefer her petition, but could only
question and wonder.

" Why should she feel thus toward this stranger ? he
was young, fine looking, pleasant and genial in his manners, well calculated in every way to win instead of
repelling.   It was all wrong, she was sure it was ; and
how could she approach God while shrinking from her
duty ?   Of course she could not : she would go back to
the house, and help her father to entertain their temporary guest.

The traveler, in the mean time, found one pretext
after another to continue the conversation, hoping thereby to gain another glimpse of the fair vision that had
greeted him at his entrance.

Finally, as he arose to go, he asked Mr. Sloan if he
could direct him to a good, quiet boarding-place.   " I
am here," said he, " for health and recreation.   I am
traveling under the patronage of a friend, who furnishes
the means upon condition that I bring back some sketches of the finest views that I can obtain of your grand
old mountains ; and I have seen none as yet equal to the
one here from your door."

" I do not know, my young friend, just what you
want, or whether, with your city habits, you could be
suited with our plain people and their common fare.
We have been having hard times up here, and the prospect ahead is no better," said the old gentleman, with a
sigh ; " but if you could be comfortable anywhere in the

place, it would be at the Widow Brown's, in the stone house beyond the church."

"Indeed, sir," said the gentleman, "if you think I should be hard to please, you are mistaken. I lived in the country myself the earlier portion of my life : my father owned a small, rocky farm, and we had to work hard to earn a livelihood. When I was about fifteen, an uncle left me a small sum of money; and then, with my father's consent, I went to the city in order to gratify the desire that I had always felt, — that of becoming an artist ; but my means are so limited, that I should not have dared to indulge myself in this trip, though needing the recreation, but for the kindness of the friend aforesaid. But why not let me stop with you ? You seem to have but a small family, and it would be so quiet : I am sure I should like nothing better.

"I hardly think it possible ; but I will talk with my daughter about it. Marion, Marion, where are you ? " he called ; and, receiving no reply, exclaimed, " Why, where has the child gone ! I never knew her to do the like ; but you must pardon her, sir, for this seeming lack of courtesy, as she is not much accustomed to seeing strangers, and is somewhat timid."

"No offense," replied the gentleman, smiling inwardly at the deference paid him by the simple-hearted old man;— no offense, sir. I will go to the village and make a few inquiries, ascertain if there are any letters for me in the office, and then return for your answer. That will give you time to talk with your daughter without the embarrassment of my presence : you have a public house in the village, I suppose ? "

"Yes, sir, and a good one for these parts."

" Good-evening, then, for the present ; " and, taking up his portfolio, he walked briskly in the direction indicated. The old man watched his retreating form till it was lost beyond the point of rocks before spoken of; and then, as he turned to take his accustomed seat, Marion came in from the back way.

" Where have you been, child ? " he asked.

" Just up the mountain a little way : has the gentleman gone ? "

" Yes ; but he is coming back again : what do you suppose he wants, Marion ? "

" I am sure I can not tell, father."

" Well, he thinks of stopping a while in the place, and wants to board here."

" O father ! " she exclaimed, as a shiver ran through her frame : you did not tell him that he might come ? "

" No : I told him that I would talk with you first ; but why not take him ? We have the spare room that he could occupy : you are a good cook ; and I see nothing to prevent."

" O father ! I don't know why ; but I feel as if he must not come, — as if there was something wrong."

" Judge not, that ye be not judged," said the old man solemnly.

" I know it, father ; and ' Be kind to the stranger that is within thy gate,' is another of the commands of that holy book. And yet I do not feel kindly toward this stranger, — did not from the first : I can not tell why it is."

" A temptation of Satan, my child : you are young, as yet, in the Christian race ; and he would try you. Pray God that your faith fail not."

" Indeed, father, I feared it was thus; and I have been out to study and pray over it: but the feeling does not leave me. O father! perhaps it is a warning; for I never felt so toward human being before."

" Perhaps," said the old man thoughtfully. Marion's eye brightened. " Then we surely ought to heed it," she said. But the scanty crops and the wants of the coming winter rose before the father's vision; and he replied, —

" No, no: it can not be that; for it was only to day that I was wondering where our winter supplies were coming from. Let us rather think, my daughter, that the Lord has sent him to rebuke my want of faith; in that case, if we do not accept what is thus put into our hands, what warrant have we of his further care?"

" I had not thought of it in that light," said Marion sadly. " You have had more experience than I have, and are more likely to be in the right. I will try to overcome these feelings; and, if you think it best to have him stop with us a while, will do what I can to make things pleasant for him."

" But I do not wish to do any thing that will make you unhappy, my child."

" Never mind me, father: you have always told me that true happiness could be found only in doing one's duty faithfully. I shall be happy enough if I feel that I am doing right." And so the matter was settled in favor of the stranger's remaining.

Something over an hour after the above conversation, the young man returned from the village to learn the result of his application.

" Has your daughter not returned yet?" he asked, glancing around the room, and not seeing Marion.

" Oh, yes ! she came in just after you left : she is not
far away," was the reply.

" And what have I to hope from her decision, Mr.
——— "

" Sloan is my name," said the old gentleman.

" And mine is Munson, — Philip Munson."

" Well, Mr. Munson, we have decided, that, if you
can put up with our poor accommodations, you can stop
with us for a while."

" Thanks, thanks," said the young man with an
alacrity that showed he was truly pleased ; and again his
eye went in search of Marion.

She, poor girl, must have felt his approach ; for she
certainly could not have seen him. Just before he
came around the ledge of rocks that hid the village from
them, she felt the same shudder running through her
frame that she had experienced before ; and, quickly
leaving the house, she found herself some rods up the
mountain before she thought what she was doing. " This
will never do," she said, as she came to herself, — " this
will never do ; " and, retracing her steps, she entered the
cottage just after the stranger had sent his second glance
in search of her.

" Mr. Munson, my daughter," said Mr. Sloan, as she
came in ; " finding that he is to stop with us a while, he
has favored us with his name."

The young man bowed low ; while she, in as cheerful
tones as she could command, bade him " good evening."

" And a very beautiful evening it is," he was about
to add ; but something in her look checked him and he
remained silent.

Marion passed a restless night, and looked so sad the

next morning, and that in spite of her too evident attempts to appear cheerful, that her father was troubled by it. " My child," said he, as soon as he had the opportunity of speaking with her alone, " is the presence of this stranger really making you unhappy ? "

" O father ! " she replied, bursting into tears, " I can not help it : indeed I can not. I try to think it all right ; but the feeling that it is so will not come. I wish that we had not consented to take him. I saw mother last night, and she looked so sorrowful."

" Saw your mother ? "

" Yes : as plainly as I ever saw her in life."

" Tut, tut : you make too much of these visions of yours, as you call them. You make too much account of them : they will lead you astray yet. You were dreaming, and thought you saw her."

" No, father : I was as wide awake as ever I was."

" I do not doubt that you think so : but the idea that your mother should leave her home in glory, and come here to be saddened by the affairs of this life, is simply preposterous : and not only that, but wicked ; for where would be the rest promised to the people of God if this were the case ? "

" Alas ! I know not, dear father : it is all a mystery to me ; but I know what I see," she replied sadly, as she turned to her accustomed duties.

The morning passed quickly. Mr. Munson spent it in looking about the valley, and in ascending the mountain some distance at several points, to find, as he said, the best views, intending to sketch them at his leisure.

He talked of this with the old gentleman while at dinner, scarcely addressing a remark to Marion till the meal was nearly finished, when, turning to her, he said, —

"Perhaps, Miss Sloan, you would favor me by pointing out some of the places from whence choice views can be had? I am sure I am not mistaken in believing that you have an eye for the beautiful."

"The view that pleases me best is from our west window," said she quietly; "and that just as the sun flings his last glance upon the village-steeple."

"And will you be so kind as to show to me the exact position in which the best effect can be obtained?" he asked.

"I will," she replied in a tone which showed that she shrank from further conversation; and, dinner over, the gentleman retired to his room. Taking a privilege that he would hardly have been willing to grant, we will follow him thither; for, by so doing, we, perhaps, may ascertain if there is really any foundation for Marion's dislike.

See! he has taken pen, ink, and paper, and seems to be writing a letter. We will peep over his shoulder, and learn for ourselves: —

EATON, Sept. 9.

Hail, friend and fellow-craftsmen of the Lodge of Loyal Brothers to the idea of doing as you please!

A long prefix, Mark; but I think it expresses your character and mine, to say the least. True, there are many things in the way, — much that tends to prevent our living out the full spirit of our creed; but we must expect to be tried. It is only the brave and persistent ones that win in a race like this; and, if we meet with opposition, we must learn to be as wise as serpents, and as harmless as—as—d—ls. I would write the whole word, but it would not look well on paper; and you well know that looks go a great way toward success. As you are pretty good at deciphering abreviations, I think that you can make out my meaning without much trouble.

"But where is Eaton ? " I hear you ask.

"Here, right here, my good brother, in the shadow of one of the tallest of the Green Mountains; and close to the village is a rural retreat, where a rheumatic old man resides with his pretty daughter; and snugly esconsced in that retreat is your humble servant. Zounds! could I have carried out my principles, I should, 'ere this, have given this mountain-nymph some strong proofs of my affection for her lovely self. I shall do it some day. Mind, I say *I shall;* and you know me well enough to have learned that I have stricken the word fail from my vocabulary.

She evidently dislikes me, but I care not for that: the harder the task, the more glorious the success. I shall have to play shy, however, — shy, pious, and all of that, which you know I can do to perfection.

But enough of this till I can report further progress. They believe me to be a poor artist, depending upon the money that a rich friend pays me for my sketches. Ha, ha, ha! isn't that rich ? Don't let any one know where I am till the excitement about that last little affair blows over; and don't write till you hear from me again.

Yours, &c.,   PHILIP.

And thus we learn what manner of man it was that had found a place in the home of the Sloans. With

the revealings and demonstrations of modern Spiritualism to aid us, we can readily see why it was that Marion
shrank from his presence, and why the spirit-mother
looked sad. We can see also to what power Munson
trusted for success, — the power of a strong will, acting
upon a susceptible organization, or, as we say, psychologi-
cally. He probably knew it not by that name; but he
knew its power.

Had Marion and her father known what we know,
they would have heeded the warning given; but, lacking
this, they passed on and suffered.

For the first two or three weeks Munson said but
little to Marion, further than common politeness required, unless occasion offered to ask a favor, as in the
case of the best view. Whenever this occurred, he
was sure to avail himself of it; but he sometimes fixed
upon her a sad, reproachful look, as if conscious of her
aversion, and deprecating its existence.

This could not fail to have its effect upon a nature
like her's, — a nature that would not knowingly wrong
the least of God's creatures; and, accusing herself of
injustice, she would strive to make amends by pleasant
smiles, and redoubled attention to his wants. Under the
influence of efforts like these, her aversion gradually
wore away, till she came, at length, to wonder that she
had ever felt any.

In the mean time, this wolf in sheep's clothing was
not idle. Steadily he toiled toward the accomplishment of his purpose; storming the outposts, and working his way gradually toward the citadel. He talked
theology to Mr. Sloan, agreeing with him on just the
points that would please the old man most; listened

deferentially to the minister, and made the deacons believe that he was almost persuaded to study for the ministry himself, only the sacredness of the office, and a sense of his own unworthiness, prevented.

But why follow the serpentine windings of this human fiend ? — fiend through the false teachings, and consequent false customs, of society, — why follow him step by step as he nears his victim ? We will not attempt further to portray the hellish arts by means of which he triumphed ; for our soul sickens at the recital. Suffice it to say, that he made good his boast, and left the roof that had sheltered him with its most treasured inmate betrayed, ruined so far as this life was concerned.

True, she believed herself wedded to him, — that in three months at most, perhaps in as many weeks, he would return and acknowledge her before the world. This he had solemnly pledged himself to do ; for, with all his boasted power over woman, he dared not even make the attempt to lead her other than through Hymen's pathway.

> But the torch, it was a false one,
> Held by hands as basely false :
> Power assumed by one who had none, —
> Priestly robe and saintly face.

Yet even here he had so covered his tracks, that she could not show this much to be true, — not a trace to serve in the eyes of her friends as a palliation for her condition.

When Philip Munson left the village of Eaton, he had played the hypocrite so successfully, that he carried with him the hearts of both young and old ; and Marion, as she listened to his praises, was for a time happy. But

gradually the psychological glamor that had been thrown
around her began to fade; her old aversion came back,
and with it the most terrible doubts. She continued
to hope, however, till the extreme limit of the time set
for his return had passed: then doubt gave place to a
feeling akin to despair.

And how fared it with this poor lamb in the church
of which she was so loved a member? Did they stand
by her in pitying sympathy in this the hour of her
sorest need? Far from it. *The sheep that went not
astray* met in solemn conclave, and expelled her from
their fold. Even the father who had argued so strongly
against the aversion she had felt toward the stranger as
to gain her consent that he should become an inmate
of their home, — even he said that there was no excuse
for her sin, and, cursing her for dishonoring his gray
hairs, took to his bed a broken-hearted man, leaving it
only for the grave.

Left alone with her mighty sorrow, Marion's only
consolation was in those visions that had once been
looked upon as evidence of God's favor, but were now
considered proof of insanity by some, and of willful deception by others. She thinks thus to gain sympathy,
they said; but she has shown herself too vile, too des-
perately wicked, to be trusted at all. And thus the
pressure became stronger and stronger.

Helpless and despised, left a pauper to be cared for
in her approaching hour of trial by those who would
have no sympathy for her whatever, — the places where
she had wandered with her betrayer, the scenes that
she had looked upon from childhood, and the faces she
had always known, becoming hateful to her, the poor

girl could bear it no longer. Reason at last really gave way, while the idea of escaping from all she had ever known took full possession of her mind. With a maniac's cunning, she laid her plans, and carried them out so effectually that the people of Eaton never knew what became of her. Yea, even some of those who had once been loudest in commendation, going to the opposite extreme, said that the devil had helped her away.

In the mean time, the little village in which our story opens was startled one July morning with the report that a young and beautiful woman had been found on Deacon Smith's doorstep in a condition that demanded immediate assistance.

Who was she? and from whence did she come? were the questions that flew from lip to lip: but no one could answer them, for none knew; and all that they ever learned of her was what transpired in the few days that she lived after she came among them. They saw that her mind was unsettled; but whether it had been caused by trouble, or otherwise, they could not tell. She said but little: and from that little they could learn neither her name, nor place of residence; and dying, of course her boy was left a heritage to the town.

I said they learned nothing from what she said, — nothing but her father's first name; for she had said of her child, " Call him Peter, after my father."

Such were the antecedents of Crazy Pete, — such the causes that made him what he was. Inheriting his mother's susceptibility, or, as we should say, medium- istic powers, intensified, he manifested them from early childhood, saw what those about him could not see, heard that of which their ears could catch no note ; and so they called him crazy.

Though perfectly harmless, his talk of seeing angels, his mother, and others who were known to be dead, made him an object of fear and awe to the younger portion of the community, and of contempt to the others. Is it strange, then, that it should call forth remark, when, instead of shrinking away, as others of her years did, Alice Vale would spend hours in his company, asserting, when spoken to upon the subject, that he was no more crazy than other folks ?

CHAPTER III.

THE PROPHECY.

LIZA COOK wrote a poem called "The Teachings of the Idiot-born;" and another writer, in speaking of her poems, says, —

"Thine idiot-born, O God of love!
How little do we know,
Who, in that world to come, shall prove
The high ones, or the low!
Then let us never dare to scorn
The teachings of the idiot-born."

Peter Stiverton, — he took his last name from those who cared for him the first years of his life, — Peter Stiverton was a pauper, and, as such, would not, of course, be judged by the same rule that more favored children are. He was always peculiar; but what would have been considered as evidence of smartness in others was counted as a tendency to insanity in him, and more especially as his mother's mind had evidently been unsettled. He was about twelve years of age when his peculiarities began to increase upon him; and, by the time he was fourteen, it was a conceded fact in the minds of the people generally, that he was really crazy: and they would as soon have thought of heeding the teachings of the "idiot-born," as to have paid any particular attention to aught that he told them; but, to Alice, there was a meaning in all his strange sayings.

"Peter, why do you look so sad?" said she to him one day, as she found him in his accustomed seat beneath the broad spreading elm, in the grove below the old mill.

"Because I have been doing wrong, Miss Alice."

"Why do you always say Miss? I am not Miss, but only Alice."

"You are Miss Alice; and I shall always call you so."

"Then I will call you Mr. Peter. But what have you been doing wrong?"

"I have been angry, — oh! so angry; and it makes me unhappy to think of it."

"What was it that made you angry, Mr. Peter?"

"That big boy who has lately come into the place called me a pauper, and my mother a bad woman."

"Well, I wouldn't mind it, Peter."

"I don't now, Miss Alice: I am only sorry that I was so wicked as to get angry; of all the people in the world, Peter Stiverton should have known better."

"Why?"

"Because I have been taught by the angels," he replied solemnly.

Alice looked at him with wondering, earnest eyes; and there was an expression in them which showed that she, too, would like to be taught by the angels.

After a moment's silence, as if in answer to her thoughts, he continued, "Wait, wait: it will come at last."

"What will come?" she said.

"I can not tell you what, for they have not told me; but they say it will come." And, as if he could not forget that he had been angry, he murmured, "Oh! it was so wrong: the birds and the bees tell me of it; the flies laugh at me; and even the mosquitoes sing, 'You got mad, Peter. Peter, you got mad.'"

"Fie, fie, Peter! that is all nonsense: you only imagine it."

Turning his blue eyes full upon her, he waited at least a minute without speaking. Alice began to fear that she had grieved him, when he asked, "Do you not believe that all things have a language?"

"Certainly I do, Peter."

"What is the use of a language that is not understood?"

"They may understand each other, — doubtless do, Peter."

"The trees and the flowers?"

"I never thought of it before; but, if they have a language, they must, of course."

"And does not God understand them all?"

"God knows all things, Peter."

"And can give to his creatures such gifts as he chooses?"

"No one doubts his power," said Alice.

"Why, then, could he not give me ears to hear what the bees and the birds, the flies and the mosquitoes, say?"

"It must be so, Peter: I feel that you are right; and yet it seems so strange. I never look upon a beautiful flower, or a grand old tree, but they seem to be talking to me: only I can not understand what they say."

" Neither can I understand what the French people say who come here sometimes."

" Oh! but you could learn if you had a teacher."

" Do you not believe, Miss Alice, that the angels understand the language of the flowers, and the trees, and of all living things ? "

" I suppose they must."

" And did I not tell you I had been taught by the angels ? "

" You did, Peter ; but I did not think of that."

" I have something more to tell you, too, Miss Alice. I am going away ; and, where I go, they will be sad if I get angry."

" Going away! Where ? "

" I am going to live with my mother: she told me last night that she was coming after me soon."

" Going to die! "

" My mother is not dead."

" She is what they call dead: we can not see her."

" I can see her when she comes to me ; I can hear her when she talks to me ; and she tells me that their songs have a note of sadness in them when those they love do that which is not right: but come, let us go down among the pebbles at the foot of the great rock, just where the little brook flows into the creek. I want to talk to you about them ; for, after I go with mother, it will be a long time before I can talk with you again."

" And will you come and talk to me as your mother does to you ? "

" I don't know how nor when ; but I shall talk with you, for mother says so. You will live to see and hear wonderful things, Miss Alice : but there is a cloud between now and then, — a big, dark cloud, with bright lightnings and rolling thunders. Oh! those bright lightnings are to clear your eyesight, and the thunder to make you hear better. You will see and hear, — you will see and hear. But here we are among the pebbles: let us talk about them."

A few days after the above conversation, Peter was taken very sick, and, after a few hours of severe suffering, went, as he had said, to his mother. The event made a deep impression on the mind of Alice; for she thought, if one part of what he said becomes true, why not the other?

From this time forth, Alice Vale seemed a changed being. She wandered in the fields and woods as before but seldom; and, when she did, she appeared to take but little pleasure in her accustomed haunts. When rallied upon the subject by her young companions, she replied, " What is the use? I never go but I see something I do not understand; and there is no one to tell me about it now."

" Only listen to her!" exclaimed half a dozen voices at once: " one would think, to hear her talk, that Crazy Pete knew every thing."

" I wish I knew half as much," said she, in a tone that forbade further remark upon the subject. And for years afterward she never referred to him in any manner whatever; and, when others did, she was silent. She became very thoughtful; was more attentive to the wishes of her parents; and people said, " It is a good thing for Alice that Pete is dead; for he held a strange influence over . her, one that was evidently injuring her."

Mistaken mortals, to think that influence at an end!

Alice was in her sixteenth year the summer that Peter died; and, beginning to grow rapidly about this time, in a few months the change was so great, that her friends would hardly have known her, had they met her elsewhere. From being small for her age, and with a child-like manner that caused people to think her younger than she was, the reverse became true. With her growth to womanhood came that quiet dignity which commanded the respect of all who saw her.

But there was one thing in which she was not changed; and that was in her individuality of character. True, it was no longer the individuality of childhood, which acts, or seems to act, more from instinct than reason: still, it was none of the less marked. She thought and acted for herself, as the following incident will show. Something more than two years had passed since she last went with Pete in search of rare flowers and curious specimens of stone. She was nearing her eighteenth birthday; and her mother said, —

" Alice, I think I must give you a party on the tenth."

" And why on the tenth, mother ? "

" Why, don't you remember that it is your birthday?"

" Indeed, I had forgotten it; but will it be convenient, mother, for us to have it at that time ? "

" As much so as at any other; but what a strange girl you are, Alice ! Another than yourself would have been delighted at the bare mention of the thing, instead of stopping to start objections."

" I am pleased with the idea, mother, — glad that you think me worthy of such a favor; but, if the party is to be for me, I shall claim the privilege of selecting the guests."

" All right, child ; go and make out your list, and I will talk with your father this evening about the necessary preparations."

" Thank you, mother," said she ; and, sitting down at the desk, the required list was soon ready, and handed to Mrs. Vale for her inspection.

" Why, Alice, I do not see Edward Winchester's name here."

" It is not there : I do not intend to invite him."

" Not invite Edward Winchester ! "

" Upon one condition I will."

" And what is that ? "

" That Addie Graves be invited also."

" Addie Graves ! You are crazy, Alice : every other girl would leave, should she come."

" Why, mother ? "

" Why ! A girl that is a mother and, not a wife ! "

" And Edward Winchester, is a father, and not a husband."

" Oh ! but that is different."

" Different only in the fact that he is the aggressive party, and therefore the most to blame. Addie never sought him ; and, if he had left her alone in her innocence, she would not now be a mother, and an outcast from society."

" But the world does not look upon it in that light."

" The question is, not what the world thinks, but what is right."

" But it will never do, Alice, to make a party and not invite Edward. He belongs to one of the first families in the place : and, more than that, your father has lately had some heavy business transactions with Winchester

& Son ; and, if we offend them, it might injure us in a pecuniary point of view."

" Then, mother, we will not have the party at all ; and the expense of it can be saved for other purposes."

" But what will people say ?   I have already told two or three that I intended to give you a party upon your eighteenth birthday ; and, as you are invited to other places, it looks as though we were afraid of a little trouble, or a little expense, if we do not return the compliment."

" If my going to parties places us under a bondage like that, I will stay at home after this."

" O Alice ! you are incorrigible."

" I do not mean to be, mother : I only wish to do what is right."

" But what shall I say to those who are expecting the party ? "

" Tell them the truth, or say that you have good reasons for giving it up."

Just at this juncture, Nellie Parton, Alice's most intimate friend, called.   Almost the first question that she asked was about the party.

" We are not going to have one," said Alice.

" Do not say we : say I, for it is all your own fault, Alice ; " and then, under the influence of the irritation caused by her daughter's cool disposal of the matter, Mrs. Vale told Nellie why Alice would not have the party.

Now, Nellie, or little Miss Parton, as she was sometimes called from her diminutive size, was a right-feeling little body ; but she had not the courage to assert herself as Alice had.   Still she always stood by Alice, and gloried in her independence.

"Good! good for you, Alice! I wish all the girls would take the same stand; for, if ever a poor girl was shamefully wronged, it is Addie Graves. I am going right to Miss Manning, to tell her all about it. Winchester is paying her some attention; and she shall know how things stand, and what at least one person thinks of him. I do not think she knows about Addie, for she has not been in the place long."

"Don't tell her about the party, Nellie," said Mrs. Vale: "for, if you do, she will tell some one else; and, the first thing we know, Winchester will hear of it, and that will make hard feelings."

"Let him feel hard. I shouldn't care. He ought to know it: it might serve to lower his self-esteem a little," exclaimed Nellie; while Alice quietly remarked, "I have no objection to Mr. Winchester's knowing my opinion of him."

Nellie was as good as her word. She not only told Miss Manning, but others; and twenty-four hours had not elapsed before it came to young Winchester's ears. He smiled quietly, and, with an air of the most consummate self-conceit, said, "I see where the trouble lies: I have not paid that attention to Miss Alice that I might have done, and she takes this mode of showing her resentment. Say nothing, John, and I can soon make that all right;" and John, the obedient shadow of this boastful libertine, said nothing, but waited further developments.

Some three weeks afterward, Mrs. Roland, the lady whose remarks about Alice three years previous opens this story, gave out invitations for a party; inviting only the gentlemen, and leaving them to select the ladies.

The next evening after these invitations were given out, the Vales were much surprised at receiving a call from young Winchester. After a few minutes' general conversation, he turned to Alice and said, "Miss Vale, I called to ask the pleasure of your company to Mrs. Roland's party."

"Do the gentlemen have the privilege of taking more than one lady?" asked Alice quietly.

"I suppose they do if they wish," said he, with a look of extreme surprise upon his countenance. "But why do you ask?"

"For no particular reason," she replied in the same quiet tones: "only I had thought of spending that evening with Addie Graves; but, if you will take her too, I will go."

The young man arose to his feet with a face flushed with passion, and so excited that he trembled from head to foot. "Miss Vale, you shall repent this insult to the latest day of your life."

Alice preserved her self-possession. "Mr. Winchester," said she, "you once thought it no disgrace to be seen in public with Miss Graves; and, if she is not what she then was, it is your own work."

Winchester strove to make some reply: but rage choked his utterance; and, turning upon his heel, he abruptly left the house. Mr. and Mrs. Vale were both present, but were too much surprised at the turn things had taken to make any remark till Mr. Winchester had gone.

"O Alice!" cried Mrs. Vale, "what have you done!" while her father said, "You are a brave girl, Alice: would to heaven there were more such! but you have made a bitter enemy, — one who will stop at nothing that promises to gratify his revenge. I fear that you will yet suffer for this."

" I can afford to suffer in the cause of right, my father," she replied.

" And to see others suffer also ? " he asked.

" That would indeed be hard ; but I could bear even that better than the loss of self-respect."

" God grant that you may be called upon to bear neither ! " said he earnestly, but in a tone which showed that he felt depressed.

After Mr. Vale had gone to his place of business, Mrs. Vale sighed, and seemed inclined to utter reproaches : but Alice looked so calm, so undisturbed, that her heart failed her ; and, with another sigh still more emphatic than the first, she retired to her room, and the true-hearted girl was left to her own reflections. And what those reflections were, let those who have dared to brave popular sins, have dared to defend the weak against the strong, the victim against the destroyer, — let such imagine.

Nelly Parton came in the next day, as usual; and when she said, " Al, I never stop for ceremony, as you see," Alice replied, " Neither do humming-birds."

" Now, Al, you are too bad to compare me to so insignificant a thing as that, even if it is beautiful."

" Choice goods are done up in small parcels," continued Alice smiling.

" Hush, flatterer ! but what was Ed Winchester doing here last night : Charley said he saw him go out of here, and he looked as if lightning had struck him."

" He came to invite me to Mrs. Roland's party."

Nelly opened her blue eyes to their utmost capacity, and uttered the single ejaculation, " You ! "

" Yes, me, little puss: what is there so strange in that ? "

" But you are not going with him ? "

" I told him I would if he would take Addie Graves too ; but that idea did not seem to suit him, so he declined the honor."

" That accounts for it."

" Accounts for what ? "

" The way he looked when he left here. Charley said he never saw such an expression on one's face in his life."

" It was not a light evening : I don't see how Charley could have seen him so plainly," said Alice.

" I did not ask him : but he had a lantern in his hand when he came in, and I suppose it must have been by the means of that. Meeting him coming out of your gate, he would naturally hold the light so as to see who it was. What reply did he make to your proposal ? "

" He was very angry, and said I should repent the insult."

" Insult ! I don't wonder he is ashamed of his own work."

" He does not act as if he was."

"Well, he ought to be, the contemptible fellow ! But why is it, Alice, that a man can crush a woman thus, and the blame be all laid to her ? I am sure I could never see any justice in it."

" There is none ; but it will always be thus so long as men are a privileged class."

" A privileged class ! what do you mean by that ? "

"I mean that they have rights under the law that woman has not. If there is a law that does not suit them, they can vote to have it changed; if one of them commits a crime, the sheriff, judges, jury, and all, are men. Can a woman vote to have bad laws made better? Can a woman, if she has done a wrong that the law can take hold of, — can she have the case tried by women? and this is but a small part of what I might mention as evidence that men are a privileged class."

"I didn't know, Alice, that you were for 'Woman's Rights.'"

"Neither am I in the sense that most people understand that term. I would have woman as God made her, — woman, and not man; but I would have her man's equal before the law: now she is not. She may be —

> 'His empress, or his slave,
> Or his discarded jest,' —

but never his equal in aught wherein she can actively put forth her energies: it is only when she is to be punished or taxed that the equality comes in. Man by his own showing, is not to be trusted; and yet he claims and holds the right to make laws for woman to protect and control her."

"And how does he show that he is not to be trusted? I have never seen any thing to make me think that men were less truthful than women," said Nelly thoughtfully.

"Perhaps not: but what does such treatment as Addie Graves has received at the hands of Edward Winchester and of society say? Why, that society at large recognizes the fact, that man's word is not to be trusted where matters of vital importance to woman are concerned; yea, that his solemn oath, his strongest asseverations, are so worthless, that the woman who shows sufficient confidence therein to place herself in his power is looked upon as a weak fool. I say that society everywhere recognizes this as a fact; and man, instead of resenting the insinuation, glories in it, says by his acts, Why, really, here is a woman who believed I spoke the truth, who actually thought that I could be trusted. Ha, ha, ha, what a fool!"

"Why, Alice, you would make a good lawyer!"

"And I should not object to being one, if I might thus aid the right, might plead the cause of the helpless; but this is one of the privileges that woman may not share: man makes law, man pleads law; woman only obeys."

"Hark! What is that?" exclaimed Nelly, starting to her feet, and listening intently.

"What? I heard nothing."

"I thought I heard a shriek — there it is again;" and both girls rushed to the door to behold a sight that chilled their blood with horror.

CHAPTER IV.

COALS OF FIRE.

" If thine enemy hunger, feed him ; for in so doing thou shalt heap coals of fire upon his head." — *Bible.*

HEN Edward Winchester left Mr. Vale's, the night before, his anger amounted almost to phrensy. The coolness of Alice, and the justice of her remarks, maddened him to that degree that he hardly knew what he was doing. " The proud minx ! " exclaimed he aloud, as soon as he had reached his room ; " I'll humble her yet ; I'll teach her that she can not insult me with impunity."

" But did she not tell you the truth ? " whispered conscience : " was it not your own work that she held up to your view ? "

" My work ! damn a woman that can't take care of herself," he continued in the same excited tones, as he walked rapidly back and forth across the room.

" How now, Winchester ! what's up ? "

" That's my business," he replied, scarcely waiting to see who the speaker was.

" I beg your pardon for intruding; but I found your door open, and you did not answer my rap," said the young man, in tones which showed that he was offended.

4

Winchester looked up. "Excuse me, Bronson; but I am vexed to-night : I meant no offense to you."

"Then I will leave you till you are in better humor."

"There," said Winchester, as the door closed behind his friend, — "there, I have offended a friend as the first step toward accomplishing my object. I must keep cool, or I shall spoil every thing ;" and, locking the door to prevent further intrusion, he sat far into the night, revolving plans that would help him to triumph over the girl who had dared to tell him the truth.

The next morning he arose with the same restless feeling upon him ; and, after trying in vain to fasten his mind upon business, he resolved to take an excursion into the country. Going to one of the stables to get a horse, he was told that they had none for him except one that was so fractious and high-lifed that he was not considered safe for any but the most experienced riders.

"Let me have him : I am not afraid of him."

"If you take him, Winchester, you do so at your own risk ; but I would advise you not to try to ride him," said the groom.

"I tell you I am not afraid of him : bring him out," was the impatient reply ; and then to himself, "I want something that has some fire : it will do me good." The horse was brought out, but behaved so badly that he was again urged not to ride him.

But Winchester replied, "I will ride him, or die in the attempt ;" and, mounting the determined-looking beast, he started off with a brisk trot. The horse went very well for about half a mile ; but, in crossing a small bridge, some hogs started up from beneath it. Making this an excuse for a scare, the creature, who had all along showed mischief in his eye, turned, and started upon a full run for town. So fleet was his motion, that Winchester could hardly keep his seat, much less check and turn back the fiery animal. Just as they reached the main part of the village, the horse made a quick movement, that threw his rider from his back; but his feet catching in the stirrup, he was dragged along at a rate that threatened instant death; and this was what Alice and Nelly saw as they reached the door.

As fate would have it, Addie Graves came around the corner just at the moment her false lover was thrown; and it was her shriek that Nelly had heard.

"O Alice, Alice, he will be killed!" exclaimed Nelly.

"I fear he is that already," replied Alice, as she looked at the pale bleeding form, which was at the moment freed from contact with the stirrup, and left lying close by their gate.

By this time quite a crowd had collected; and Addie was slipping away, when Alice, seeing the movement, stepped quickly to her side and said, " Go into the house Addie, and stay in my room till I can come to you."

The poor girl looked the thanks she could not speak, as she availed herself of this opportunity of being near the man she still loved, though he had so cruelly wronged her, till it could be ascertained what his injuries really were. As the mother of his child, she should have been by his side: but no, that might not be; for the curious, questioning eyes of those who condemned her because he had led her into wrong, and then forsaken her, was more than her sensitive nature could endure.

" Gracious heaven, what an anomaly is this! In all other cases, the tempter is looked upon as the most to blame, and is treated accordingly; but here he is exonerated, or mostly so, while the weight of public indignation falls upon the tempted. There is a reason for this somewhere; but who shall find and hold it up successfully to the view of the world?" Such were the thoughts of Alice as she marked the looks of contempt cast upon Addie during the few moments that she mingled with the crowd.

Young Winchester was taken up in a senseless condition, and carried into Mr. Vale's; while the hastily-summoned physician proceeded to examine his wounds. He reported one broken ankle, one dislocated wrist, beside bruises external and internal.

" Can he live?" was the anxious question that was next asked.

" I see nothing to prevent it if he has careful nursing: but he can not be moved for a month at the least; and if fever sets in, as I fear it will, it may be longer."

" What if his friends call to see him?" asked Alice.

" His parents will be admitted of course, but none others; for he must be kept as quiet as possible."

" His parents are not in town."

" Where are they?"

" They started last week on a visiting tour through New England, and do not expect to return under two months."

The doctor looked anxious.

" Do not be uneasy, doctor," said Mrs. Vale: "he shall be cared for as if he were my own son. Henry, our boy of all work, if he is but sixteen, is as good as a wo nan to wait upon the sick ; and Alice, I am sure, will do her best."

"I certainly shall," said Alice ; "but, doctor, I would like to talk with you a minute."

He stepped aside ; and his countenance brightened at the few words that were spoken in his ear. "I wish it could be so," said he : "but it would occasion remark ; and, if not, he would not consent to it."

"Are not persons in his condition apt to be deranged when fever sets in ?" she inquired.

"Very apt to be ; and his head is so jarred, that he is not exactly himself now. Indeed, I don't think he realized, at any time while I was dressing his wounds, what the trouble was."

"If you will leave it to me, doctor, I will manage it so that he will not be excited ; neither shall there be any remarks made. All I ask is, positive orders from you that there shall be no one admitted to his room except those who have the care of him."

"I shall certainly do that, for the necessity of the case demands it ; and will promise silence, and my aid in carrying out your plan as far as is possible."

"Thank you, doctor."

Alice next went to her mother. Here she found more opposition. "What will people say ?" she asked.

"I do not intend that they shall know it, — not at present, at least."

"Ah! but they will find it out," said Mrs. Vale, shaking her head : "you can not keep such things from the public."

"And what if they do, mother."

"What if they do ? Why, we shall lose our reputation. People will say that we justify such conduct, Alice. I tell you I don't want her in the house."

" But she is here, mother; and I don't want her to leave.

" Is here : where ? "

" In my room."

" O Alice ! Alice ! Who ever saw such a girl ! I thought, after Crazy Pete died, that you were learning some sense ; but I had as soon you would run in the woods, and climb trees, as to do as you are doing now."

" When I was a child, I behaved like a child, was true to my child-nature ; but now that I am a woman, with all due deference to you, mother, I wish to be true to my womanhood," said Alice, tears filling her eyes.

" And do you call it being true to your womanhood, — this sustaining those that have been false to theirs ? "

" But, mother, suppose it was your own daughter ? "

" She should no longer be a daughter of mine ? "

" But you would take her destroyer into the house, and care for him ? "

" No : I don't think I could quite do that," said Mrs. Vale, softening a little at the thought of such a contingency.

" Well, remember, mother dear, that poor Addie lost her mother just at the time that she needed her the most."

" I know it : I know it, child ; and I have always felt sorry for her : but I can not, on that account, permit you to take a step that would compromise you. No, no, it can not be : I shall not consent to it," she continued, in response to the pleading look that was cast upon her.

Alice began to fear that she was to be defeated; but just then her father came in. "What is all this that I hear of Winchester's being nearly killed?" said he.

Mrs. Vale told him the state of the case as near as she could, and then added, —

"And Alice, foolish child, is determined to have Addie Graves here to help take care of him."

"And why not?" said Mr. Vale.

"Why not! You men never do have any sense: it will not do at all, and you ought to know it."

"I must confess, wife, that I can not see why it will not do. Alice, my child, what is your object in wishing Addie here?"

"Why, father, I have always noticed, that, when people were suffering, they are apt to be more tender-hearted, more ready to feel for the sufferings of others and " —

"And you thought, perhaps, that if he could see Addie now, — could know she was ready to care for him, notwithstanding all that has passed, — that his heart might soften toward her, and he be willing to do her justice by making her his wife?"

"I had thought of that, father; but there is another thing. The doctor says that he must have the best of nursing, or he will not live: now, what is there that will make so good a nurse of one as devoted love?"

"You are right, my child; and it shall be as you wish " — .

"But " —

"No buts in the matter, Mrs. Vale. I do not often oppose your plans, nor interfere with your wishes; but this thing shall be as I say."

" O father ! ' said Alice deprecatingly.

"I am not angry, child, only in earnest: now go your way, and your father will see that there shall no blame fall on your head."

Thus dismissed, Alice hastened to her own room, where she found poor Addie lying upon the bed with her face nearly as white as the pillow upon which her head rested.

" O Alice ! is he alive ? " she gasped, staggering to her feet.

" Yes, alive, and with good nursing will recover; so the doctor says."

" Thank God! thank God!" she exclaimed; and, sinking back upon the bed, burst into a passion of weeping.

" Addie," said Alice, when she had grown somewhat calm, — " Addie, do you still love that man ? "

" Love him ! I would give my soul for his to-day, as cruelly as he has wronged me," was her quick and emphatic reply.

" He is not worthy of such love," said Alice; " but, Addie, the doctor said that he would get well with good nursing: where shall we find a good nurse ? "

Looking a moment into Alice's face, as if to gather her full meaning, the poor girl clasped her hands and said, " O Alice ! if I only might."

" And so you shall : you and I together; for you can not do it all. It is all arranged : the doctor says he must see no one only those who have the care of him. I have pledged them all to silence, except Betty the kitchen-girl; and she will do any thing I wish. You can come, and the neighbors will be none the wiser."

" What shall I do with my baby ? "

" Have you weaned him ? "

" No; but it is time that I had."

" Well, then, send him out to Aunt Chloe for that purpose."

" Aunt Chloe who ? "

" Why, don't you know ? the black woman who lives up by the steam-mill. It is only a mile from town. I will write a note for you, and you can take your baby there this afternoon: it will be all right."

" All right if I can get father's consent; but he is so incensed against Edward that I fear he will not give it."

" I will go and see him myself," said Alice. " I believe I am rather a favorite with him, and I don't think he will refuse me."

Alice had a harder task than she had supposed: but she succeeded at last; and the next night found Addie Graves watching beside the bed of the man, who, of all others, should have been her best and truest friend. But, alas! past events had proved him far otherwise.

The sick man was in a high fever, tossing hither and thither, as much as his wounds would permit, — at times moaning piteously with pain, and then again living over the scenes of the past, as was shown by disconnected sentences and incoherent mutterings.

At one time he would be talking to Addie, pleading, in soft insinuating tones, the promises that had worked her ruin; and at others he would curse her for being such a weak fool as to believe him.

Sometimes, when she rested her soft hand upon his forehead, or passed it gently across his temples, in her efforts to soothe him, he would say, " That feels like

Addie's hand: I wonder if she loves me well enough
to follow me to hell. Surely this is hell. How hot it
is! nothing — nothing cool but this soft hand." And
then he would curse Alice for minding that which was
none cf her business. But — but she told me the truth
— the truth — the truth," he would fairly shriek; till,
falling back upon his pillow, his voice sank lower and
lower, and was lost at last in fitful slumber.

Poor Addie. It was a hard place for her; but
bravely did she fill it, till, at length, he would not be
content without her. No one but her could give him
his food: no hand but hers could smooth his pillow to
suit him.

Alice watched the progress of things, and hoped
much therefrom: still, she trembled as well as longed
for the moment when he should awake to consciousness, as so much depended upon the first impression
made upon his mind then.

His symptoms were growing better, his sleep less
disturbed and of longer duration; and the physician said
that he was liable to awake at any time, perfectly sane.

One day, when he had slept unusually long, Addie,
who had not slept the night before, fell into a drowse
herself. A slight movement on his part aroused her;
and, looking up, she beheld his eyes fixed upon her with
the old look of intelligence in them.

Her presence of mind forsook her; and she could not
utter a word, but sat for one moment like to one para-
lyzed, and the next arose, and glided from the room.

He did not speak, nor attempt to detain her; and,
when Alice came in just after, he responded to her sal-
utation, and inquiries after his health, as if it was the

most natural t .ing in the world that he should be there, and in the con lition he was.

After a few moments' silence on both sides, he said, " Miss Vale, I need not ask you how I came here : the last recollection I have is of being thrown to the ground, and dragged furiously along. I suppose, that, by some means, I must have got loose from the stirrup, and have been brought in here. All after that seems like a frightful dream, in which I thought I was in hell, and that an angel was trying to get me out."

" Well, that is past, and you are better now," said Alice, more agitated than at any time previous, — even more so than when she had seen him taken up for dead at her father's gate.

" Yes : I am better now," he responded, and, turning his head away, indicated no disposition to converse further.

Alice slipped through the door, where Addie stood in a suspense that hardly permitted her to breathe. " Wait! be patient," said she in a hurried whisper, " and it will all be right ; " and then returned again to her post.

After lying quiet for perhaps twenty minutes, he turned toward Alice again, and said, " I have been conscious longer than you are aware of, Miss Vale: now, why did you get Miss Graves to help take care of me ? "

" I had several reasons, Mr. Winchester ; one of which was, the doctor said, that, unless you had careful nursing, you would not recover."

" And you think she could take better care of me than others ? '

" I know, Mr. Winchester, that love is the most faithful of watchers," replied Alice, having so far recovered her self-possession as to look him calmly in the face.

" Do you believe that she loves me still ? "

" I know that she does," was the reply.

" And another reason ? " he continued.

" I hoped to see your better nature so aroused that you would do her justice," was the firm response.

" Then you do not think me wholly bad ? " he asked, with an air of humility in his tones so unlike his former self that Alice could hardly believe her own ears.

" Not by any means, Mr. Winchester."

He sighed, lay silent again for a time ; and, when he next looked up, it was to ask, —

" Will you send Miss Graves here, Miss Vale ? "

What passed in that room for the next hour is too sacred for the public ear : but, ere the sun had withdrawn the last evidence of his smiling face, Addie Graves was a wife ; and, from thenceforth, there was no need of concealment, for the world acknowledged her right to watch by the bedside of her husband. When *he had done her justice*, then others were willing to.

CHAPTER V.

THE CLOUD RISING.

Not larger than the human hand ;
And yet the prophet's eye
Could, in its swiftly moving form,
The coming tempest spy.

LICE," said Mr. Vale to his daughter, one evening some three months after the marriage of Winchester and Addie,— " Alice, it seems to me that you and Brown's clerk are getting quite too friendly."

" Which one ? " asked Alice demurely : " he has three, and I am acquainted with them all."

" Which one! you know well enough, without asking, you jade ; and you had better not let me catch John Shepherd here again very soon."

" What harm is there in him, father ? "

" Harm ! none that I know of, only he will be wanting to marry you next."

" And what if he should, father ? " said Alice, in those quiet tones that mean so much.

Mr. Vale looked at her a moment in silence. Should he arouse the opposition of her determined spirit by laying his commands upon her ? or should he take some other c urse to separate them ? These were the questions that he was debating in his mind. He feared the

effect of the former course, but shrank from taking the
latter   for he despised every thing that looked like underhanded dealing.   At length he said, —

"Alice, you will never marry that man with my
consent."

"I am sorry, father," she replied; "for then I shall
have to marry him without it."

"If you do, you are no longer a child of mine," he
exclaimed excitedly; for her cool self-possession so
maddened him that he entirely forgot his resolutions of
prudence.

"Husband, O husband! don't say that," said Mrs.
Vale entreatingly; but he turned upon her such a look
that she dared not say more.

Mr. Vale was a singular man, — in many respects an
excellent one.   He was usually an indulgent husband
and a kind father: but there was a streak of tyranny in
his nature, which, when aroused, brooked no opposition; and his wife had long since learned this fact.
And, withal, he had a species of pride that was none
the less real because it did not appear upon the surface.
He had, as I have said in the opening chapter, figured
once as a merchant of some note in New-York City;
but, having failed there, came and settled in this little
village, to continue the same business on a small scale.
Notwithstanding his suavity of manner, he had always
felt a sort of contempt for the people of the place; and
this was one reason why he had cared so little when
Alice, in carrying out her own ideas of things, had
provoked their remarks, and brought their criticisms
down upon her.

True, he liked to see independence of character, when

such independence did not interfere with his cherished plans. And, more than this, what difference did it make if they did find fault with his child? They were not her equals. Such were his most secret feelings, though hardly acknowledged even to himself.

Some of their old acquaintances from the city — sons of wealthy men, who had been the schoolmates of Alice in childhood — often came to the country in the summer; and one or more of them frequently spent weeks at his house. And the proudly fond father had secretly hoped that some one of them would marry Alice, and reinstate her in her old position in society, or, rather, in the one she would have occupied had he remained in the city and continued successful.

He saw no reason why this should not be; and, through the influence of such a marriage, he might regain, partially at least, an *entrée* into the social circles from which he now felt himself excluded. But, should Alice wed a poor clerk, these hopes would be dashed to the ground: hence his excitability upon the subject.

It was not ten minutes after the above conversation before young Shepherd himself appeared upon the scene.

"Mr. Shepherd," said Mr. Vale, turning fiercely upon him, "I find that you are presuming upon the hand of my daughter. Leave this house, sir, and never dare to enter it again."

"Does your daughter acquiesce in this decision," inquired the young man, turning to Alice.

"My daughter will do as I say," exclaimed Mr. Vale, pointing to the door.

Alice was about to speak, but a second thought restrained her: she gave her lover a look, however, which so far satisfied him that he left without another word.

" There, that matter is settled : now, don't let me hear of any more such nonsense, Miss Alice ; " but, as he looked into her quiet face, he felt a doubt as to the matter's being really settled, after all. He expected either a storm of reproaches, or a flood of tears ; but he met neither. " I must watch her," was his mental resolve, " or she will be too much for me yet."

The next morning, soon after breakfast, Alice called on Mrs. Winchester. Addie met her with a glowing face of welcome. " O Alice ! I am so glad to see you ; but what makes you look so sober : is any one sick ? "

" No: we are all as well as usual," replied Alice ; " but father has forbidden John Shepherd the house ; and I want you to help me a little, that is all."

Addie lifted up her hands in astonishment. " Forbidden him the house !   What does that mean ? "

" He thinks I am going to marry him, which I certainly intend to do."

" But how can I help you, Alice ? "

" In the first place, say nothing of this, not even to your husband, till I give you permission ; and, in the next, find means to put this note into Mr. Shepherd's hands as soon as possible."

" I will do both with all my heart ; for I can never half repay the obligation I am under for your past kindness."

" Do not speak of that: I am more than paid for the past ; 'tis the present we have to deal with," said Alice smiling ; " but I must return home, or I shall be missed."

That afternoon, when Mrs. Winchester went into Mr. Brown's store, she so managed it that it was John Shepherd who waited upon her, instead of the clerk who usually claimed that honor; and, when she left, the young man found himself in the possession of the following note: —

DEAR JOHN, — Be patient, and all will yet be right. Do not seek me at present, but rest assured that I shall prove true to you. Destroy this when you have read it, to prevent accidents; for my father will leave no stone unturned in seeking to know if we hold any correspondence.

From your own

ALICE.

"Bless her true heart!" was the lover's mental exclamation, as he looked the note over carefully for the second time, and then, putting it into his mouth, commenced the process of destruction by masticating it finely. "Bless her true heart! still, this underhanded way of doing business goes against my feelings. How much better it would be to have every thing open and above board!"

"Hallo, there, Jack! are you learning to chew tobacco?" said a fellow-clerk to him, as he returned to his post.

"Not exactly," was the reply; but, in saying this, he drew in his breath in such a manner that the paper choked and set him to coughing. With the first cough, it was thrown half way across the room. Shepherd and the other young man, whose name was Holten, both

started for it; but Holten reached it first, and refused to
give it up.

It was in vain that Shepherd coaxed and threatened
by turns. The paper was so mutilated that it could not
be read; but Shepherd did not know this, and Holten
kept it for a purpose of his own. "It is some love-
letter, I will warrant," said Holten laughingly; "and
he could not get enough of it without eating it."

Shepherd colored so violently at this, that Mr. Brown
and the other clerk joined with Holten in teasing him,
till the day was far spent before the subject was forgotten; and it would not have been dropped even then,
but a rush of custom put it out of their minds.

They did not revert to it again: still, Shepherd could
not help feeling anxious; but as day after day passed,
and nothing further was heard from it, he at length
concluded that Holten had not been able to read aught
that the note contained, and ceased worrying about the
matter. In the mean time, how fared it with Alice?

To all outward appearances about as usual. She
neither moped nor fretted, but went cheerfully about
her accustomed duties, as though nothing had happened
out of the ordinary course of things; but one who
could have looked beneath the surface would have seen
there a calm determination, a firmness of purpose, that
it were not well to oppose.

Her father watched her closely. "It can not be,"
said he to himself, "that she is going to yield so easily:
I must keep my eye upon her, for I fear she means
mischief;" but as week after week passed, and he saw
no signs of any communication between her and Shepherd, he gradually relaxed his vigilance.

Something more than a month after Shepherd had been thus summarily ejected from the house, the elder Vales were agreeably surprised by a visit from the only son of an old friend, who was one of the wealthiest of their circle of acquaintances in the city; and, what was more, Mr. Vale was well aware that the elder Sawtelle desired good substantial personal qualities, more than he did wealth, as the portion of the woman who should become the wife of his son.

"Just the thing! just the thing!" ejaculated Mr. Vale, rubbing his hands. "Young Sawtelle is unexceptionable in every way, — rich, handsome, intelligent: and I'll warrant old Sawtelle has sent him here on purpose; for those city girls are of no account, and he knows it. Wife, if we manage this thing right, we can go back to the city, and take our old place in society yet."

"If it could only be, Mr. Vale, I should like it very much," she replied; "but Alice is hard to manage. I feel very certain that she has not given up Shepherd yet, as quiet as she is."

"Why? What have you seen?"

"Not a thing; but, if she does not carry her point, I am mistaken in her."

"She shall not! She shall not! I would rather bury her!" he exclaimed, starting up and walking rapidly back and forth across the room.

"O husband! Don't say such terrible things. Think how you would feel to see her in her coffin, and she our only remaining one."

"Better thus than married to that beggar," was the irate reply. Mrs. Vale said nothing further, for she saw that it was of no use ; but her heart was with her child. . Though a weak woman in some respects, she was all right upon this point.   Experience had taught her the lesson, that wealth alone can not bring happiness. She had, in her girlhood, loved one who was considered beneath her, — had given him up, and married to please her parents, while her heart cried out at the sacrifice ; consequently, her life had been one of endurance, instead of happiness.   Under the influence of such a memory, she hoped, in her secret soul, that Alice would not yield, as she had done.

Her husband seemed to. feel something of this ; for, suddenly facing her, he said, " Wife, if I know of your countenancing that girl in her folly, you will go too ; for I will not be defeated in this thing, — I tell you I will not."

Mrs. Vale had never seen her husband in quite such a state of excitement ; and it alarmed her.   She hastened to quiet him, by giving him every assurance in her power that she would do nothing to thwart, but what she could to aid him.

Alice was an unintentional listener to the above conversation between her parents ; and she laid her plans accordingly.   She watched Mr. Sawtelle closely ; taking care, at the same time, not to give him the least encouragement.   It was not long before she perceived that he was interested : so much so that the love-light began to flash from his eye at her approach ; and she felt that it would not be long ere he would ask her father for permission to address her.   And then another note found its way into the han's of John Shepherd.   It ran thus, —

DEAR JOHN, — The crisis must come. If Mr. Sawtelle asks my father for my hand (as I feel that he
will), and I refuse, his anger will be terrible. I had
hoped, by quiet waiting, to soften down his opposition
to our union : but I see that it is useless ; and the best
thing that can be done is to put it beyond his power to
separate us. Have every thing in readiness, and meet
me at Edward Winchester's to-morrow evening at eight
o'clock, or. half-past. Be very cautious in your movements ; for, if discovered before it is too late, father will
stop at nothing that in his estimation would effectually
prevent our marriage.

Faithfully yours,   ALICE.

This note found its destination in the same way that
the first one did. Shepherd, of course, retired as soon
as possible, in order. to ascertain its contents. Holten
was watching him, for he suspected what was going on.
Not that he cared ; but, as I have said, he had a purpose
of his own to serve. The first one John had put into
his mouth ; and, having been ejected therefrom in the
manner related, Holten had got possession of it. And,
though so mutilated that it could not be read, there were
two words, that, when examined closely, were quite
legible ; and they were, " Destroy this."

With this, the second one, Shepherd was even more
unfortunate. " I will see this time," said he to himself,
" that it is fully destroyed ; " and, lighting a match, he
set it on fire. Just at this moment Holten called, —

" Shepherd, Shepherd, come here, quick ! " John,
thinking the paper beyond recovery, dropped it upon the
stove, and hastened to see what was wanted.

" Oh, you are too late ! they have gone around the corner."

" Who ? "

" Why, the oddest-looking couple that you ever saw : I should think they had just come out of Noah's Ark."

" Who is it that you are speaking of ? I saw no one of that description," said the other clerk, who was standing outside of the door at the time.

" Oh ! you never see any thing, old Sobersides," replied Holten laughing. He then managed to get the two into earnest conversation, when, slipping into the back room, he found the piece of burnt paper upon the stove-hearth. He gathered it up quickly but carefully, and placed it in his pocket-book ; and, taking another piece, lighted it, and, putting it exactly on the spot from which he had taken Alice's note, watched it till it was consumed.

He had barely left the room when Shepherd returned. Seeing the ashes of burnt paper lying where he had left paper burning, he supposed that all was right, and gave no further thought to the matter.

Holten, as soon as he had the opportunity, examined that which he had saved, and found only these words legible : " Be very cautious in your movements ; for, if discovered " —

" I'm in luck," said he to himself, as he put it carefully aside.

It was less than a week after these events, that Sawtelle sought Alice for the purpose of asking her to be his wife. She read his purpose in his eye, as he approached her, and sought to avoid him.

" Do not turn from me, dear girl," said he. " I have

the permission of your parents to address you; and it only needs that you consent to be mine to make me the happiest of men."

"I am sorry to disappoint you, Mr. Sawtelle; but what you ask can never be," she replied calmly but firmly.

"Oh, do not say that! Take back your cruel words," he exclaimed, with a passionate earnestness that fairly startled her. Still, her self-possession did not forsake her; and she answered as calmly as before, —

"It would be cruel for me to say otherwise, or in any manner to give you the least hope. Mr. Sawtelle, I have striven to avoid this; for it is not a pleasant position for me to be placed in. The thought of giving you pain is, of itself, painful, for I know of no one that I more fully respect; but added to this is my father's certain displeasure, — a displeasure so deep that I expect he will forbid me his house, perhaps disown and cast me off for ever. Indeed, sir, you are not the only sufferer."

"But why need either of us suffer?"

"Mr. Sawtelle, would you take to your bosom an unloving wife?"

"I certainly should not wish to; but why not give me a chance to win your love?"

"I have none to give you, for it is bestowed upon another."

"Irrevocably?"

"So irrevocably that nought but death can separate us."

"Nothing but death?" said the young man, with a look of inquiry.

"Those are the conditions of marriage, — are they not?" she asked.

"You do not mean to tell me that you are married, Miss Vale!"

"I do," she replied.

The young man covered his face with his hands, and groaned aloud; while Alice, feeling that her presence was no longer needed, sought her room, and began to make preparations for the storm of wrath that she knew must so soon burst upon her.

Her first impulse was to tell her mother; but, on second thought, concluded that it was not best to trouble her sooner than was necessary. Quickly packing her best clothing and a few choice keepsakes into as small a compass as possible, she dropped them out of the window into the back-yard; and then, descending thither herself, she hid them in a safe place in the loft of the stable: "For," said she to herself, "father will be so angry that he will not permit me to take a thing, and mother will not dare to interfere in my behalf." This done, she sat down to wait the course of events.

In the mean time, Mr. Sawtelle, having recovered somewhat from the shock that her announcement gave him, began to make preparations for his departure to the city; and Mr. Vale, coming home earlier than usual, found him thus employed.

"What does this mean, Robert?" he asked.

"It means that there is no hope for me."

"She has not refused you?"

"She has."

"Tut, tut, man: you are too easily disheartened. Wait: she will come to terms yet." He had forced himself to speak calmly; but the flash of his eye, and the palor about his lips, told of the storm within.

The young man looked up, and opened his lips to speak: then, as if upon second thought, closed them again, and went on with his work.

"What is it, man? speak out."

Sawtelle shook his head; but, upon further importuning, said, —

"You must learn it sooner or later, Mr. Vale: she tells me that she is already married."

Had an earthquake opened at his feet, or a thunderbolt exploded in their midst, the effect could not have been more startling than was this announcement upon Mr. Vale.

He reeled as though struck by a heavy blow, staggered to the nearest seat, and fell rather than sat down. "Married!" he repeated, like one bewildered, — "married!"

"That is what she told me," answered Sawtelle, forgetting his own disappointment in pity for the father.

However, this mood lasted but a minute; and then anger took the sway. "The disobedient jade!" he exclaimed. "I told her I would do it; and I will. This is no longer a home for her." And going immediately to her room, he confronted her with, —

"Alice, are you a married woman?"

"I am, father."

"Leave this house, then, and never dare to enter it again."

"I will obey you, father, until you see proper to recall your stern mandate," said she, commencing to gather up her things.

" Not a thing, — not a thing, — my lady.   Go as you are, and let the beggar you have married provide for you."

" Would you have me go bareheaded through the streets, father ? "

" What is that to me ? you are no longer a child of mine."

Alice paled. She had expected this, but the reality was worse than the anticipation. Forcing a calmness she did not feel, she turned, and walked out of the room and down the stairs. Her father followed her ; and, as she was about to go into her mother's room, he said, " Not there ! not there ! " pointing at the same time to the outer door.

This last act aroused her anger. What ! not even permitted to speak one farewell to her mother? With flashing eye, she confronted him. " You will regret this, sir, when it is too late ; " then, with a firm step, she walked out the front door, down the walk, through the gate, into the street.

Mr. Vale watched her till he saw the gate closed behind her, and then he sought his wife's room. " Mrs. Vale," said he, in a tone which showed that he thought she derived all her importance from the fact that she was Mrs. Vale, — " Mrs. Vale," — then pausing till he could get her eye fully, — " did you know aught of this ? " he continued.

" Know aught of what ? " she asked wonderingly.

" Did you know that Alice was married ? "

" Married : no, it can't be possible ! When ? where ? "

" I did not ask her when, nor where. It was enough that she acknowledged the fact. It is well for you that you had no hand in it, or I would have sent you after her."

" After her? where is she? "

" In the street; and she will stay there unless she finds shelter elsewhere."

Mrs. Vale arose to her feet. For the first time in her married life, her spirit was fully aroused. Walking up to her husband, she laid her hand on his arm, and, looking him full in the face, she said, —

" William Vale, you have not turned our child, our only one, into the street? "

" I certainly have; and you will follow her if you are not careful."

" As I certainly shall if you do not recall her."

This was more than the man had dreamed of. Not only had his child defeated his plans, but his wife defied him, — the woman who had always submitted to his will, and from whom he had expected only submission, — that woman was daring to have a will of her own.

" William," said she, seeing him hesitate, " I have always been a good, faithful wife to you, as you well know; and have I no rights here that you are bound to respect, that you should thus turn our child, my child, from our door, without permitting her even to see her mother? Surely, it is not your own proper self that acts: you are blind with excitement. Oh, say that you will recall her before this thing goes any further! "

" Recall her, — never? " he fairly shouted. " You are just fit, both of you, to go out lecturing upon woman's rights; and I'll have no such fanatical nonsense about my house. Why didn't you say *my door*, as well as *my child?* "

" Mr. Vale, you say *my house ;* and, if man and wife
are one, I have as good a right to say it as you: but I
ask once more, and for the last time, will you permit
our child to return ? "

" And for the last time, madam, I tell you I never
will."

" Then I, too, shall go ; but first I will tell you that
which I never intended to reveal to any one, much less
to yourself. William Vale, you have, for the most
part, been a kind husband, as the world calls kindness.
When one has their own way, it is easy to be good ; and
you have always had it as far as I am concerned : but
had I been as true to my own heart as our child has
been to hers, I had never married you.

" I followed the wishes of my parents, instead of my
own ; and oh ! how many, many times during the first
years of our marriage, did I say to myself, ' If I had it
to do again, my hand should go with my heart. I had
sealed my own fate, however ; and there was no going
back from the sacrifice I had made : but our child has
been firm, and from my inmost soul I am glad of it."

" And pray who was it upon whom you had placed
your virgin affections ? " asked he with a sneer.

She looked at him a moment, as if debating the question, and then replied, " Robert Sawtelle's father ; and
now farewell, for this is no place for me after the revelation I have made." Saying this, she walked deliberately out of the room ; but, just as she had closed the
door behind her, her steps were arrested by the sound
of a heavy fall. On going back to learn the cause, she
found Mr. Vale lying upon the floor, with the blood gush-
ing from his nostrils. The excitement had been too in-

tense : nature had given way, and the strong man was prostrate.

The screams of Mrs. Vale brought the neighbors. The doctor was called ; but it was too late. He had broken a blood-vessel ; and Alice had not been absent more than three-quarters of an hour before she was summoned back to look upon her father's corpse.

CHAPTER VI.

TELLING TALES.

"Dead men can tell no tales," 'tis said;
When lo ! the voice of nature cries,
"Mistaken man, there are no dead."

AR away on the borders of some Western prairie, where to-day there is no habitation but such as the wolf or the fox, and kindred animals, furnish for themselves, to-morrow there may be a rude cabin, and the next day four or five; the next week a score; and, ere a year has rolled around, the wilderness of flowers will have given place to a wilderness of houses.

It is to such a place as this, — one that had sprung up almost in a night, but not, like Jonah's gourd, to wither in a night, — that I would now call your attention.

People were coming from all directions. North, South, East, and West, each furnished its quota. The shrewd Yankee, the phlegmatic Englishman, the lively Frenchman, the honest German, the witty Irishman, — all, all, from whatever source they came, — found a welcome here.

All, did I say? I am not quite so sure of that; for there was one, a motherless girl, who had journeyed from the hills of old Massachusetts to find a home in this Western city, who gave the good people thereof a great deal of uneasiness. There was nothing formidable in her appearance. Her mild blue eye gave no indication of evil: still, they were troubled at her presence, watched her closely, and said many things of her that had no foundation in truth.

Church-people asserted that she was in league with the Devil, or rather under his control; others that she was insane, or fast becoming so; still others, that she was a cheat, a sort of juggler, a hypocrite, one who pretended that which was not, or which had no other origin than her own cunning: in fact, the whole city was moved by the presence of this one feeble woman, and questioned one with another as to the result of her coming.

But what said she of herself? what was her testimony in the case?

Why, that she was a mediator, or medium of communication between the two worlds, — the physical and the spiritual; that those who once lived upon the earth, but are now in the world of spirits, — that such could control her person, take possession of her organs of speech, and talk with those who were still in the flesh.

Such was her claim; and such is the hunger of the masses for some knowledge of the great hereafter, for some word from the to them silent ones, that the anathemas of the church, the cry of Devil, the charge of insanity, nor the laugh of derision, often the most potent of all, could keep her rooms from being thronged. The Nicodemuses came by night; while sad, sinning, sorrowing ones — those who had little of the world's favor to lose — came boldly and at all hours;

and, like the Na zarene of old, she received them all.
And like him, too, she was scandalized for so doing.

Those who came by night were generally from the
churches. At one time it would be the minister, who,
sitting with closed doors, would apologize for the secrecy
desired, by saying, " I am willing to investigate this
subject, but do not wish to lose my influence over my
people ; and the masses are so easily prejudiced."   The
next evening, perhaps, or at some hour when they
thought they would not be seen, some of the members
would make their way thither with, —

" We want to understand this matter for ourselves ;
but don't say any thing about it, for I don't know what
our minister would think."

But of the many *séances* held, and the many convincing tests given of the reality of spirit presence, we
will look in upon, and make public, the occurrences of
but one evening.   It is a select circle of six that have
met.   They have sat together from time to time, till the
conditions of harmony have been established ; and, by
the especial request of the controlling spirit, some two
or three strangers have been admitted to the room.
Amongst these is an old man of perhaps sixty years of
age, who had come into the place that very day, and
was stopping at the house where the circle was held ;
and another, who had been in the city only a week, and
might have been five or six years younger.   Of the
first, those present knew absolutely nothing, but that he
had given his name as Waldo. The second one had
given a false name on purpose, as he said, to test the
matter.

There was still a third, a young man ; but with him

tl.ey were slightly acquainted. These were not in the circle, but only in the room. The circle was formed; the medium was controlled; and the very first movement she made was to rise from the table, take the attitude of a half-drunken bar-room bully, and pour forth a volume of oaths.

The members of the circle were astonished, for they had seen nothing of this kind before; while the strangers could hardly restrain their feelings of contempt; and he who had given a false name was heard to whisper, " That is the devil, I know."

And, indeed, it did look hard to hear the big oath coming from these lovely lips; but presently there was a change. The medium approached the gentleman who had given his name as Waldo, seeming desirous to speak to him, but afraid to do so; while the look was no longer bold and defiant, but that of a humble suppliant.

There was such an evident shrinking, that a member of the circle said, " You need not be afraid of that gentleman: speak to him if you wish."

Thus encouraged, the following conversation was held between the controlling spirit and the aged stranger: —

" Do you recollect keeping a public house in Cherry Green some years since, Mr. Waldo? "

" I do," was the reply.

" Do you remember a young man by the name of James Jordan, who used to visit your bar, and drink, not to drunkenness, but till so boisterous that you had to put him out? "

" I remember it well," said the old gentleman.

" Do you remember that your barns were burned shortly after, and you never knew who did it? "

6

" Certainly I do : that fire so nearly broke me up, that I have not recovered from its effects yet."

" Well, I am that young man," was continued, in tones of deep contrition : " I burned your barns. I have been in the spirit-world four years, and have been look-ing constantly for some means of reaching you, in order to confess my wrong-doing, and beg your forgiveness; for I could not get away from earth and earth-scenes, could not progress one step, till I had done so."

Deep solemnity had by this time taken the place of other feelings in the circle : while he who had sneered turned pale, even to the lips ; for his most secret thought was, " If they can come and confess their own sins, they can, if they choose, point out ours ; " and, as if in re-sponse to these thoughts, the medium turned directly toward him, and said, " Yes, they can."

There was silence for a few moments ; and then one of the circle said, " Compensation, compensation : as far as the condition of things make it possible, such seems to be the order of the universe. Never did I see such force in the words of Jesus, ' If thou bringest thy gift to the altar, and rememberest that thy brother hath aught against thee, go thy way, first be reconciled to thy brother, and then come and offer thy gift.' Never did I see such force in them as now. They seem to hold good of both worlds."

" But why," asked another, " was it necessary that the manifestation should commence as it did ? Why those oaths ? "

" We think there are various reasons for this; but we will question the spirit on this subject. James, can you tell us why this is ? " said the leader of the circle.

" I will try, sir. Did you never get to thinking so intently upon some exciting scene in your past life, that you seemed really to live it all over, even to the minutest incident ? "

" I certainly have ; and I think that most people have experienced the same," was the response.

" Do you not know, also, that those persons who can enter most fully into the feelings of those they represent make the best actors ? "

" True, true," was uttered simultaneously by some three or four.

" Well," continued the spirit, " the difference between us and actors is this : they act out the feelings of another through their own bodies ; we act out our feelings through the body of another. Now, it is a difficult matter for one to act through the body of another, as you can readily imagine ; and, to communicate what we wish, it becomes necessary that we go back and live over those scenes so thoroughly that we can send the same sensations through the body of the medium ; and, further, we are the more readily recognized by acting our own selves than by simple statements."

" That is true, as far as identity is concerned," said Mr. Waldo : " for another, who knew of the facts, might have made the same statement, and claimed to be the same person ; but it would take an accomplished actor to personate James Jordan as thoroughly as did the medium when she was first controlled."

" I thought you had not progressed, James," said another of the circle : " it seems to me that you must have learned considerable, to be able to explain this subject to us as you have "

"I said I could not progress till I had made all the reparation in my power : neither could I, in the common acceptation of the term; but, in order to communicate, I must learn to control for myself or have assistance. Now, my organization, my relation to the one wronged, and other conditions that I can not now explain, made it necessary for my best good that I should not have help : consequently I had to learn the law of control; and, having learned, can tell, as it was a characteristic of mine, that of being able to tell what I knew."

"That is true," said Mr. Waldo; "for it was a common saying, that Jim Jordan could tell all he knew, and more too."

"But I can not, in this case, see the force of the argument, that acting out his old character was better proof of his identity than his simple statement would have been; for who would be likely to confess to wrongs that he never did?" said the one who had given a false name.

"I would," said a voice that was the very expression of duplicity and meanness. All turned to look at the medium, and were surprised at the transformation. She had taken a seat, and was pegging away as if her life depended upon the immediate finishing of the work in hand, while her features were those of a little weazen-faced old man.

The young man, who was not a member of the circle, had not spoken until now; but, upon hearing this, he laughed aloud, and then asked, "Why would you do that, Bob?"

"Because I should like to fool the people. But who is it that calls me Bob? I would have you know, sir, that I am Roger Sherman, the most famous shoemaker that ever lived in this country."

" You are unfortunate, then, in your attempts to make yourself known : for I say that you are Robert Perigrene, my father's cousin, commonly called Bob ; and, when here, you were such a liar, that ' Lies as bad as Bob Perigrene,' was a common saying in the neighborhood; but what brought you here to-night ? "

" That man," was the reply, as the finger of the medium pointed toward the stranger with a false name. " I like good company, and thought I had a right to tell a lie as well as he."

The stranger turned very red in the face. " I will own," said he, " that I have not given my true name : still, I have seen nothing here to-night that is convincing to me ; for I do not know but there may be collusion. If they will tell me my true name, I will believe."

" No, you wouldn't," said Bob, in his own peculiar tones ; " but there is one here who says he will tell you when the lady comes."

" What lady ? "

" I don't know ; but she will come."

" When ? "

" I don't know that, either ; but I don't like this uniform, and I must leave."

" Why do you not like it ? "

" Because it is hard work to tell a lie in it : it wasn't made for such as me, and the truth will come out when I have it on. Good-by. If you want any shoes made, call on me, and they will certainly be done at the time promised ; for I never disappoint a customer."

This last caused a general laugh, while the influence

changed again. This time there was nothing said; but the medium seized a pencil and wrote, —

" Come here again when you return. — M. S." And handed it to the one who had asked for his true name.

" And who is M. S. ? " asked he, when he had read it.

Again the pencil was taken; and it was written, " You will know in good time." He seemed about to question further; but, at the moment, a. change went over his countenance, as though —

> Memory's cords were swept by hands unseen,—
> By hands that rudely tore aside the vail
> Which covered the forgotten past, —
> By him forgotten : God remembers all.

The influence now left the medium; and the circle was closed till the time appointed for another meeting.

The stranger last referred to left the next day to go still farther west : was absent for several months ; but, when he returned, he again sought the circle. What then occurred is reserved for a future chapter.

CHAPTER VII.

A RIFT IN THE CLOUD.

AVE you not seen, when the thunder had sped its bolt, the storm roll back from one side of the heavens, letting in the sunshine to build a rainbow bridge upon which hope could travel from one end of the earth to the other?

And thus it was with Alice for a few months after the death of her father. True, the storm was not past; pearly drops fell plentifully and often: but the beautiful reflection of as true a love as ever warmed the human heart arched the blackness that was past, and hope promised brightly for the future.

We find, however, that, in the physical world, sunshine and rain together indicate another storm, and that not far away; but we must not anticipate.

In a preceding chapter, we left Alice beside her father's corpse. Let us enter more minutely into the particulars of that sorrowful hour, that we may thus, one by one, trace the links that connected her life with the future.

Mrs. Vale was nearly frantic when she found that her husband was really dead. The temporary strength that had caused her self-assertion forsook her entirely, and she reproached herself most bitterly for the part she had acted.

"Oh! why," she moaned, " did I not suffer on in silence? It was not his fault that I married him, not loving him. I wronged him cruelly in so doing; and I deserved to suffer."

Alice was, as usual, self-possessed : still, her heart sank within her when she looked upon the result of her perseverance, of her assertion of her own personal rights ; but what she thus gathered of her mother's heart-history through the broken and half-incoherent sentences uttered in that hour of anguish made her feel that it was better, even thus, than that she had sacrificed herself and wronged another by entering into the holiest of life's relations in such a manner as would have made her whole life a living lie.

It was found, upon the examination of Mr. Vale's business affairs, that he was insolvent, or so nearly so that it would take every thing there was to meet the obligations against him. This was doubtless one reason why he was so intent upon a wealthy marriage for Alice. It was his last hope, — his *left bower ;* and, when she covered it with the *right* one of her own personal independence, the game was lost, and it was more than he could endure.

It was a sad thought to the affectionate but firm-hearted daughter, but still more sad to witness the condition to which his sudden death had brought her mother ; for living trouble is harder to be borne than that which death has placed beyond our reach.

Mrs. Vale was so completely broken down, so under the dominion of self-reproach, that it required all of Alice's tact and self-possession to keep that last scene in the room when Mr. Vale fell from being made public. John Shepherd, as the husband of Alice, as a matter of course, took charge of affairs; and, when all was settled, it was found that there was very little, except his own salary as a clerk, for the support of both Alice and her mother.

This troubled him: not on his own account; but he feared, that, with the mother also to care for, he should not be able to make both as comfortable as he would like. But Alice smilingly said, —

" Poverty is not the worst thing in the world, John. ' Better is a dinner of herbs where love is, than a stalled ox and hatred therewith.' If mother can have what she needs, I shall not care for myself."

" Bless you, my own dear wife ! " he replied ; " but when I think of the wealth that would have been yours had you married Sawtelle, I " —

" You wish I had married him," said Alice mischievously.

" No, no, not that ; for what would my life have been without you ! But surely I were a wretch, did I not feel that I could never sufficiently prize the love that chose poverty with me to wealth with him."

" Nonsense, John : don't go to getting up any heroics now. I am sure there was no great credit in taking that which I preferred when I had my choice," she replied, in a tone of deprecation that was perfectly enchanting to the young husband ; and, catching her to his heart, he exclaimed, —

" God do so to me, and more also, my darling wife, if I ever prove otherwise than a kind and faithful husband to you ! "

Edward Winchester and Addie stood their firm friends

in this their hour of trial ; and, after due deliberation, it was decided that it would be better for them to leave the place connected with such unpleasant associations, and start anew elsewhere.

Winchester had friends living in the village of Bates-ville, some fifty miles distant ; and through his influence a clerkship was secured for Shepherd in the largest store there, and at a better salary than he was getting at Brown's. In a few weeks, they were established in their new home, where Mrs. Vale, under the influence of new surroundings and new cares, became compara-tively cheerful, while Alice, but for the too recent sad memories, would have been as blithe as a bird.

An intimate friend of Shepherd's had taken his old place ; and, from the correspondence held with him and the Winchesters, they were kept well informed as to what was going on in Ellsville. Things prospered with them in their new home. Alice, by economy and indus-try, added to their weekly gains ; and, as the past slipped farther away, the present continued to grow brighter, till at length the dark cloud lay only on the confines of the horizon, — not even high enough for a background to the rainbow that was no longer needed.

But how often have we seen a storm, that had spent but a portion of its fury, pass on, only to return with redoubled violence ; and thus it was in their case. The dark cloud that " Crazy Pete " had told Alice of so long before had cast only a portion of its shadow upon her spirit : the depth of its blackness was yet to come.

The first indication she received that the " indigna-tion " was not past was in the steady failure of her mother's health. Mrs. Vale's nervous system had received such a shock that it could not recover its tone again. True, there was a temporary rally during the excitement consequent upon changing her residence, going among new scenes, making new acquaintances, &c.; but, this over, there came the reaction. It was so gradual, however, that Alice for a long time did not notice it; and, when she did, she would fain believe that it was nothing serious, — nothing but what medicine and tender care would relieve; but, when the doctor was spoken of to the invalid, she utterly refused to see him.

"It will do no good," she said: "he can not minister to a mind diseased."

"O mother!" said Alice, "why will you talk thus? You were not to blame; and the past can not be remedied."

"I was more to blame, my child, than you think. It is the last drop that makes the cup overflow; and, in my love for you, I forgot that he, too, had claims upon me. I know that he was doing wrong: but he was excited and bitterly disappointed; and what right had I, at such a time above all others, to tell him that I had perjured myself at the altar, — had given him my hand without my heart?"

"But you were excited, too, mother: why not make some allowance for yourself for doing wrong under excitement, as well as for others?"

"But mine was a life-long wrong, carefully concealed till the time that he could least bear it. O Alice! your father was not to blame in this: he did not know that he had wedded an unwilling bride. If I had only been firm, had been true to myself, he might have found one who did love him, and have been happy with her now."

" You are sick, dear mother, and your fancies are morbid: put such thoughts away from you, and all will yet be well." Mrs. Vale shook her head, but made no further reply; and from this time forth she sank rapidly.

About a week after this, Alice said to her husband one night, after her mother had retired, " I think, John, that we had better call the doctor for mother, even if she is not willing; for she is failing so fast I fear that we shall not keep her long unless something can be done for her."

" Certainly, certainly, wife : I should have called one before now had the matter rested with me."

" Then stop on your way to the store in the morning, and request Dr. Wilson to step in some time in the course of the day," said Alice, in conclusion ; and then other subjects of conversation were introduced.

Upon retiring for the night, she went, as usual, to her mother's room to see if any thing was needed. Upon speaking to her, however, she received no reply. As she lay with her face turned away, Alice thought that she was asleep ; and, not liking to wake her, left without further effort at getting a response. In the morning she went again to her room ; but, upon opening the door, she found that her mother was lying exactly as she was the evening previous. With trembling steps, and a terrible fear at her heart, she went to the bedside to find but the cold form from which the spirit had fled.

She had evidently been dead for several hours : her cheek rested upon her right hand, and a pleasant smile showed that there had been no struggle.

I will not attempt to portray the grief of Alice at the loss of this, her only remaining parent.

"O John! I have no one but you now," said she, as she lay sobbing upon his breast; and he only kissed her in reply, for his heart was too full for speech.

They took the body back to Ellsville, and laid it beside that of her husband. As they were passing Brown's store, Holten, the clerk before spoken of, was standing in the door, and remarked to some one within, and loud enough for Alice to hear, —

"Miss Alice has had her own way, and has killed both of her parents by the means." It was too much for the stricken one; and she fainted. Shepherd made no remark at the time, but called upon Holten before leaving the place, and, referring to the circumstance, said, —

"You will see the day, sir, that you will be sorry for that remark."

Holten smiled maliciously, and asked, "When you are inside the walls of a prison?"

"You are too contemptible for chastisement," said Shepherd, as he walked away.

"What do you mean by that, Holten?" asked the clerk who had taken Shepherd's place in the store.

"That is my business," was the curt reply; and, taking his hat, he left the store. Brown, the merchant, came in soon after, when Taylor, the clerk before spoken of, asked, —

"What is the matter with Holten, that he is so spiteful toward Shepherd and his wife?"

"I don't know, unless he wanted Alice himself," replied Brown.

"That may be," said Taylor smiling, and made no further remark : but he did not forget; for, taken in connection with some events that had already transpired, but which we have not as yet related, he feared that there was trouble ahead.

CHAPTER VIII.

MIDNIGHT BLACKNESS.

" The night cometh, and also the morning."

HEY called you crazy, Peter, because you saw too much, because your spiritual eyes were open; but did the cloud that you beheld in the distant horizon of your playmate and companion fling no shadow upon your spirit? Or was it the shadow that was cast upon you from before birth which gave you clearer vision to penetrate the future?

Be that as it may, the cloud grows blacker, and the midnight deepens over the pathway of our Alice. Kind spirits of love, are you watching? will you sustain her when the surges of the tempest would flood her soul?

Cheerful, yet saddened, the bereaved ones went back to their lonely home, and again adjusted themselves to the tasks of duty and of love. Each was all to the other now, for Mr. Shepherd had been an orphan from boyhood; and each strove, with love's purest intent, to fill the needs of the other's being.

A lonely day had given place to the softened glory of the brightest of nights; the duties of the evening were done; John Shepherd and his wife were sitting together, talking of the past and planning for the future, when a rap at the door indicated that others were near.

"I wonder who it can be at this hour," said Alice, while John went forward to ascertain. Upon looking out, he saw three men, strangers, standing together upon the step.

"What is wanted, gentlemen?" he asked.

"Are you John Shepherd, formerly clerk in E. P. Brown's store in Ellsville?" said one of the party; and, as he did so, he made a step forward, when Shepherd saw that he wore an officer's insignia.

"I am," was the reply.

"Then, sir, you are my prisoner," said he, placing one hand upon John's shoulder.

"Prisoner!"

"Yes: will you go with me peaceably?"

"Certainly, but upon what charge am I arrested?"

"Upon the charge of embezzling from your employer, in person while there, and since then through the aid of, and in conjunction with, Robert Taylor, who took your place when you left, and who is now under arrest."

"When, and by whom, was this charge first concocted?" asked Shepherd indignantly.

"Young man, I can not stop to argue with you," said the sheriff: "it is my business to take you back to Ellsville. You will there be tried, and, if innocent, will most likely be able to make it appear. Will you go with us quietly, or shall we have to use force?"

"I have told you already what I would do, and I see no cause for insult, sir; but will you walk in, gentlemen, while I get my hat and overcoat, and speak a word with my wife. O God! how can I tell her?" he groaned inwardly.

But of this last there was no need, for Alice had heard every word.

With firm tones, though blanched cheek, she now stepped forward.

" You will take me too ? " she said.

" We can not, madam : we have orders for only your husband."

" Orders that you shall permit no one to accompany him ? " she questioned.

" Not exactly that," was the reply ; " but a press of other business makes it necessary that we should ride all night. And, besides, we have no comfortable conveyance for a lady, and no room in it if we had : there are seats but for four."

"" Enough," she replied. " I see that you do not want me along; but my place is beside my husband, and I shall go." And, whispering a word in John's ear, she threw a shawl over her shoulders, and started for the street.

" Don't go to-night, Alice," he said : " wait till morning, and I will not object."

" I shall go to-night," was her firm response. " Do you think I could stay here quietly till morning, and live?" And, hurrying quickly forward, she soon reached the only livery-stable in town. The keeper was just about to close it for the night, when she accosted him with, —

" Mr. Jennings, for the love of Heaven, furnish me a horse, buggy, and driver, to go to Ellsville with, as soon as possible ; and here is my watch and chain to secure you for the payment till I return."

" What in the world is the matter, Mrs. Shepherd ?

is anybody dead or dying?" asked the man in astonishment.

"No: but be quick; for there will be if they take
away my husband, and I can't go too."

Jennings looked into her face, and, seeing the terrible
earnestness depicted there, called to the boy to harness
as quick as possible, while he questioned further, —

"What are they taking your husband away for?"

"Upon the charge of robbing his former employer;
but, for Heaven's sake, don't detain me a moment!
Send the horse around to our gate as soon as possible,
and I will go and get ready."   And away she went with
the speed of a deer, reaching her own home just as the
sheriff and his posse were about to start.

"I shall be right after you, John," said she, kissing
her hand to him.   "Keep up good courage ; for, if there
is such a thing in the world as justice, you will soon be
free."

They had not gone more than two miles when Alice
overtook them; and, after that, she kept close behind
them the most of the way.   Notwithstanding their
haste, with bad roads, and stopping a few hours for rest,
they did not reach Ellsville till toward evening of the
next day.   When they were within six or seven miles
of town, Alice drove ahead, and had the Winchesters
apprised of what was going on.   As she passed the store,
Holten saw her, and seemed much surprised ; but, as
her clear, full eye met his, his countenance fell, and,
with a muttered curse, he turned away.

It will be necessary, here, to go back a little, and explain some of the causes that led to this arrest; and, to
do so fully, we must give something of Holten's history
ere he came to Ellsville.

He was the illegitimate child of a gentleman of leisure, who lived by his wits, and inherited both the expertness and duplicity of his father. He had lived in the city till he was twenty-one years of age, and in that time had acquired just that kind of education that Christian cities furnish for their outcast sons. He had often been caught in petty scrapes, and as often suspected of more grave offenses, but always managed to escape any serious punishment. But at length, becoming more bold in crime, he essayed his hand at forgery, and came so near being caught, that he resolved to quit for ever the scene of his old haunts, seek some retired place, and see what fortune would do for him in the way of his earning an honest living.

In pursuance of this resolution, he had come to the little village of Ellsville, some three years previous, and taken up his abode there. He had enough of his ill-gotten gains left to support him, till, by his suavity of address, pleasing manners, and a well-concocted account of his previous life, he secured the position of clerk in the store of E. P. Brown, who was the largest merchant and one of the most influential men in all that region of country.

This situation secured, and all was clear before him; at least, so he thought: but there is no condition in life for either man or woman, in which they will not be *tried;* and that is not virtue which does not stand the test. All went well with him till he saw Alice Vale; but, from that moment, his bosom was torn with a feeling to which he had hitherto been a stranger. To become acquainted with and win her for his wife was now the sole thought that occupied his mind; but, when he found that his fellow-clerk was the favored one, hatred took possession of his soul, and from that hour he resolved to accomplish the ruin of John Shepherd.

He had learned the relation in which John and Alice stood to each other before he had made his own feelings known ; and he understood human nature too well to think for a moment that one like Alice could be won from her allegiance. There was no hope for him only in vengeance upon the innocent rival who had won her heart before he had had the opportunity of doing so.

The pure instincts of Alice's soul would have prevented his success, even had her affections been unengaged ; but this he could not know. He had not, as yet, learned that there were those from whom he could not be hidden, let him cover himself ever so deeply.

Resolved on the wrong, there was not long wanting the occasion. The incident of the note suggested the first step in his afterward matured plan for success ; and, from that time forth until he left the store, William Holten hovered, like the shadow of the imp of darkness, over every movement of John Shepherd's.

From the getting possession of that first note, and finding those few legible words thereon, he had commenced a system of embezzlement from the money-drawer, resolving, when the right moment arrived, to fasten suspicion upon Shepherd, and use this, in connection with whatever else he could gather, toward insuring his conviction.

The sums taken were at first small and infrequent, but so planned, that, suspicion once aroused, they could be readily disco ered. These sums were gradually increased, both in size and frequency as though the perpetrator, in the absence of discovery, was growing bolder in crime.

When John and Alice were married, and left the place, this at first disconcerted, but upon further thought really facilitated, Holten's plans: for he had only to make it appear that Taylor was an associate, and that it was he who had written the notes that had enjoined care for fear of discovery; and, for this purpose, he took to copying Taylor's handwriting.

He was naturally good at imitating; and it was not long till he had succeeded so perfectly, that Taylor himself would not have suspected the difference, had something that he had really written been presented to him after it had been copied by Holten. This done, he next took those remnants of notes, and, by careful efforts, succeeded, at length, in substituting others in their place, so chewed and burned that the difference could not have been told between them and the originals, only that the legible words in the copies were in the handwriting of Taylor, instead of the feminine one belonging to Alice.

Beside, as is always the case, there were many little incidents, nothing in themselves, but weights when put into the balance of suspicion. And, added to all, was a note of his own preparing, kept to be left, as if by accident, where Brown would be certain to find it when the right time came for putting his plans into execution. Upon these forged links, so connected with the accidental ones as to present one unbroken chain, did Holten depend for the success of his Satanic scheme.

The chain was complete, all but the hook; and the visit of the Shepherds to Ellsville at the time of the funeral of Alice's mother furnished the occasion for

forging that. Holten, as soon as he knew of their presence in town, took an unusually large sum from the
drawer, and was the first to miss and draw Brown's
attention to it. Brown had been in once that morning,
and gone out again; and, upon his return, Holten
asked, —

"Mr. Brown, have you taken a sum of money from
the drawer this morning?"

"I have not: why?"

"Nothing, only there is some missing; but perhaps
Taylor knows where it is."

"Where is Taylor?"

"He went out a few minutes ago with Shepherd."

"Yes: I heard that Shepherd was in town," said
Brown, and then added, "I presume Taylor has paid
out the money, for there were some small bills due
to-day."

"Perhaps he has," was Holten's reply. "He could
have done so without my noticing it, for I have been
very busy."

Taylor returned in about half an hour; and, soon
after, the bills that Brown had spoken of were presented
for payment.

"How is this, Taylor?" said his employer: "I supposed that these were paid?"

"What made you think they were paid?" asked
Taylor.

"Why, Holten said that there was some money gone
from the drawer; and we concluded that you had paid
it out."

"No: I have paid out no money. I have had no
occasion to pay out any," said Taylor, looking a little
surprised.

" I must look into this : how much is there missing, Holten ? " said the merchant with a look of anxiety upon his face.

" Fifty dollars. Smith paid it in last night just before we closed."

" Are you certain that you did not put it in some other place ? "

" I am. Taylor saw him pay it to me, and saw where I put it."

" Yes," said Taylor: " I remember it the more particularly, as he paid me fifty at the same time ; and I noticed that the bills were of the same denomination, and upon the same bank, as those paid to Holten."

" Was he owing you ? " asked Brown.

" Yes, for money borrowed three months ago."

" I fear we have a thief amongst us," said the merchant: " did you take the numbers of the bills, Holten ? "

" I did: I have been in the habit of doing so when any bill as high as five dollars was paid in, ever since there has been so much counterfeit money afloat."

" That is well: perhaps we may be able to trace them, and catch the rogue."

" I hope so," said Taylor ; " for, if there is any thing that I despise, it is a thief."

" And so do I, " said Holten, " Still, when I think of the suffering thus caused to friends and relatives, I almost wish that the guilty could escape for the sake of the innocent."

" A sentiment very creditable to the heart : but it will not do for the head in the present state of society," said Brown, as he took the number, date, and denomination of the bills in question, from Holten's memorandum, preparatory to going out for the purpose of instituting measures that should lead to the detention of the guilty party.

Holten had noticed the evening previous, that, with the exception of dates and numbers, the bills paid to Taylor were the same as those paid to him for Brown, and had said to himself, " Here is just the trap I need, if I can only set and spring it aright." It was his intention to get hold of Taylor's pocket-book, and, taking his, substitute the ones of which he had taken the numbers and dates ; but, as yet, he had had no opportunity.

He had accomplished enough that morning, however, to make him think it safe to speak to his employer ; for when Shepherd came in, and asked Taylor to give him two fives and a ten for a twenty, after the change had been made, he had said, " Let me look at those bills, Shepherd."

Taking them in his hand, and examining them a moment, he looked at Taylor with, " Those that Smith paid you last night ? "

" The same," said Taylor.

They are upon the same bank that those were he paid me," remarked Holten carelessly, handing back, as the other supposed, the same money. But, in the mean time, it had been changed ; and, all unconscious of wrong, Shepherd carried away three of the missing bills. The next night, Holten succeeded in getting hold of Taylor's pocket-book, and the balance of the exchange was made.

Shepherd had paid out a portion of his — a ten and a five — to Winchester. Indeed, it was for this very purpose that he had had his larger bill broken; and, the morning after he left, Taylor paid out ten dollars of that which was in his possession to a farmer from the country. He took it home, and paid it to a neighbor; and that neighbor came back the very next day, and paid it into Brown's own hands. This, being traced up, led to the arrest of Taylor; and Winchester, the morning after paying out that which he had received from Shepherd into the hands of one of the parties that Brown had set upon the watch, caused his suspicion to be turned in that direction; but Holten said,—

"I can't believe it possible, Mr. Brown, that Shepherd is guilty. I saw Taylor pay him some money, and I think this must be a portion of it:" at the same time, however, he managed that the letter he had so artfully concocted should fall into Brown's hands.

"Somebody has lost a letter," said the merchant, picking it up from the end of the step at the front door of the store, where it lay with pieces of loose paper, and all seemed to have fallen there as if by accident.

Holten looked up. "Is it sealed?" he asked, at the same time putting his hand to his own pocket, as though he feared that it was his.

Brown laughed aloud. "Been writing a love-letter," said he, "and was afraid you had lost it?" And then, looking at the letter in his hand, he continued, "Yes: it is sealed, and directed to John Shepherd; but it has not been mailed, and, as I live, it is Taylor's handwriting. I must see what is in this!"

The result of the reading of that letter was the arrest of Shepherd. That evening Holten said, "Had we not better look over the books, Mr. Brown: perhaps this thing has been going on longer than we think."

The merchant readily consented; and Holten, giving him the clew so cunningly that he never suspected but that he had discovered it himself, he traced it back to the very first petty sum taken. The next morning Holten made up a bundle of his old clothes, and desired the errand-boy of the store to take them to a poor woman up town, handing him a dime to pay him for his trouble

"Wait a moment," said he, as the boy was about to start: "I believe I have not looked in all of the pockets; and, taking them from the boy's hand, he looked them over one after another. "There is nothing," said he; "but I always like to be certain," turning towards Brown as he spoke, as though half excusing himself for being so particular. He was about to relinquish the bundle into the hands of the boy again, when he drew it back with, "Hold — here is a pocket I had not seen; and, thrusting his hand into it, he drew forth the copied remnants of the notes that Alice had sent to John more than a year before. Glancing at them, he laughed, and said, "The fragments of those notes, — I had forgotten all about them."

"What notes?" asked Brown.

"Don't you recollect the time we had with Shepherd, when he coughed, and threw that piece of paper from his mouth; and I picked it up, telling him that he was in a great strait if he could not get enough of his love-letters without eating them; and the other one is the remnant of one that I saw him set on fire, and throw down on the stove-hearth, a short time afterward."

" How happened you to keep them ? "

" To tease him about ; but his speedy marriage and old Vale's tragic death put an end to that."

" Let me see them, will you ? "

Holten handed them to the merchant, with a countenance as innocent as that of an angel. Surely, if ever mortal stole " the livery of the court of heaven to serve the Devil in," he had.

Brown looked at the scarred and mutilated remains a moment, and then, turning to Holten, said, " More evidence."

" More evidence ! how, sir ? " said Holten, in a well-feigned tone of surprise.

" Who do you suppose wrote this ? "

" I am sure I do not know ; but I always supposed it was Alice, and that was why I wished to tease him."

" But why should she be so careful about discovery ? "

" On account of her father's opposition. I tell you, Mr. Brown, Mr. Vale would have stopped at nothing that would have separated them ; and Alice knew it," said Holton earnestly.

" But Alice never wrote this. Look at the handwriting, and see if you don't know whose it is."

Holton took the papers from Brown's hand, and looked at them carefully. " It is Taylor's," said he ; " but I had never thought of such a thing."

" I wonder that you did not recognize it before."

" You know, Mr. Brown, that I was not familiar with Taylor's handwriting at the time ; and I hardly looked at them now before I gave them to you, sir."

" True," said Brown. " I had forgotten that Taylor did

not come here till after Shepherd left; but it really seems providential that these fragments should turn up just at this time."

" Providential! " yes, in the same sense as that of the ancient Jew, when he said, " Is there evil in the city, and the Lord hath not done it? " Surely, it needs the light of eternity to illuminate the dark places of this life.

And thus the evidence accumulated. A portion of the missing money was traced to those two men, and the remainder was found upon their persons. Taylor and Shepherd were fast friends; had long been known to be such; and, when Shepherd left Brown's employ, it was through his influence that Taylor had secured the place.

The letter found had the appearance of being written with the intention of sending it to Batesville by mail: but it had not been mailed; and the supposition was, that, upon Shepherd's coming to the place, Taylor had handed it to him, and he had dropped it. This letter was so written, that, in connection with other events, it revealed what it seemed intended to conceal from all but the parties themselves. A stranger could have understood nothing from its contents.

And, lastly, these fragments. It seemed to the prisoners at the bar, as they listened to all this testimony, that the prince of darkness himself could not have concocted a more thoroughly connected chain. They felt morally sure that Holten was at the bottom of it; and yet there was not a single circumstance by means of which they could make others think so.

The evidence was so strong, that no one but Winchester and his wife doubted their guilt; and even they hardly knew what to believe. Of course they were convicted, and sentenced to prison. Words would be useless in attempting to portray the agony of Alice; still, she restrained every expression of it, further than what her compressed and bloodless lips would betray· for, with woman's instinct, she not only felt that this was Holten's work, but she felt the why; and she determined that he should not have the triumph of seeing any manifestation of weakness on her part.

She kept up bravely also in the presence of her husband. "He has enough to bear," she said to Addie Winchester, "without my adding to his load." "There will be a righting to this wrong sometime, my husband," were almost her last words, ere he started on his way to Albany; "and we shall not be wholly separated, for I shall follow you soon, shall stay in the vicinity, and see you as often as possible.'

"God bless you, my own sweet wife! it is my greatest comfort that you believe me innocent," said he, speaking as calmly as his emotion would permit.

"Not so great as the consciousness that you are so," she replied smiling.

"Your approval would not only be worthless, but torture, without that: your innocent confidence would be a greater reproach to me than even the crime itself." And thus each sustained the other, with loving words and noble sentiments, till the hour of parting came. Alice then returned to her home, boxed up her bedding and such other things as she could keep best, sent them to Ellsville, to Winchester's, for safe-keeping, disposed of whatever else there was to the best advantage she could, and putting the money on interest, all but a few dollars for present need, she started for the city whose limits held the gloomy prison-walls that had shut her husband from the outer world ; and here, for the present, we will leave her.

CHAPTER IX.

GOD'S ELECT.

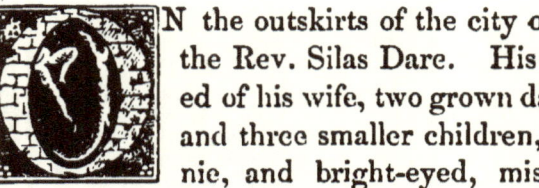N the outskirts of the city o. Albany lived the Rev. Silas Dare. His family consisted of his wife, two grown daughters, a son, and three smaller children, — Susie, Jennie, and bright-eyed, mischievous little Eddie, aged respectively twelve, nine, and seven years.

Their home was a neat white cottage, very tastefully adorned, and standing in the center of a plot of ground laid off in walks, and filled with flowers and choice shrubbery, the whole of which was so artistically planned, and so well kept, that many a stranger, passing by other places of greater pretensions, would stop to admire this.

Mr. Dare, when he believed that at least half of the poor creatures who were confined within prison walls would finally become heirs of eternal torture, — objects of God's vengeance for ever; when he believed and taught the doctrines of election, reprobation, &c., — had been chosen, year by year, to act as chaplain for the prison; but now, when his ideas had become so enlarged as to believe that God would eventually wipe the tears from off all faces, the place was shut against him.

His organ of what phrenologists call human nature was large. He studied men and things closely; and his long experience with those who are held in bonds as criminals had convinced him that human justice is so short-sighted, so mole-eyed, that the innocent are about as often condemned as the guilty, and that, when otherwise, it was more often from weakness, from the force of circumstances, than from real wickedness, that the acts were committed which incarcerated their unhappy victims.

Largely sympathetic, he came at last to pity more than to blame even the worst offenders. The more closely he observed, the less sympathy he had with those lines of Young, —

> " From all beings but himself
> God hides that worst of sights,
> A naked human heart," —

till finally thus, step by step, he was led out of the great darkness that had hung so like an incubus upon his soul. He saw the way clear for all ; and not only that, but that all would at last find it. And, without a thought of worldly policy, he boldly proclaimed that which gave him so much joy ; for, in the earnestness and honesty of his own heart, he did not once imagine but that others would rejoice with him.

Alas ! he had not measured the strength of superstition and prejudice : he little anticipated the storm that was thus brought upon his devoted head. What had he done, that he should be disfellowshiped, cast out of the band of brotherhood where he had so long been a faithful worker ? What crime had he committed ? What moral law had he broken ? None, — not one ; but he had had the audacity to think for himself,

till so imbued with the spirit of Jesus, that he could say
from the heart, " Neither do I condemn thee : go and
sin no more ; " and the angel of progress, seeing this evidence of fitness, had touched his eyes with magnetic
fingers, causing him to see truths that they could not
see : therefore they thrust him out.   And this was well.
It is a law of nature, that those who are in advance
should move on and prepare the way for the coming
multitude.   But to Silas Dare it would have been quite
a serious affair, so far as a visible means of support was
concerned, had not a legacy of several thousands fallen
to his wife about this time.

The sun had set on a beautiful October day, and the
stars were shining as only stars can at that season of the
year, when a lady, simply but neatly attired, rang the
bell at the door of Mr. Dare's pleasant cottage.   It was
opened by the tidy servant.

" Does the Rev. Silas Dare reside here ? "

" He does."

" Will you please say that a lady would like to see
him."

" Any name ? " asked the thoughtful servant.

" None : I am a stranger," was the reply ; " but
stop : you may hand him this if you please," said she,
giving the servant what proved to be a letter of introduction.

" Very well : take a seat in the parlor, and I will inform Mr. Dare."

" The lady walked into the room indicated, took a
seat, and waited, — waited like one fully absorbed in
some painful subject ; for, though several choice pain t-
ings adorned the walls, and evidences of taste were upon

8

all sides, she never once glanced at any of them, but sat
with her head resting upon one hand, and the other
pressed tightly over her heart.   Presently, however, the
sound of footsteps aroused her to a sense of her present
condition.   The door opened; and with quiet grace she
arose to her feet, as a benevolent-looking gentleman ad-
vanced to meet her.

"Mrs. Shepherd, I am happy to meet you," said he,
frankly extending his hand.   "I have long and favor-
ably known your friends the Winchesters.   Indeed,
the old gentleman was a classmate of mine; and whoever comes from them is sure of a welcome in my
house."

"Thank you, sir," said Alice, scarcely able to suppress her emotions; for kindness more often touches the
fountain of tears than coldness or severity.

"Then one of those fine-looking fellows that was incarcerated here a few days since was your husband,"
said Mr. Dare, thinking that the sooner the trial of
speaking of this was over the better; and then, without waiting for a reply, he continued, —

"I was at the prison, and saw them when they were
brought in; and I told Mrs. Dare, upon my return home,
that, if ever innocent men were shut up within those
walls, they were such."

"Oh! thank you, sir: you" —; but she could say
no more: the fountain of tears was completely broken
up, and she wept and sobbed like a child.

"Weep away," said the good man, while a suspicious
moisture gathered in his own eyes, — "weep away: it
will do you good.   I will leave you to yourself a littl-,
till I prepare my wife and daughters for your acquaint-

ance : in the mean time, take off your things ; for you will not leave us to-night, and, if I mistake not, for many days to come. Your friends tell me that you wish a situation where you can support yourself and be near your husband ; and we need some one very much just now as governess for our three youngest children."

And thus did this man, who was considered no longer good enough to teach those who were deemed neither fit nor safe to mingle in society, — thus did he pour the oil of consolation into this bruised and almost broken heart ; and thus did Alice find a home, friends, and the tenderest sympathy, among strangers.

It was the custom of Mr. Dare to read a portion of Scripture each morning, and afterward to invoke the divine blessing upon himself and family. He had been educated to this ; had kept it up for many years ; and had, till recently, done so more from the force of habit than any thing else. But, having perused several progressive works of late, he was able to take a broader, a more extensive view of things : so much so, that what had once seemed to overshadow eternity, he now found touched only upon points of time. The significance of the present grew greater, — so much greater, that it needed what he had once supposed referred only to a future world to meet the demands and explain the phenomena of to-day.

Under the influence of these awakened views, the chapter read from morning to morning assumed a new interest to him ; the pages of the Bible gleamed with a new light, which showed the darkness of the past, as well as of the present, — the dark chambers of its inspired minds, as dark where not illuminated as were the minds of those who made no such claims. Thus he thought, not realizing that the light came from his own soul, — that all things are dark to him whose eyes are closed.

Some six weeks after Alice came there, the morning lesson was the eighth chapter of Paul's Epistle to the Romans : and, in the remarks made, the doctrine of election very naturally came up for discussion.

" If these, and similar texts taken to prove the doctrine of election, really referred to an eternal life beyond the grave," said Mrs. Dare, " what thinking being could look upon God as other than an infinite tyrant ? "

" And still, wife, my observation goes to prove that every generally, or even largely received opinion has its foundation in truth ; and, such being the case, what think you, Mabel, is the real meaning of the term ' God's elect,' " said Mr. Dare, turning to his oldest daughter.

" I think, father, that the term, as it is now understood, has its foundation in man's ignorance," she replied.

" We are not speaking of the term as now understood, my daughter, but of the law in nature, the reflection of which has given rise to the idea."

" I think," said mild-eyed Maud, " that all are God's elect, each for the place they can best fill ; and the consciousness of this truth shining brighter in some souls than in others has led to the especializing of a universal principle."

" Pretty well expressed, little Maud," said her father ; " but I hardly think it will cover the whole ground."

" Father," said Susie, " every one can not be president, or there were no private citizens, no government: now, we elect our president, governor, and other officers of state; but that does not prove that those who are not elected are lost, cast out from the benefits of the government. And why may not God thus elect certain persons, or certain nations, to perform some important part in the economy of his government, and still hold all under his living care, as heirs to life eternal."

"Out of the mouth of babes and sucklings," murmured the mother; while the father said, "The best explanation I ever heard, Susie. William, have you nothing to say upon this question?"

"I was thinking, father," said the young man, "of the many examples we have of things that are alike being chosen for different purposes, and the different treatment to which they are subjected on that account. Take, for instance, a field of wheat: from the sowing to the harvesting, — yes, till after it is threshed, it is treated as one; but, after that, look at the difference. The largest portion is set apart for present use, but the best portion as seed for a future harvest. Now, that which is for present use could glory, were it conscious, in ministering to our wants; in finding a place upon our tables; resting upon china, perhaps as snowy biscuits; eaten by the *élite* of the land in the form of crust for the richly-made pie; or forming the substantial part of the delicate bride's cake, — places of honor all; — while that which has been selected for seed lies in darkness and silence, decaying, dying, that its fruit may appear in the future.

"Now, is it not thus in human life? Do not the greater portion of the race meet and mingle upon the

plane of the present, — some in high, and some in low
positions, even as flour from wheat is found in the poor
man's cot upon the wooden trencher, as well as upon
the millionaire's massive plate: and so of the human
masses ; each ministering, as they have the power, to
the needs of the sphere in which they are found. But
there is still another class, few in number, and not ap-
preciated in the present, because their work is not for
the present.

"Now, it seems to me, that, if there is a class upon
earth who can justly be called God's elect, these are
the ones."

"A good illustration, my son," said Mr. Dare : "still,
no one view, no one illustration, can cover the entire
ground.   Truth so pervades nature, that her shadow is
reflected from every point : but it is only the shadow ;
and we, as reasoning beings, must trace them to their
source to find the substance. Mrs. Dare, will you not
give us something·upon this question ? "

"I will try; but I do not think I can improve upon
what the children have said. I shall go to the forest
for my illustration. We find a great variety of trees
here ; and they can be put to a great variety of uses, —
uses that each shall fill in its own time. But the owner
desires to accomplish some especial object, — an object
in which some of this timber must bear a part; so he
goes through the forest, and elects, chooses, such trees
as will best suit his purpose, passing the others by.
Now, those that are chosen are not saved, nor the others
lost, in any true sense of that term."

"I think your illustration better than William's, wife,
from the fact that it can be carried out more fully. In

the grinding, the bolting, or, to make the application, the discipline, the suffering, come upon the wrong side."

" You think, then, that suffering in the present is the portion of the elect ? " said Alice, now speaking for the first time.

" I believe that ' whom the Lord loveth he chasteneth,' in the same sense that the man chasteneth the tree he has chosen. He needs it for a purpose : he sees within it that which will meet his need, but not in its present condition. Choosing it from the rest, he may, in a sense, be said to love it : still, the very next step is the ponderous axe cleaving its side, blow after blow, with no heed to its echoing groans, till it yields at last, and comes to the earth with a crash."

" O papa ! " said little Eddie, " if that is the way God loves people, I don't want him to love me ! "

The father smiled as he looked upon this, his youngest darling. " Did you ever draw your sled to the top of the hill for the sake of riding down upon it, my son ? "

" Oh, yes, papa, many a time : it is such fun."

" What, drawing the sled up the hill ? "

" No, not that : I don't like that part ; but the going down again, — oh ! it is so nice, and especially if the track is long and smooth."

"'The longer the track, the farther you have to walk and draw your sled."

" Yes ; but we don't mind that."

" Why ? "

" Why ! Because we are thinking all the time of the ride back, to be sure."

" Suppose that you did not know of the ride back ;

suppose the slide was upon the opposite side of the hill, and you could not know of it till you reached the top: what then ? "

" Indeed, papa, I think the sled would draw rather hard."

" Now, suppose the work to be done was ten, twenty, or even fifty times as hard, and you were told that you should be fully compensated, but how or when you could not know."

" Papa, may I answer that ? " said Jennie.

" Certainly, my child."

" We should have to believe, to walk by faith, or be very miserable."

" What, then, does faith save us from, present or future misery ? "

" From present misery, — does it not ? "

" It does, my child ; and yet the most of people believe that faith is necessary in order to salvation from eternal misery : but the teachings of nature are, that faith in the future is needed to secure, not future, but present happiness."

" This office of faith is so very plain that I don't see how any one can misunderstand it," said Mabel.

" Still, they do, as we have abundant evidence ; but have we not wandered from the subject ? I should like to have a more full application of these illustrations to the question of God's elect," replied Maud.

" Suppose you make the application yourself," said Mr. Dare.

" I would rather hear you, father ; for I think, from one remark you made, that you and I would agree : if your ideas differ from mine, I will give mine afterward. Please analyze William's first."

"Well, then, Miss Critical, the comparison of the wheat appears good on the surface, and is very suggestive : but, upon looking closer, we find that the field where the wheat is sown represents more properly the individual chosen to do a work for the future ; for, in the breaking up and tearing to pieces of the soil, we have a fit symbol of the trials, the discipline, to which such souls are sure to be subjected, while the wheat stands for the harvest of thoughts generated in their minds by these experiences, and brought forth to bless the world."

"Is that all, father ? "

"All that I have to say now, Maud : I wait for you."

"It seems to me that the seed-wheat poorly represent the thoughts of the world's great reformers, from the fact that a harvest is contemplated of the same kind and quality ; whereas, in the realm of mind, God chooses and prepares his agents for the especial purpose of their becoming channels through which broader, deeper, higher thoughts may flow from himself to the great heart of humanity."

"Little Sis," a term by which they called her, from the fact that sickness had checked her growth till her size did not correspond with her years: "Little Sis," said William, "I think I shall have to take lessons of you in logic ; but you must not, on that account, get strong-minded, and fancy that it is your business to go out and teach the world."

"'Must not ? ' Is not that strong language from pupil to teacher ? " said she archly.

"Well, please don't, then."

"And why not? I opine that I should find many people more ignorant than my brother ; and who knows but I am one of God's elect, chosen through suffering for this very purpose?"

This retort provoked a general laugh; which was changed, however, into the quiet, tender tear, as they looked upon her shrunken form and earnest face.

The moment's silence thus caused was broken by Mr. Dare's saying to Alice, —

" Mrs. Shepherd, will you not favor us by giving your opinion?"

" I am under the cloud," she replied, "and can not see clearly; therefore have none to give."

" Under the cloud, — under the cloud;" how those words lingered with her as an echo of the past! how they took her back to Pete, and the last conversation held with him!

Had he not said that she would yet see and hear, but there was a cloud between. A part of the prophecy had come true: why not the other?

CHAPTER X.

DESPAIR.

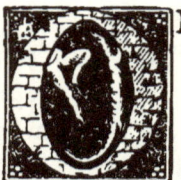NE morning, when Alice had been three months in Mr. Dare's family, Jennie came to her room with, —

"Mrs. Shepherd, there is a gentleman in the parlor who wishes to see you."

"To see me? Do you know who it is, Jennie?"

"I do not: he said he came from your old home."

Alice sat and thought a moment. "Jennie, please go and ask him to send up his name."

The child did as she was requested, and returned in a few moments with "William Holten, with best respects to Mrs. Shepherd," written upon a neat card.

Upon taking it into her hand, Alice felt a shudder running through her frame, and that before she had seen the name, as she herself wondered, as she thought of it afterward.

For a moment she hesitated, as if she dreaded to look: but, when she had read it, a cold, stern look settled upon her features; and, taking a pencil, she wrote underneath, "Mrs. Shepherd will be excused," and sent it for answer to the gentleman in waiting.

"I was frightened," said Jennie, in telling her sisters of the circumstance, "he looked so angry; ard, as he went down the steps, I heard him say, ' Curse her: she shall pay for this.'   Oh! I am afraid he w ll do our kind teacher some harm."

" Well, never mind repeating his bad words, but pray that good angels may watch over her," said the gentle Maud.

" That I do every night," replied the child; " for sometimes she looks so sad, that I fear she has something• to trouble her."

" Then we must try to make it up by being very kind; and I know that my little Jennie will be good, so as to give her as little trouble as possible."

" That I will, Sister Maud; for who could help being good, with you for a sister and her for a teacher? "

Maud kissed her lovingly, and said, " There, run away now, and see if mamma does not want you? "   Mr. Dare's younger children knew nothing of Alice's trouble, neither did their parents think it best that they should.

William Holten went from Mr. Dare's door almost choking with rage.   Naturally calm and cool, no matter how provoked, he was thus the more to be feared.   His self-possession was equal to Alice's, but used to compass evil ends; and thus even his anger generally partook more of the nature of steady heat intensified, than otherwise. But now his self-possession was so disturbed, that he could only find relief in revolving plans of vengeance.

" The proud, insulting jade," said he to himself: " I will compass heaven and earth but I will yet have her in my power."   Having a friend, an old crony, who occupied a post of trust in the prison, Holten went from Mr. Dare's directly thither; and the first thing he did on reaching it was to ask for John Shepherd and Robert Taylor.

He was left in the waiting-room while the officer in charge went for them. "I wonder," he soliloquized, "if they will treat me with the contempt that Miss Independence did? they had better not; they had better not." He had recovered his cool, calculating spirit, and, as far as the external went, was a very saint.

The appearance of the prisoners put an end to these cogitations. With his face covered with smiles, he arose, extended his hand, with, "How are you, boys: I am glad to see you, though I wish it could have been elsewhere."

"Is it you, Holten?" said Taylor, not noticing the extended hand; while Shepherd folded his arms upon his breast, and remained silent.

"Tut, tut: now, don't be holding a grudge against a friend for doing what he could not help. I am sure I would not have appeared against you could I have avoided it," said Holten, with one of his most winning smiles.

"Perhaps," said Shepherd sarcastically.

"Perhaps," repeated Holten. "I hope, John, you do not suspect me of lacking in friendship for you. I know that human nature is liable to err, and I should be sorry to cast off an old companion for one fault."

"Silence," thundered Shepherd: "don't come here calling yourself friend, and at the same time telling us that you believe us guilty;" and then, turning with the dignity of a king to the officer in charge, he said, —

"Will you conduct us back to our places?"

And thus was Holten left to himself again; but the malignant smile that lighted up his face as they passed from the room was fearful to behold.

He remained in the city, and visited his friend at the prison from time to time; sometimes staying the entire day, and sometimes only an hour or two. This friend, Frederic Stanton by name, had charge of the kitchen department; and, ten days after Holten had called upon Alice, word came to her that her husband was dead, — had died very suddenly, and from some unknown cause.

Mr. Dare was first informed, and upon him devolved the task of telling the faithful wife. She seemed to have a presentment of the coming evil; for, as she looked into his sad face, she said very calmly, "Tell me all: I can bear it better than the horror that has hung over me for the last few hours." Thus entreated, the good man, in as tender a manner as possible, told her of her bereavement.

She listened with a calmness that was surprising; and, when he was through, she only said, —

"I wish you to see, Mr. Dare, that there is an examination made as to the cause of his death. I wish the contents of his stomach analyzed."

"You do not suspect foul play, Mrs. Shepherd!" said Mr. Dare in surprise.

She raised her eyes to his for a moment, and then, with as little trace of emotion as though speaking of any ordinary circumstance, said, —

"I think the same agency that sent him to prison while innocent has now sent him out of the world."

"What! how!" said Mr. Dare, with increasing surprise: "how could that agency reach him in prison?"

"I have no tangible evidence to give," she replied; "but I feel it, I know it: will you do what I ask?"

"I will, Mrs. Shepherd; and God help you to bear this trial!"

" Help," she replied, — " help, when all is gone : will He restore my husband ? "

" The good man sighed, and left her to herself."

" How did she bear it ? " asked his wife, as he passed out of Alice's room.

" So calmly that I tremble for her reason : go to her, wife, and see that she is not left alone," was the reply.

An examination of Shepherd's stomach revealed the presence of poison, but by whom given no one seemed to have any idea but Alice; and her only reply, when interrogated was, " I have no evidence."

A prisoner who sat next to him at meals, and who had once or twice spoken rather ill-humoredly of the deceased was, it is true, subjected to a slight examination ; but his innocence was so apparent that he was soon discharged. William Holten staid till the grave covered his victim, was very officious through all, and seemed particularly desirous of thrusting himself upon Alice's notice, — not for the purpose of sympathy, as many supposed, but that he might thus the more thoroughly torture her.

But the agony upon which he had hoped to feed his soul did not manifest itself. She shed no tear, spoke no word by means of which others might judge of her real feelings; and those who had learned to love her so well during the few months that she had been with them shook their heads as they looked upon her impassive face.

When all was over, she returned with Mr. Dare's family to their home, went to her own room, and, gathering up every thing calculated to remind her of the lost one, she placed them in a little tin trunk, locked it, then went to the window, threw the key as far away as she could, and, sitting down, folded her hands as though she had nothing further to do upon earth.

The door stood ajar, and Mrs. Dare was watching her from a room across the hall; but of this she seemed unaware, or, if she knew it, cared not, but continued to gaze into vacancy —

> "Like the blank statue of despair,
> Or madness graved in stone."

Mrs. Dare kept up her unobtrusive watch till the bell sounded for supper: then, going to Alice's door, she quietly said, —

"Mrs. Shepherd, tea is ready." Alice made no reply, but arose, and followed her to the dining-room. At the table she made no remark whatever; and, when the family attempted to draw her into conversation, she paid no attention to any thing that was said to her that could not be answered by yes or no. The more they tried to direct her mind from the source of her grief, the more did she seem to shrink into herself; and this meal was but a sample of what occurred, day by day, for many weeks following.

She seemed more like one dead than otherwise. True, she breathed, walked, ate, drank, and slept, the same as ever; but these were more the mechanical movements of an inanimate object than the spontaneous efforts of a living soul.

Whatever affection could devise, or ingenuity suggest, to win her back to her former self, was tried, but without effect. Those who attempted to show her the sinfulness of undue grief were silenced by a look from

her great solemn eyes, and retired from the task, confessing that the case was beyond their reach, and must
be dealt with by a more skillful hand.

She had lived only for her husband; or, it might
rather be said that her husband was her life: and, as
the body without the soul is dead, so was she without
the object of her affection; and only he who had permitted this life of her soul to be taken from her knew
how to reinstate therein one that was higher and
better.

She maintained the same scrupulous care about her
room and person that she had ever done; but this was
so much the result of habit, that it required no exertion,
no thought for its performance. The children who had
been her care, and who had delighted in her smile, now
shunned as much as they had once sought her society.
There was something so sacred in the deep grief which
had fallen like a thick veil upon her spirit, that the
joyous laugh of youth was hushed at the sight, while
age looked on with a pitying sigh.

The months passed in quick succession. The golden
hues of summer were resting upon the ripening harvest;
but no ray of light had, as yet, found its way into the
cloud resting upon her spirit. Sunshine and storm,
cold and heat, summer and winter, were alike to one
who was insensible to outward influences.

Friends began to despair, looking upon her case as
hopeless. Addie Winchester had tried in vain to
induce her to stay a while with them; and Mr. Dare
himself said that she was incurable, unless she could
be benefited by treatment in a neighboring asylum, to
which place he was about to have her removed, when

9

an uncle, her father's youngest and only remaining brother, came to seek her.

His presence awoke the memories of childhood, and for a time she seemed partially to revive.

This uncle was but two years the senior of Alice, had been the playmate of her childhood, and the affection subsisting between them was more like that of brother and sister than aught else. She was but ten years of age when her grandparents removed to the far West; and long and bitterly did she lament the loss of her Uncle James.

She knew him, notwithstanding the change that years had made; and for the first time in all these weary months she smiled. She seemed interested when he told her of his Western home, his beautiful residence, his lovely wife, and the little daughter named for herself; but, when he attempted to draw from her something of her own history, she turned away with such a look of agony upon her face, that he never dared to approach the subject again.

After some entreaty, he induced her to go to New-York City with him, for the purpose of visiting old scenes and old friends. She had been there but two days, however, when she met Robert Sawtelle, and from that time forth she could be induced to go out no more. She relapsed gradually into her old condition, and thus were her friends doomed to disappointment.

True, she consented to go with her uncle to his Western home; but it was in a spirit of passive hope-lessness, that left no expectation of her being benefited thereby. They stopped at different points on their way westward; visited relations both on her father's and mother's side : but still the lovely sufferer was sunk in apathy, still she bowed like one benumbed beneath the stroke of her affliction.

James Vale looked on in sadness. Sorrowfully he asked within himself, " And is there nothing that will penetrate the darkness ? " and echo answered, " Nothing that human wisdom can devise."

They were but two days from their journey's end when Alice came into the sitting-room in the morning with a smile upon her face ; and, in answer to her uncle's inquiring look, said, —

" Uncle James, I have seen Pete, — Crazy Pete, they used to call him."

" Where did you see him, Alice ? " he asked.

" He came and stood beside my bed, uncle."

" Came and stood beside your bed ! What business had he in your room ? "

" Oh, you don't understand, uncle ! " said she. " Pete was the best playmate I ever had."

" Better than Uncle James ? "

" If you interrupt me again, I shall tell you nothing further," said she, with a spark of her old vivacity. " Yes : better than Uncle James ; for he told me of things that others do not seem to know any thing about. People called him crazy ; but he wasn't. Well, he died more than five years ago. He told me of it before it happened, though he didn't call it dying. He said that he was going to live with his mother, — that she came and told him so.

" He said that I should see as he did some day, — should both see and hear, — but that there was a dark cloud between. God knows that the cloud has come, and dark enough too ; " and, sinking into a chair, she broke into a passionate fit of weeping.

Blessed tears !   How they soothed the parched brain ! how they relieved the dull ache of the heart !

Mr. Vale was astonished.   Her words indicated to him an increase of her malady ; but her looks and her tears were the reverse.   He wisely resolved, however, to let her weep as long as she pleased.

It was some time before she was sufficiently calm to speak again ; and, when she did, her first words were, —

" You need not tell me, uncle, that it was a dream; for I know I was awake."

" I presume you think you were : some dreams are very vivid, Alice," he replied.

" I tell you I was not dreaming: I had not been to sleep.   I heard the clock strike one, two, three ; and, just after the last, I saw Peter standing by my bed, looking just as when I saw him last.   He did not speak, but smiled so sweetly, pointed the way we are going, shook his head, bowed, smiled again, and was gone.   I was not a bit afraid, but so glad : for, if I can see him, I shall see John some time ; " and again she fell to weeping.   This was the first time that she had spoken her husband's name since his form was buried from her sight.

Puzzled beyond his power to solve, Mr. Vale resolved to humor her fancies, as he believed them to be, and so asked, —

" What do you suppose he meant, Alice, by shaking his head, then smiling again ? "

" It seemed to me to indicate danger close at hand, but that it would be safely passed."

" Why do you think that ? "

" I don't know, uncle : I only feel that it is so."

"Well, well, we will think no more about it now: there is the bell for breakfast, and the train goes soon after. If we have no bad luck, we shall reach home to-morrow."

All that day Alice continued cheerful; and still her uncle watched her even more closely than before. Man's efforts to restore her had failed, because they had no comfort to give; but, when the angels came with their healing, they were distrusted.

CHAPTER XI.

RETRIBUTION.

ND where was Holten all of this time ?
Had the leopard changed his skin, or the
tiger his nature ? Had he given up the
object for which he had periled so much ?
Far from it.

The idea of possessing Alice Shepherd had taken
entire control of him, — was the master, and he the slave.
For this he had given up his place in Mr. Brown's store,
resolved that nothing should stand between him and the
accomplishment of his nefarious purpose. And for this
he had followed them from point to point with the per-
tinacity of a hawk in pursuit of a dove.

He had disguised himself, so that Alice did not recognize his person ; and he was careful that she should not
hear his voice, and recognize him by that. In this manner he would ride behind them in the cars for hours,
catching every word, and thus, learning their plans,
would lay his accordingly.

It is said that " like attracts like," and that if we
" seek we shall find." It is certain, that, in Holten's
case, one disguise attracted another, and that, in accept-
ing another rascal's aid as he supposed, he only plucked
the fruit grown from seed of his own planting.

Before he came to the peaceful village where Alice

had resided, he was acquainted with two boys by the names of Berton Cooley and Silas Porter. These boys, striplings just verging into manhood, looked enough alike to have been brothers; though it was not known that there was any relationship between them. But, though alike in person, it was hardly possible for two to be more unlike in disposition.

Silas Porter was an honest lad, who toiled hard to help support his mother and sister, and despised meanness of all kinds as heartily as mean, tricky boys hated him: while Berton Cooley, or " Bert," as he was called, was just the reverse; and the meaner, the more tricky, one was, the better he liked him.

Though Holten was some years the oldest, still he and Bert were fast friends, and continued so till Holten chanced to see Porter's sister. But from this time forth he assiduously cultivated Porter's friendship, and seemed to have broken entirely with Cooley; but the following conversation, which took place between them about this time, shows the true state of the case.

" Cooley, are you acquainted with Porter's sister?" said Holten one day, soon after seeing Miss Porter for the first time.

" Not much: she is too d——d proud for me."

"'Proud; and pray what has she to be proud of, I should like to know?"

" Nothing more than other folks. I think it is her brother's fault; for he seems determined that none but the good folks, the saints, shall come near her.

" God! how I should like to get her away from him, to pay him for some of his impudence! Don't you think he told me the other day, right to my face, that I wasn't fit for any decent girl to associate with."

"Why didn't you knock him down? I would have done it for you had I been there," said Holten, smothering the joy he felt at thus finding a tool ready for his purpose, under a well-feigned indignation at what he called his friend's wrongs.

"I wish you had been there, Holten. I would have knocked his teeth down his throat, only he had too many friends around."

"Yes: that's it, Cooley. Such fellows always have plenty of friends; and the only way that we can get the start of them is by stratagem. Now, I have a plan, Bert; and, if you will assist me, I think we can carry it out."

"Name it! name it! any thing to make him bite the dust, and I am with you."

"Cool, keep cool, Bert, or I shall not dare to trust you."

"Yes: I'll be as cool as an iceberg in January, if that is what you want."

"But I shall have to cut your acquaintance, call you a bad boy, &c."

"Why must you do that?"

"To make Porter and his sister think I am all right, — that I am one of the saints."

"I don't see the use of that."

"Not if I succeed in making Marion Porter what her brother would shoot any one for calling her now?"

"O Holten! that would be too bad."

"I thought you liked the girl?" said Holten with a meaning smile.

"And so I do; but I hate her brother."

"Have you any hope, any chance, of success?"

" Not in the least, that I can see."

" And all through her brother's watchfuless ? "

" Not wholly.   I don't think I could win the girl anyhow."

" Then she is proud too.   No, Bert," continued Holten : " there is no hope for you, unless she is humbled.   I can see that in her eye.   If you were not so well acquainted with her, I would advise you to play good ; but now you would be suspected if you attempted it   But, if you will remain my friend, I will win her, and then throw her into your arms.   She will be only too glad to find a friend when I leave her.

" You can thus possess her, and have your revenge on her brother.   You are but young yet : in a year you will seem much more like a man, will have a better chance with the girls ; and it will take me at least a year to get around the beauty, for I shall have to play sharp, or fail."

The lad, for he was hardly nineteen, studied a moment, and then said, " Holten, I swear I will do it."

" Your hand on it," said Holten.   .

" Yes : my hand on it ; here it is. . But I didn't think there was so much devil about you, Holten."

Holten smiled at the compliment.   " We must look out for number one, in this world of Priests and Levites," said he, " or go to the wall."

" Are you sure, Cooley," he continued, after a moment's silence, " that you can carry this thing out ? Remember, that to the outside world we are enemies, — must act as such on all occasions ; or, rather, you must be my enemy, and curse me for trying to make a good boy of you."

" Yes: I'll remember," said Cooley.   " Oh, how
hard you are trying now ! I think I shall be good soon ; "
and, throwing himself upon the grass, he laughed till the
tears rolled down his cheeks.

And thus was the compact made between these two,
and all for the purpose of ruining one innocent girl.

Holten worked faithfully for a year, and succeeded
only in breaking Marion Porter's heart.   He never had
the privilege of possessing her himself, much less that of
throwing her into his friend's arms, as he had boasted.

Marion learned to love him, believing him to be noble
and true.   When she found to the contrary, the shock
was too severe for her gentle, loving nature ; and,
broken-hearted, she sank rapidly to the grave.

Her brother said but little ; but such was the determination of his look, and the fire of his eye, that Holten
thought best to leave the place.

When Porter found he had really gone, he simply
remarked, " The atmosphere is at least free from the
poison of his presence."   Cooley, too, soon after left
the neighborhood ; but, before going, he had revealed
to a companion the compact he had made with Holten :
that friend told it to another ; and he had not been gone
two weeks, before it came to Porter's ears.

" Well for him that I did not know it sooner," said
Silas quietly ; but from that time forth he watched
and waited.   From that time two individuals stood forth
so plainly on the page of his memory, that there was
not the least danger of their being forgotten.

During the autumn that Alice and her uncle were thus
visiting from place to place, Silas Porter, now grown to
the full vigor of manhood, held a commission as travel-

ing agent for a flourishing firm in Buffalo, and several times he had been a passenger in the same train with them. Latterly he had noticed a man near them several times, whom it seemed to him that he ought to know; and still he could not remember where they had met.

He further noticed, that this strange man was sure to be near the sad-looking lady and her companion; but that, though watching them closely, he never spoke to them. "I must unravel this mystery," said he to himself; "and, if there does not prove to be mischief at the bottom of it, I am mistaken."

On the morning that Alice averred she had seen Pete, it so chanced that James Vale, Alice, Silas Porter, and this stranger went to the depot in the same hack, and took seats near each other in the same car; and, while stepping from the hack, the stranger made an impatient gesture, by means of which Porter recognized him.

"It is Holten disguised: I am right about the mischief," was his quick thought. Alice, for the first time since she started, was cheerful. Holten watched her with increased interest, and Porter watched him.

All at once, Porter remembered how much he used to resemble Berton Cooley. "I will do it," said he: "I will pass myself for Cooley, and claim his acquaintance."

With him to resolve was to do; and, taking a seat beside Holten, he said, —

"I've been thinking, sir, that I ought to know you; but, until this moment, have puzzled my brains in vain."

Holten gave him a quick-side glance, and replied, "I think you are mistaken: I have never met you, to my knowledge."

Porter put his finger to his lip, cast a quick glance toward Alice and her uncle, and then said in a low tone, "Come this way, sir, and I will talk with you.".

Holten looked surprised, then distrustful, but finally decided to go. They took a seat in the farther end of the car, when Holten demanded, "Now, sir, I wish to know what this means?"

'It means that I do not wish to frighten your game, so thought it best to get beyond their hearing," replied Porter with a laugh.

Holten scowled savagely, and placed his hand upon his pistol. "This is beyond endurance."

"Oh! don't wake up that barker now!" said Porter, laughing harder than ever: "this is a pretty greeting for an old friend, isn't it?" he continued.

"In the Devil's name, who are you?" growled Holten in reply.

"I suppose you don't remember Bert Cooley, eh?" replied Porter with the utmost coolness.

Holten's countenance changed: he scanned the man beside him closely. "It can't be," said he; "and yet I do see some resemblance."

"And I see *some resemblance* between you and William Holten," replied Porter, mimicking his tones.

"You do know me; but I was not certain of it till you called my name," said Holten, grasping Porter's hand: "but how in h—l did you recognize me?"

"Oh! I watched you. I thought there was something about you that was familiar; and I kept thinking where had I seen you? At last you made a peculiar motion that I never saw any one else make: then I knew who it was. But what is up now?" he asked, glancing toward Alice.

" Oh! nothing in particular."

" Now, you needn't think to fool me, for I know that there is: neither need you fear to trust me. Don't you remember Marion Porter, and how we planned about her. Didn't I do my part well ? "

" Well enough," replied Holten impatiently, for the subject was not a pleasant one.

" Oh, now, you needn't feel badly because you didn't succeed ! " drawled Porter : " the best of folks fail sometimes. I only spoke of it to show you that I was true blue."

" I believe you are, Cooley, and I will try you," said Holten ; " for I think I shall need some help."

" Be thankful, then, that the Old Nick has thrown some in your way," laughed Porter, while Holten proceeded to unfold his plans.

" At a farm-house ? " asked Porter.

" Yes: they stop to-day at Smith's Station. We reach there just before night. These friends of theirs live fifteen miles away, but will send a conveyance for them. It is pleasant weather, and their conveyance will be an open two-seated carriage ; and Alice can be taken from the hind seat easily if we manage right."

" To be sure she can ; but when did you learn all this, Holten ? "

" More than a week since, I heard the gentleman — uncle, she calls him — tell her what day they should reach the end of their route by rail, how far and in what direction his wife's father lived, and that he had written for him to meet them. I then went ahead to reconnoiter. I know every step of the way, have my plans all laid, and I hardly think the bird will ever reach that nest.

She has insulted me once too often; and, when I have her in my power, sha'n't she pay for it though."

"Ha, ha!" laughed Porter: "now you look like your own self, Holten. I should hate to fall into your power, were I your enemy."

"And well you might; but don't speak quite so loud. Should my lady-bird find me out before we leave the cars, it would be all day with my plans; for I really believe she can read my very thoughts when once her attention is turned toward me."

"How far beyond the farm-house does this man (Vale, I think you called him) live?" asked Porter.

"Some thirty miles, I believe: they intend to go there to-morrow."

"And is the road across the prairie away from settlements?"

"I don't really know, though I believe it is; but why do you ask?"

"I thought," said Porter, "that, if we failed to-night, we might have another chance to-morrow."

"But we must not fail, Bert."

"Not if it can be avoided; but you know, Holten, that the best laid plans of men and mice —

'Gang aft agley.'"

"I know, I know, Cooley; but I swear, by the Eternal God, that I will succeed in this, or die."

"Die, then; for succeed, you shall not," said Porter to himself; but outwardly he was as calm as a summer morning.

Holten was about to take his old post behind Alice

and her uncle; but Porter prevented him by saying,
"Let me sit there, Holten: I can plan to get into conversation with them, and my voice won't betray me as
it might you. I can question them, and find out if they
have made any change in their plans, better than you
can."

"Well, do so: but I shall watch you, Cooley; and, if
you do play me false, I will shoot you," said Holten,
looking as if he did not quite trust Porter after all.

"Nonsense! why should I play you false? What interest have I in these people?" said the pretended
Cooley, as he moved forward to take the seat indicated.

He managed to attract Mr. Vale's attention, and get
into conversation in a very short time; made himself as
agreeable as possible; and, when they had talked fifteen
or twenty minutes, he drew Alice's attention to something that could be seen from the car-window, and at
the same time thrust a piece of paper into Mr. Vale's
hand, on which was penciled, —

"Go into the smoking-car: I have something to say
to you. I will follow soon: we are watched.

.   A FRIEND." ·

Vale read it, and instantly the words of Alice, "I
think it meant danger safely passed," flashed through
his mind. But the words, "we are watched," told him
the necessity of suppressing all emotion; and he governed
himself accordingly.

Porter continued to talk to Alice for some minutes,
thus giving her uncle time to think, — to plan. Presently, as Porter turned toward him, he said, "I don't
think I have a fair chance with my niece for a rival: I

hardly get my share in the conversation. Suppose we adjourn to the smoking-car; or don't you use the weed?"

"Thank you, sir: there is nothing I like better than a good Havana; but I prefer staying here a little longer, unless you are afraid to trust me with your charge," giving him, at the same time, a significant look.

"Not at all, not at all, sir: and I shall leave you here with the lady just to show you that your suspicions are unfounded; and, rising from his seat, he sauntered away in as nonchalant a manner as he could assume.

Porter talked with Alice, perhaps five minutes after he left; and then starting up, as if suddenly recollecting something that should be done immediately, he said, —

"Excuse me, lady, but I must speak to my friend yonder a moment; and, going quickly to Holten's seat, he clapped him on the shoulder with, —

"Things are going on swimmingly; but I remember the promise you made me in regard to Marion, and shall claim its fulfillment in this case, for she is lovely enough to quicken the pulse of a Stoic."

"What promise?" said Holten, affecting not to remember.

"What promise! just as if you had forgotten; but I see how it is: you wish to keep this one all to yourself."

"I see what you are driving at now, and it shall be as you say; but I shall have ample revenge first."

"Why, man, that will be but a continuation of your revenge; but I must see Mr. Vale again: he don't seem just willing to talk freely before the lady. He invited me to have a smoke with him, and I refused; but I will make an excuse to look after my baggage, and stop on my way back. And, without waiting for further comment from Holten, he hastened to find Vale.

"Now, what does all this mean?" inquired that gentleman, as soon as Porter was seated.

"I can not tell you all it means now; for it would take too long, and would excite suspicion in the mind of the villain whose plans I wish to defeat. But this much I will say. If you have no pistol, get one; and, when you cross the ravine five miles this side of where you stop to-night, keep both eyes open, and shoot the first man who lays hands on the lady."

"But I have no pistol, and don't know where I can get one," said Mr. Vale in astonishment. "And, further, I can see no reason why any one should wish to disturb my niece."

"A defeated lover will sometimes do any thing," replied Porter.

"Ay, ay, I begin to see. I think I will not go on till to-morrow, and thus avoid the danger. I"—

"And leave him to carry out his scheme when you are not warned?"

"There is something in that," said Mr. Vale thoughtfully.

"He is disguised," continued Porter: "otherwise Mrs. Shepherd would know him immediately; he dare not even trust his voice in her hearing."

"If I was sure that there would be no danger"—

"No danger at all, Mr. Vale: I will let you have my pistol. I shall not need it; and we can thus bring the knave to justice."

"Why are you so anxious in the matter?" asked Mr. Vale, looking Porter full in the eye.

"An only sister went to the grave broken-hearted, sir;" and, pausing a moment to suppress his emotion, he continued, "He does not know who I am, or he would not trust me: he believes me to be another person entirely. If you have occasion to address me, call me Cooley; but that is not my true name.

"Promise me, sir, that you will go on, as you have intended," added Porter, after waiting for something further from his companion.

"Will you be there?" asked Mr. Vale.

"I shall, and shall seize the horses by the bits; so don't fire that way."

Still Mr. Vale hesitated.

"I wait your answer," said Porter anxiously; "for I must not remain here longer."

"Danger safely passed," again came to Mr. Vale's mind; and he replied, "I will go on."

"Thanks, but don't alarm the lady," said Porter, as he hastily made his exit.

He found Holten looking moody, but soon put him in good humor again, with, —

"I was d—d 'fraid that they would not go on till morning; but it's all right now, and you may thank me for it."

"How?" asked Holten. Porter drew upon his imagination for a fitting reply, and to keep his companion entertained as the cars sped onward to their destination.

The train was behind time; and it was nearly sundown when they reached the station where Alice and her uncle were to stop. "It is a bright moonlight night, and it will be a fine ride that we shall have across the prairie," said Mr. Vale to Alice.

"Is it all prairie, uncle?" she asked.

" No : there is a ravine, through which runs a creek, and a patch of timber some five miles this side our journey's end," was the reply.

" I am glad it is late," said Holten to Porter, " as it will be all the better for us ; " and, making a hasty meal while two fine horses were being saddled, they were soon speeding their way over the prairie in a somewhat different direction from that which Mr. Vale was to take.

He took things more leisurely ; and it was at least half an hour after Holten and Porter left before he was ready to start. " The road is perfectly plain, I hope," said Alice to the boy who had been sent with the carriage.

" Perfectly so," was the reply.

" Why do you ask that, Alice ? I hope you are not getting timid," said her uncle, smiling.

" No, uncle ; but there is danger somewhere, and I did not know but it might be on the prairie. I have been told that people get lost sometimes on account of there being so many different roads."

" Nonsense about your danger : you are getting to be a coward, that is all."

" You will see, uncle."

" Danger to-night, do you mean ? "

" I do, sir," she replied.

" If your prediction proves true, we shall count Alice among the prophets," said Mr. Vale, laughing to hide the surprise he felt.

" As you please, uncle ; " and for a time they rode on in silence. Indeed, each seemed to be busy with their own thoughts, and little inclined for conversation ;

but, as they neared the ravine, Alice turned to Mr.
Vale, and said, —

"Do you think I am asleep now, uncle?"

"Certainly not: why do you ask?"

"Because you say I was dreaming last night, when
I tell you that I saw Pete."

"Alice, what do you mean?" he exclaimed in a
startled tone.

"I mean that he is here now, and John is with him,"
she answered as quietly as though it was an every-day
occurrence.

"Will wonders never cease?" was his inward comment; and to her, "Do they say any thing, Alice?"

"Pete says, 'Fear not:' John only smiles."

They were now fairly in the ravine. Mr. Vale had
taken Porter's pistol from his pocket, and was holding
it firmly in his hand; for, in spite of his pretended disbelief, the words of Alice gave him courage.

"They crossed the stream, and were about to ascend
upon the other side, when two horsemen dashed into
the road ahead of them. One of them grasped the
horses by the bits, and the other made for the side of
the carriage where Alice sat; but, just as he gathered
his arm about her, a ball penetrated his shoulder.

Holten — for it was him of course — had not anticipated such a reception; for he supposed that Mr. Vale
was not armed. The shock was so sudden that he lost
his balance; and, at the same moment, Vale's driver
struck his horse with the whip-handle, causing the animal to dash aside, and thus complete his rider's fall.
He tried to hold on to the brid'e; but the frightened
beast reared, wheeled, and then started forward, throwing

him so violently against a tree as to kn)ck him sense-less, tearing his foot from the stirrup, an1 breaking his leg at the same time.

Porter now loosed his hold of the bits; and the driver was about to lash his horses into a run, when Mr. Vale's voice arrested the movement.

"The danger is over; the other is a friend," said he: "let us stop, and look after this one."

Alice had not spoken till now, neither had she mani-fested the least fear; but, as Porter and her uncle dis-mounted to look after the fallen man, she calmly re-marked, "William Holten, I thought your turn would come some time."

Her uncle looked up inquiringly. "Pete told me," she said; and he questioned no further.

Holten was alive, but badly injured; and, as they found it impossible to take him with them, they were con-sulting as to what was best to be done, when another team came in sight. This proved to be a farmer, with a good farm-wagon, in which there were two or three bundles of straw.

Into this they lifted Holten, Porter staying behind to help care for him, while Mr. Vale rode Porter's horse, and Alice went on with the driver, a lad of fifteen, and brother to Mrs. Vale.

Mr. Vale and his party reached their destination an hour before the wounded man was brought thither; for the latter had partially revived, and the motion of the wagon gave him so much pain that they could move but slowly.

By the time they reached Mr. Shelton's, Holten was so far conscious as to recognize the place. "In the name of God, where are you taking me, Cooley?" he asked.

"My name is not Cooley. I have deceived you; and, when I tell you that I am Silas Porter, you will know why," was the reply that greeted his ears.

A deep groan was the only response to this announcement. The doctor arrived presently, for he had been sent for as soon as Mr. Vale reached his father-in-law's house; and, upon examination, pronounced it impossible for the wounded man to live more than two or three days. For, besides the shoulder and broken limb, there were internal injuries that could not be reached.

When Alice learned this, she went to his bedside, fixed her eyes upon him, and stood some moments without speaking. At last she said, "William Holten, the dead are beyond your reach; but there is still time to do justice to the living."

"What do you mean, Mrs. Shepherd?" he asked, turning toward her a face where pain and fear were striving for the mastery.

"The doctor says that you can not live, and there is one languishing in prison whom you can set free: that is what I mean," was her reply.

"Mrs. Shepherd, you do not suppose that I know aught of that theft?"

"Yes; and of a murder too."

He turned his face away, and lay quiet, as far as his sufferings would permit, for perhaps ten minutes. At length he asked, —

"Doctor, how long can I live?"

"You are pretty sure of twenty-four hours, and have one chance out of three of lasting two or three days longer," was the response.

"Very exact in your calculations, sir," said Holten, with something of his old spirit.

"I suppose that was what you wanted," replied the doctor.

Another silence.

"If you have any business matters to arrange, had you not better attend to it immediately?" asked Mr. Vale; and, for reply, Holten called for a justice of the peace.

"Would you not like to see a minister too?" asked Mr. Shelton.

"Not yet, not yet," was the reply. "There is something else to be done first: where is Porter?"

"Here," was the response, as Porter stepped around where the dying man could see him.

"Silas Porter," said he, "you have deceived and betrayed me; but I can not blame you, for I murdered your only sister. I do not mean that I poisoned or stabbed her; but I deliberately planned her ruin, — won her heart for that purpose: failed, it is true; but she loved me, and the knowledge of my perfidy sent her to the grave. It seems like mockery to ask your forgiveness; but how can I die without it?"

"If my forgiveness were all that was needed to secure you a place where her pure spirit dwells, you would never get it," was Porter's stern reply.

"Forgive as you would be forgiven," said Mr. Shelton solemnly.

"Work out your own salvation," responded Porter. "This last is Scripture as much as the other, and far more in accordance with the principles of justice."

"Mercy is God's favorite attribute," continued Mr. Shelton.

"And justice is mine," replied Porter : "accord to us justice, and we shall need less mercy."

" It is a fearful thing to fall into the hands of the living God," persisted Mr. Shelton, with a sigh at what seemed to him the young man's perverseness.

" And I should say that it was more fearful to fall out of them. Mr. Shelton, you, no doubt, think me a wicked wretch ; but I want no heaven that I do not earn."

Mr. Shelton held up both hands in horror. " And you would count the blood of the covenant an unholy thing ! Young man, if such are your sentiments, this is no place for you, by the bedside of the dying. Talk about forgiving him : you are the more wicked of the two."

" More wicked to doubt the prevailing theology than to rob, murder, or ravish innocence : no wonder that the world is sunk in wickedness ! " murmured Porter to himself, as he passed from the room.

" Infidelity of the worst form," groaned Mr. Shelton : " and I am told that there is a class of persons who claim to hold communion with the departed; and they assert that the spirits of our friends and neighbors, even those who were good Christians here, come back and teach the same doctrine. ' Anathema maran-atha ; anathema maran-atha.' "

" ' Let him be accursed.' Is that what you say of the young man who has just left the room ? " asked Alice.

" Why not, if he teaches the doctrine of devils ? "

" If, by that, you refer to those who come back to us from the other side of the grave, they are not all devils,

Mr. Shelton. Peter Stiverton is no devil, and I know John Shepherd is not; and I have seen them both."

" Mr. Shelton looked at his son-in-law, and the latter touched his forehead significantly."

": I thought so, I thought so," said the old gentleman to himself.

Holten had listened to the conversation with a good deal of interest; and his face flushed with satisfaction when Mr. Shelton pronounced Porter more wicked than himself.

The justice had now arrived; and steps were taken to have the dying man's deposition taken as soon as possible.

It was thought that Alice was having too much excitement, and had better leave the room: but she objected; and, as Holten desired her to stay, she was permitted to remain. Holten was first sworn, and then proceeded to give the details of the plot by means of which John Shepherd and his friend had been convicted and sent to prison; ending with the confession that he had murdered Shepherd by means of poison dropped into his food, after it was dealt out, and before Shepherd had taken his seat.

He then told of his determination to possess Alice at all events; how he had a place prepared where her friends could not have found her, &c. " And I should have succeeded but for Porter. Still, that gentleman," pointing to Mr. Shelton, "says that he is more wicked than I am; so perhaps there may be hope for such as me."

Mr. Shelton flushed, but asked, " You do not expect to go to heaven upon your own merits, Mr. Holten? "

" Certainly not: how could I ? '

" You are willing to accept pardon through the merits of Christ Jesus?"

" I am, if I could only be sure that he would accept me."

" Young man, there is hope for you. He says, ' Come unto me all ye that labor and are heavy laden, and I will give you rest.' Are you not one of the heavy laden?"

" Laden with a life-long load of sin," replied Holten with a sigh.

" But you are sorry for it?"

" Could I blot it out, I certainly would."

" Go to Jesus, young man; cast yourself upon his mercy: it was for such as you that he died," said Mr. Shelton, his face lighting up at the prospect of saving a soul. " Examine your own heart well, though; for death-bed repentance is apt to be deceptive," he continued, after a moment's pause; " but we will leave you now to the care of those who are to watch with you, and to your own thoughts. In the morning, we will send for the Rev. Mr. Stevens: he can instruct you in the right way better than I can?"

Accordingly Mr. Stevens was sent for. He read and prayed with the repentant sinner, as he called Holten, and left him with high hopes that he would be as a brand plucked from the burning.

Mr. Porter, having nothing further to detain him, went his way; but more than one comment was made upon his unforgiving disposition, and more than one shake of the head in reference to his infidelity.

Holten was hurt on Wednesday evening, died on Friday about the same hour, and was buried on Sun day. Mr. Stevens attended him to the last; preached his funeral sermon, taking the words of Jesus to the thief on the cross, as his text; and carrying the idea to his audience, that William Holten had given sufficient evidence of a change of heart to warrant the belief that he was then with Jesus in paradise.

Mr. Shelton, when he reached home after the funeral services were over, found one of his youngest boys, a lad of some eight summers, very busily engaged in play.

" Fie, fie, my son ! " said he, " What do you suppose will become of you if you play on Sunday ? "

" Oh ! I love to play," said the little fellow ; " but I will get very sorry for it just before I die, and then it will all be right."

The father was too much surprised to reply ; while Alice, like Mary of old, pondered all these things in her heart.

Mr. Vale, having tarried at his father-in-law's longer than he intended, started early the following morning for his own home.   Alice was quietly cheerful ; for the loved ones from the shores of life immortal had made their presence known to her, thus pouring comfort into her despairing soul.   But her uncle looked upon her with far more anxiety than when sunk in gloom ; for surely none but the insane talked as she did.

CHAPTER XII.

MORE THEOLOGY.

ILAS PORTER'S business led him to the town in which Mr. Vale resided; and he, of course, received an invitation to call there as often as was convenient while he remained in the place, — an invitation that he was not slow to accept: for, in all his travels, he had never met a lady who interested him as Alice did.

Mrs. Vale, Mr. Shelton's daughter, was a church-member of the Methodist persuasion, and very zealous in her profession; while her husband belonged to that numerous class who do not claim to be Christians, but feel that they ought to be. Such, standing self-condemned before their own souls, are ever earnest in defending the doctrines of the church, fully intending, some day, to make preaching and practice correspond.

Mr. Vale, as I have said, belonged to this class; and, having heard the remarks made by Porter at Holten's bedside, their conversation very naturally turned in that direction.

"What did you mean, Mr. Porter, by saying that you wanted no heaven but what you earned?" he asked, upon the second evening of Porter's calling at his house.

Mrs. Vale looked up with surprise, not unmingled

with horror, depicted upon her countenance, " Why, Mr. Porter, you did not say that ? " she exclaimed.

" I did, madam ; and I meant it too."

" But why ? What are your reasons for so strange an assertion ? " said her husband.

" Because I believe it to be a law of God, founded in the very nature of things. Another can not eat for us, can not drink for us ; and, if we remain inactive while another works for us, that other becomes healthy and strong, enjoys both food and sleep ; while we, on the contrary, shrivel up, grow weak in body and in mind.

" Another may possess a knowledge of the laws of life, and try to impart that knowledge to us ; but if we fail to learn, fail to act thereon, we can not enjoy the benefits " —

" That is just what we teach," interrupted Mrs. Vale : " we must come to Christ, or we can not enjoy the benefits of his salvation."

" You believe, if I understand you rightly," said Porter, " that God, for the sake of Jesus, in virtue of his sufferings and death, will forgive us our sins if we ask him."

" Most assuredly I do : it is my only hope."

Mr. Porter turned to Mr. Vale : " I understand, sir, that you are superintendent of the public schools in this place ? "

" I am," he replied.

" Did you ever have any one come and ask you for a certificate that they were qualified to teach because their brother had a splendid education, and had studied enough for both ? "

" Certainly not ; but this is trifling, Mr. Porter."

"I can not see it so, sir; and, for my part, I was never more in earnest in my life. Study is a weariness to the flesh; and, if we could have the benefits of an edu: ation simply by confessing that we were lazy wretches depending upon another to do the labor for us, I think there would be but few who would do much studying."

"But the cases are not parallel at all," said Mrs. Vale.

"I think they are, madam: could you enjoy food without the sense of taste?"

"Certainly not."

"And you must have that taste yourself, and not another for you?"

"Most certainly."

"If you inhale the miasma of fever, can another be sick for you, and you escape the suffering because that other has not inhaled the poison, but still has been sick?"

"I tell you, Mr. Porter, that I can not see the analogy at all," replied Mrs. Vale.

"I can," said Alice. "Mr. Porter means to say that heaven is not something that can be wrapped around us like a garment, but that it must be wrought out through the forces of our own being, even as the leaves, buds, blossoms, and fruit of a tree are produced, wrought out through the innate forces of the tree."

"You have the right idea, Mrs. Shepherd; for how much good would it do a barren tree to have the credit of another's fruitfulness imputed to it?"

"Not much, I am thinking," replied Alice laughing. "And yet Christians talk of imputed righteousness, of Christ our righteousness, of his obeying in our stead, &c., &c. Now, I must confess that I can see no possibility for such a thing to be true. It is contrary to the laws of nature; and, if God violates his own law, why punish us for doing the same?"

Porter waited a moment for a reply, but none came. Mr. and Mrs. Vale seemed as much surprised to meet an independent thinker, one who dared to question what others accepted, as they would have been had a thunder-clap burst upon them from a cloudless sky.

. "And then look at the influence of such a theory," he continued: "William Holten acknowledged himself a seducer, a perjurer, and a murderer; he pursued his wicked course up to within a few hours of his death, stopping then only because he was forced to do so. Nothing left for him in this world; and is it any wonder that he should seize hold of any thing that afforded the least pretext for hope in the next.

"It would be strange if he did not: and yet this is called conversion; and the idea is held out that this man has gone to heaven, to a state of perfect happiness. What, I ask, is the influence of such an idea upon the minds of the young?"

"I will tell you," said Alice. "Johnnie Shelton was at play when we went home from the funeral; and, when his father reproved him for breaking the sabbath, he said, —

"'I love to play, father; but I will get very sorry for it before I die, and then it will all be right.'"

"Precisely that," said Porter; "and how can it be otherwise when belief is put before acts; when a man who has violated every law, human and divine, but who claims to believe in Jesus, — when such a one is called better than one who has tried to live according to the dictates of right, but who does not believe as the church and the minister say is necessary ? "

" I hardly think that this is so," said Mrs. Vale. " I am sure that for my part I should prefer the latter to the former for a neighbor."

" Individuals often hold in theory that which they can not put into practice ; but I have often heard it asserted, both by minister and people, that a strictly moral man, who trusted in his morality, was the very worst man in the community ; and your father, Mrs. Vale, when expressing my opinion in the presence of Holten, told me that I was the more wicked of the two. Poor encouragement that to live right, if such as he is accounted the best simply because of belief."

" But what can one do when situated like Holten ? There is nothing left to them but to believe ; and shall we deny them even the comfort of that ? shall we tell them that there is no hope ? "

" No: I would not do that, Mrs. Vale. I would tell them that God's laws were the same in all worlds ; that there was the same chance for improvement there as here ; and that only as one suffered the consequences of sin, thus learning the evil thereof, could he truly hate and forsake it, and by a higher and better life earn the rewards of such a life."

" Strange sentiments these, Mr. Porter: may I ask you where you got hold of such ideas ? " asked Mr. Vale.

" I feel in my soul that God is just, and that he is also love ; and I can reconcile his love and justice in no other way than by giving justice her full demands, — not for the purpose of vengeance, but that we may be perfected thereby, — may be brought into a condition that will admit of the blessings of his love."

"But justice demands the condemnation of the sinner," said Mrs. Vale.

"Yes, but not his eternal condemnation," replied Porter: "only to the utmost farthing; and how can a finite being contract an infinite debt?"

"Does not man sin against an Infinite Being, Mr. Porter?"

"No: he sins against himself; and help must come from within, not from without."

"How do you show that?" asked Alice.

"From the book of nature: if I burn my hand, the recuperating power is in the body, not outside of it. If I break my limb, it is the same: in both instances I have violated the law of my physical being, and must suffer the consequences, and suffer them for myself too: but I do not suffer as long with a slight burn as with a broken limb; and I believe that it is the same with the moral as with the physical, with the soul as with the body. It seems to me just as impossible to escape the consequences of a broken moral law as of a broken physical law, — as of a broken limb."

"No forgiveness of sin!" exclaimed Mrs. Vale.

"No forgiveness of sin," replied Porter.

"God help us, then!" she ejaculated.

"God helps those who help themselves, dear lady; and, 'Work out your own salvation; for it is God that worketh in you, both to will and to do,' is a favorite text of mine, — the God within, not the God without; God all and in all blessed for evermore."

Mr. Vale and his wife seemed astonished to hear such

11

tones of reverence from one who was such an infidel, as they counted infidelity; but Alice seemed like one endowed with new life, as she listened to the reasoning of the earnest-hearted young man.

"God's ways are wonderful," she said; "and, unless we recognize him as all and in all, as directing all things in wisdom, we are lost in the labyrinth of an uncertainty that too often leads to the gulf of despair."

"Do you think deception is ever justifiable, even for the sake of self-defense?" asked Mrs. Vale, as if to change the subject.

Porter flushed. "Do you mean to ask me if I think I did right in deceiving Holten, and thereby preventing the consummation of his plans, Mrs. Vale?"

"I did not intend to be personal," she replied, "for this may be among the theories that we are too weak to put into practice; but, taking the strict sense of the command, 'Thou shalt not lie,' is it right in any case to practice deception?"

"I am not partial to either gnats or camels," said Porter impatiently; while Alice added, —

"It was certainly a good thing for me, Mr. Porter, that you took the course you did: otherwise I tremble to think what might have been my fate."

"And the consciousness of having been of use to you, Mrs. Shepherd, is reward enough to compensate for a great deal of suffering," he replied in a tone that brought the blood to Alice's cheek.

"I have thought of it so often since," she continued: "how strange it was that retribution for the wrongs of one should prove such a blessing to another!"

"The law of compensation, Mrs. Shepherd, — compensation to her and me too; for I have no doubt that my darling sister rejoices with me in your safety."

"I know now," said Mr. Vale, "where you got your ideas, Porter. You are more than half Spiritualist."

"Altogether one, Mr. Vale; that is, so far as I understand their views."

"And do you really believe that the dead can come back, Mr. Porter?"

"I do, sir; and I further believe that my sister assisted me in penetrating Holten's disguise."

"Nonsense: we shall have to send you and Alice both to the insane asylum."

"I am sure I shall not object to my company if we can go together," replied Porter smiling.

"By the way, we have a medium (I believe that is what you call them) here; and her house is thronged, so people say. Suppose we all go to see her some time."

"O husband!" exclaimed Mrs. Vale, "you certainly will not go there?"

"Why not, wife? how can we prove a thing unless we investigate it? and we are commanded to prove all things."

"But we must not put ourselves in the power of the Devil if we want God's protection."

"If it is the Devil's work, so much the more need that good people should investigate and expose it; and, if God will not protect his children in exposing that which is evil, how can we trust him in any thing? I, for one, am going to find out for myself: who will go with me?"

"I will," said Alice. "And I, too," said Porter: then, turning to Mrs. Vale, he added, —

"Come, madam, I think you had better go: perhaps we three can keep the Devil from catching you; and, if we leave you here all alone, he might possibly slip around and get the advantage of you."

Mrs. Vale laughed in spite of herself, and finally concluded that she would go if the rest did. And so it was decided that they should attend a circle.

CHAPTER XIII.

THE CIRCLE.

R. PORTER thought it best to carry out the suggestion of attending a circle before objections could be brought forward by interested parties to prevent it: so he called upon the medium the next day, and obtained permission to be present at their next meeting, which was on the following evening.

Mrs. Vale demurred somewhat when the hour came, but finally went with the others. And here we are again, gentle reader, in the circle-room. Things look somewhat familiar; for it is in the same room, the same medium, and nearly the same company, that we met before. The honest-hearted gentleman, whose barns were burned, is not present; neither is the young man who recognized Bob Perigrene: but the gentleman who gave a false name has returned, and waits the fulfillment of the promise then made him. The members of the circle are the same, and only our company are new to the place.

Mrs. Vale watches things with a sort of fearful interest, — interested in spite of her determination not to be, and fearful lest she should see a cloven foot somewhere.

The members of the circle took their places, our party

and the gentleman before spoken of remaining upon the outside. The words commencing, —

"Come, Holy Spirit, Heavenly Dove," —

were sung; the leader of the circle remarking that we needed, not only one, but many, holy spirits to watch over us, and then giving a short invocation, the burden of which was, that, while both needing and desiring the protection of good spirits, he implored a sufficiency of the sweet charity that would receive and try to benefit all who came. A few moments' silence, and the medium was controlled.

Again that fair young form took on the semblance of a little weazen-faced old man; again the movements of shoe-making were gone through with; while the metamorphosed form nodded, smiled, and said, —

"How do you do, good friends? Hard at work, as you see; but honesty and industry are indispensable to success, — indispensable, good friends, or I had never gone from the shoemaker's bench to a place in the councils of my country."

"Here is Bob Perigrene again, pretending to be Roger Sherman," remarked one of the circle.

"My name is Robert, not Bob; and I would thank you, sir, to call me Mr. Perigrene."

"Excuse me, Mr. Perigrene: I acknowledge my fault; for all should be treated with respect, especially if we wish to benefit them."

"Benefit them! Do you intend that as an insinuation, sir?"

"An insinuation?"

" Yes : it looks as though you thought I needed benefiting."

" Well, don't you ? "

" No : I am well enough off."

" The best of us can be made better, Mr. Perigrene."

" True, true : I don't think much of those saints who
imagine that they are so much better than other people."

" Who is it that thinks so ? "

" It looks as if you did when you talk of benefiting
me, Mr. Mentor."

" Not at all, Mr. Perigrene, not at all ; for I presume
you could benefit me, and I am certain that you could
benefit yourself."

" Just tell me how, will you, Mr. Consequence ? "

" You are not giving me my right name in either case,
sir ; but I will answer your question. You can benefit
yourself very much by learning to be truthful."

" An insult, an insult, Mr. Impudence ! If I only had
my old body, I would thrash you for that. Truthful,
indeed ! Pray, when have I been otherwise ? "

" You have come to this circle twice now, and pretended, either directly or indirectly, to be Roger Sherman ; which you know is false."

" Well, it's in me ; and I think I have as good a right
to tell a lie as my neighbor there," said he, pointing to
the stranger with a false name.

" Come, husband, let us go home," said Mrs. Vale,
at this point. " They are lying spirits, by their own
confession ; and I don't think it right to encourage them
by our presence."

" If you go, you will have to go alone," was the reply ; " for I am going to see the play out, now I am
here."

" Look," said Porter : " the influence is changing : we shall have something different now."

" Something better, I hope," was Mrs. Vale's impatient response ; and then, as her eye turned in that direction, " Look at Alice, will you ? "

" Alice, what is it ? your face is radiant."

" Wait, uncle," was her only response.

Presently the medium turned slowly toward her, extended a hand, and said, " Miss Alice, is it not as I told you ? "

" Yes, Peter, it is," she replied.

" Call me Pete, please : it makes me feel more as if we were back in that little village, or rambling in the woods, or by the streams around it."

" Yes, Pete : those were happy days ; but dark, dark ones have been mine since then."

" Did I not tell you of the cloud, Miss Alice ? I saw that it must come, and it has, — a cloud so dense, that no light but that from our side of the river could penetrate it."

" True ; and thank God with me that such a light was permitted to shine upon me. And the other part of your prophecy was true, too, Pete ; for I have seen you, and now I hear your voice once more. You said that I should see and hear."

" Yes ; but you can not hold those blessings for yourself alone, Miss Alice. You have a work to do, — one which will bring a storm about your ears."

" A storm ? "

" Yes. Before it was a cloud ; now it will be a storm."

" Well, let it come : it can not put out the lamp I carry now. Is your mother with you, Pete ? "

" She is, and she tells me that my father is here present to-night."

" Your father!" exclaimed the stranger gentleman.

" Yes, sir: she tells me that you are my father."

" 'Tis false!" he vociferated, springing to his feet; " all false. I thought it was from the Devil; and I know it is now, for I never had a son."

The influence changed almost instantaneously; and a voice of peculiar sweetness said, " Philip, have you forgotten your Vermont trip, and the poor girl whom you trapped into a false marriage?"

The irate man sank back into his seat, with pallid cheek and quaking limbs. " Who speaks? whose voice is that?" he asked, in tones which showed that he was touched to the soul.

" It is I, — Marion Sloan; and he who has just spoken is your own son. You have given a false name here, and you gave me a false name then; that is, the last name: your true one is Maldren, — Philip Maldren."

" This is psychology, — mind-reading: there are no spirits in the case; and those who claim that there are, are humbugs," said Mr. Maldren, who, having recovered his self-possession, seemed determined to contend to the end.

" Have we not given you your true name?"

" You have; but you read it from my mind."

" Did you not tell us, when here before, that you would believe if we could tell you what your name was?"

" True; but I did not think then of the time you would have to trace it out. It has been months since, — long enough to learn my whole history: had you told me then, it would have been different"

" Did you leave any clew, by means of which we could do this ? "

" No : I took good care of that; but I tell you that you took it from my mind."

" You were wont to take good care, Philip. You have been accustomed all your life to covering your tracks; but there are eyes that can penetrate all disguises. I was not the first one that you deceived and betrayed : you have another son here."

" Indeed ! you will make me a man of family pretty soon. Perhaps you can tell me the name of this other victim ? "

" I can : it was Maria Holten ; and she called her son William."

Here Vale and his wife gave each other glances of astonishment; while the controlling spirit continued, " Did I take that from your mind, Philip? "

" No ; for I had forgotten it."

" You acknowledge its truth then ? "

" I don't see as that follows."

" How could you forget that which you never knew ? "

" Well, well, have your own way about it," said Maldren ; for his bold bearing was fast giving way to the pallidness of guilt and fear: " but where is she now, — this Maria of whom you speak ? "

" Where she never would have been but for you, Philip, — the keeper of an assignation in —— Street, New York. You start ; and well you may, for you were there the last time you were in the city. You did not recognize her ; but she knew you, and would have murdered you but for my influence. You remember the circumstances : it is not necessary for me to enter into details."

" O my God ! " groaned the unhappy man : " it is all too true ; but I never thought to meet these things till the judgment-day."

" No uncommon mistake, Philip : there were those in the days of Jesus who thought they were tormented before their time."

" O Marion ! " said he, " and did you indeed watch over me for good ? "

" I did, Philip, and have for years done all that I could to restrain you from evil, and lead you to the right."

The attention of the company had been so taken up, that they did not notice the change coming over Alice ; consequently were somewhat startled to hear a heavy bass voice say, —

" For years I have striven to get possession of this body ; received my death-wound in my last earthly attempt, but I have succeeded at last. Yes : I have succeeded ; but oh, under what different circumstances from what I anticipated or desired ! " Then turning to Maldren, he — for you have already recognized William Holten — continued, " The lady may watch over you for good ; but I will " — the medium's hand was quickly placed upon Alice's lips ; and she who had called herself Marion Sloan said, —

" No, no, William : you must not curse him ; for, in so doing, you will only injure yourself."

" And what if I do, lady ? I can not be much worse off than I am."

" But you can be better off if you desire it."

" How, pray ? "

" By returning good for evil ; by striving to benefit others, even those who have wronged you the most."

" Do you imagine, lady, that wrongs such as he has committed can ever be forgiven ? Only think what my life has been, and all through him."

" I was not talking of forgiveness in any such sense as to do away with the consequences of his acts. It is because he must suffer these consequences, — because he can not escape them, — that I ask for him your pity and kind feeling. I also ask it for your own sake, because it will be better for you," was the reply.

Maldren looked and listened with an expression of the keenest anguish upon his countenance. And was this indeed the Marion that he had so deeply wronged ? Had she really come from the land of the blessed to plead for him ? Such were the thoughts of this wretched man ; while William Holten, still controlling the form of Alice, laughed in derision at the gentle counselings of the pure spirit who sought to lead him upward.

" Ha, ha, ha !" he exclaimed : " wouldn't I look well now, in trying to benefit the man who ruined my mother, and left me a waif upon the world's mercy ? "

" And have not you wronged others ? " asked the spirit.

" It is his fault if I have," was the reply.

" In one sense it was, William ; and in another sense it was your own fault. There was a cause for his doing as he did, as well as for your doing as you did." ·

" I don't care if there was : I'll have my revenge, and upon you too," turning to Porter. " You deceived and betrayed me, and I'll make you suffer for it yet."

Mrs. Vale had watched Alice during the above colloquy, with a half-frightened, half-horrified look, till, unable to contain her feelings longer, she begged her husband to take her home.

"It is the Devil: I am sure it is the Dev.l," she said; "and he takes this course to make us believe that the blood of Christ is not sufficient for us. William Holten died trusting in Jesus; and I am certain he would not be here talking in this way."

"It's the Devil, is it? You want to go home, do you?" said the one claiming to be William, turning fiercely toward her; while the influence controlling the regular medium changed very quickly, and a voice full of solemn warning said, —

"Madam, you are right: these influences come from the Devil and his angels. I, Paul, the servant of Jesus Christ, am mercifully permitted to tell you this, to the end that you may be without excuse if you have further to do with this wickedness."

The spirit controlling Alice looked up as if surprised, and then, giving expression to a hearty laugh, left; while Alice, with a bewildered air, said, —

"Strange that I should go to sleep."

"Not asleep, but under the influence of an evil spirit, madam," said the one claiming to be Paul; and then, turning to the company, he continued, "You see, beloved, how soon these vile spirits fly when one of God's commissioned ones appears."

Mrs. Vale now insisted upon going, and her husband went with her. Alice refused to leave, however, till the circle closed; and Porter remained also. Mr. and Mrs. Vale had no sooner left the room than the dignified, devout Paul changed his base entirely. The face of the medium broadened and shortened considerably, while the eyes twinkled with mischief, or, rather, the muscles around the eyes, for the latter were closed.

" Well, wasn't that well done ? " was uttered in tones
of triumph.

" Wasn't what well done ? " asked Porter.

" Making that woman believe it was the Devil.　Ha,
ha ! "

" And why did you do that ? " continued Porter.

" Why, the poor woman was hunting for a devil, and
I thought I would help her to find one.　Doesn't the
Book say that we must help such as want help, and be
kind ? "

" It says something to that effect; but you are per-
verting its meaning, and wronging others at the same
time."

" How ? "

" It will make trouble for this lady, who is staying
with them, as it will only intensify their opposition."

" I can't help that : I answered her according to her
folly.　What I said came through the same channel as
did the good advice to William Holten ; and if she
chooses to think that my lies were from God, and
Marion Sloan's truth from the Devil, why, let her have
her own choice.　People generally get what they are
looking for: she was looking for a devil, and she got
some d——lish lies."

" Tut, tut ! " said Porter : " that's rather rough."

" Well, I was a rough, jolly sort of a fellow when I
was here, and I haven't got polished yet ; shall, though,
in good time, — that is, if I don't meet too many like
her ; but, when I see such folly, it arouses all my old
spirit of mischief, and I do love to play off upon them."

" Will you not tell us who you really are ? " asked
Alice.

"One who will never harm you, lady: as to my name, it can make no difference if you do not know it; but you may call me Jack, for sho.t, and so good-night."

As there was no further manifestation, the circle was closed; and each, as they went to their homes, pondered in their hearts as to what these things meant.

CHAPTER XIV.

CONSULTATION.

PON leaving the circle, M . and Mrs. Vale walked on a while in silence. It was at length broken by Mr. Vale's saying, " This will never do, wife."

" I thought you would be scrry : I wish we had not gone," she replied.

" But I am not sorry : I am glad we went," said he ; " for it will help us to avoid what might otherwise have occurred."

" What do you mean, Mr. Vale ? " asked the lady in accents of surprise.

" Why, in reference to Alice. Don't you see that she is a medium too ; and, in her present state of mind, she can be easily influenced to do what she otherwise would not ? Porter is really a believer in these things ; is enthusiastic in what he undertakes ; and he, together with the medium, will try to make Alice think that she must devote herself to the cause."

" Oh, I never thought of that ! I would not have her do it for the world ! " exclaimed Mrs. Vale.

" Neither would I," he replied ; " for, in the rebound of her mind from the extreme of grief in which she has been plunged, she would be sure to go to the opposite extreme, and perhaps become really insane."

"I hardly think there would be any danger of that; but only think of the disgrace of having a relative of ours, a member of our family, take such a course. To be insane on another subject would not be so bad as being sane on this; for the first would be looked upon as a misfortune only, but the latter is infamous."

"Well, wife, we see the danger now, as we should not have done had we not visited the circle to-night; and we must take steps to prevent such a catastrophe. I love Alice as if she were my own sister; and it shall be no fault of mine if she is not saved from this new danger."

"But how? What course shall we take?"

"I can not tell as yet; but something must be done, and one thing is certain: we must not seem to oppose her, not strongly at least, or she will call it the storm that Pete spoke of, and it will only make her the more determined. Your father will be here in the course of the week, and we will consult him as to the course to be taken."

"I was surprised at you, James, when you consented to go to such a place; but now I see that there was a purpose in it. The Bible says that 'The hearts of the children of men are in the hands of the Lord; and he turneth them like rivers of water, whithersoever he will;' and I think it has been so in this case. O James! I wish you were indeed a Christian."

"And so I shall be, little wife, when the Lord turns my heart in that direction," he replied, half in jest, and half in earnest.

"O husband! now you are making fun of the

12

Bible," she said, with an earnestness that broug'it tears
to her own eyes, if not to his.

"Indeed I am not, wife; but I must confess that I can
not quite understand the theories that you church people advocate, — some of them at least."

"Not theories, Mr. Vale; not theories, but truths."

"Well, truths, then, but truths that are only theo-
retical with a large proportion of those who profess to
understand and accept them; for I see but very little of
the practical results."

They had now reached their own door; and the honest little woman made no further reply, but only offered
up a silent prayer that God would indeed turn the heart
of her husband in the right direction.

When the nurse had been summoned, and the little
one duly kissed and caressed, Mrs. Vale said, "Shall we
sit up for Alice and Porter?"

"Most certainly," was the reply; "for Alice feels
that she owes more than life to Porter. It will not do
to treat him rudely; but we must give them no more
opportunity for conversation than we can help, and get
her from under his influence as soon as possible. But
here they come: now, keep cool, wife: be careful what
you say, and how you say it; for, if Alice once gets an
idea that we are working to break up this thing, we can
do nothing with her."

"Not gone to bed yet?" said Alice as they came in.

"No," replied Mr. Vale, "but were just talking of
it. I thought, though, that we would wait a little, and
learn what further manifestations you had."

"O chameleon-hued Curiosity!" said Porter, laughing, "verily, thy forms are legion: want to learn what

happened after you left? Don't think you deserve to know after running off as you did."

" You must blame Mrs. Vale for that: I would have staid had she been willing."

" Eve did it," cried Alice. " Now, aunt, I would not put up with that if I were you ; for I believe that that solemn-faced admonition frightened him as badly as it did you."

" Hush, Alice ! don't speak so lightly upon so solemn a subject," said Mrs. Vale.

Alice looked into her aunt's face, and, catching its awed expression, was fairly convulsed with laughter when she remembered the cause of it. " Excuse me, aunt," said she, as soon as she could speak ; " but, could you have seen the ending of the quondam Paul's solemn farce, I am sure that you would feel differently from what you do."

" Why do you speak thus, Alice ? What evidence have you that it was not Paul ? " said Mrs. Vale in a tone which showed that she had the same human nature as others, even if, according to her idea, she had been born again.

" Just like the rest of us," said Porter : " don't want that proved false which we desire to be true ; but come now, Mrs. Vale, let us lay aside prejudice, and decide in accordance with the evidence."

" I shall not stop to argue with you, Mr. Porter : the Bible forbids us to have any thing to do with familiar spirits, and that is enough for me."

" Why, then, was Paul sent to you, Mrs. Vale ? " asked he, with a merry twinkle of the eye.

" I see that you do not believe it was Paul," she replied ; "but what was claimed to have com: from William Holten, that was all right, of course."

"Mrs. Vale, you mistake me entirely," said Porter. "In the first place, the fact that a spirit claims to be or not to be a certain person does not prove that it is so, — that they tell the truth. Still, if there is no opposing evidence, we accept their testimony, unless there is that in the very nature of the case which is calculated to do us an injury. If a spirit tells me to be good and true, to live a pure and progressive life, I accept his teachings, no matter who it is from. It is what, not who. On the contrary, if one who claims to be Paul, Peter, Isaiah, or any one else, tells me to do that which I feel to be wrong, I should reject the teaching, no matter if it was proven to have come from the person claimed."

"I don't believe in doing evil that good may come."

"Neither do I, madam."

"Why, then, have any thing to do with these things ? What do they add to what we already know ? and, if violating a plain command under pretense that good may come is not doing evil, I don't know what is," said Mrs. Vale in a tone which showed that she thought her position impregnable.

"Why have any thing to do with these things ? because they come to us as a manifestation of God's providence, demanding our attention. In the burning-bush of life's intensity they find their place, and we hear God's voice therein ; and, as to adding to what we already know, they are among the cloud of witnesses who demonstrate eternal life, are of the innumerable company of angels that Paul speaks of, are of the just made perfect, and also of the spirits in prison that the Christ of love is ever ready to receive and benefit."

" But what do you do with God's command?" persisted Mrs. Vale.

" What command?" asked Porter.

" The one given through Moses."

" To whom was it given?"

" To the children of Israel, of course."

" Moses did, so we are told, give such a command to those under his control. But we have no proof, except his word, that God told him to give it; and, further, we are not Israelites."

" God gives his commands to one age for all time, and to one people for all people; and you have shown yourself an infidel by your own admission. You do not believe the Bible, Mr. Porter?"

" If God's commands to one people are for all people, why do you eat pork, Mrs. Vale? The command that the Jews should not eat pork is just as emphatic as in the other case."

" Come, come, wife, this is all nonsense: you and Mr. Porter might talk all night, and you wouldn't agree."

" Thank you, Mr. Vale, for reminding me of the hour," said Porter; " for I must leave early in the morning, and shall need some sleep."

" How long will you be absent?" asked Vale, in a tone so interested that Alice noticed it, and understood it afterward; but it puzzled her at the time.

" About a month, I think; but I hope to find you all here, and all well and happy, when I return; so good-night."

Alice retired immediately; for the experience of the evening had placed her in a frame of mind that required solitude, — solitude and reflection, for her soul was too deeply stirred for sleep.

"That takes one difficulty out of our path," said Vale to his wife, as soon as Alice had left the room.

Mrs. Vale looked up inquiringly.

"Porter's going away," he continued. "We could hardly do any thing toward removing Alice while he was here; for he would be certain to find some means of preventing it."

"I am glad he is going," said Mrs Vale; "for he is really a very dangerous man. Why is it, husband, that those who hold such ruinous sentiments are generally so correct in their lives as far as acts are concerned?"

"Because they trust in works, of course: I should not think that you would need to ask that, wife."

"True, true, — works, self-righteousness."

"And then there is the stealing of the livery of the court of heaven to serve the Devil in."

"Yes; but why should trusting in works lead to a more correct life than trusting in Jesus?" said she, with a puzzled expression upon her face.

Mr. Vale regarded her for a moment with a half-serious, half-amused look. "Look out, little wife," said he, "or you will ask one question too many, and thus find yourself doubting before you know it."

She colored, sighed, and said no more; but she could not stop thinking.

"A storm?" said Alice to herself, after she had retired, "a storm? I wonder what kind of one."

A voice from the unseen seemed to reply, "Not so

properly a storm as a prison where the sun is reflected from ice, — a something that will inclose you for a season, but will give you no warmth."

" And can you not save me from this ? " she asked.

" Were it best, we could," was the response.

For a moment her soul shrank from the coming ordeal; but when she remembered that the angel side of her life could not be inclosed, that light and warmth from the summer land would still be hers, she grew strong again to do and to bear, and, laying her head upon her pillow, slept as sweetly as an infant on its mother's breast.

The next morning, at the breakfast-table, the conversation naturally turned upon what had occurred the previous evening; and Mrs. Vale said to Alice, " Your uncle thinks that you will turn medium yet."

" And why not ? " she asked quietly.

" Why not! and would you really do such a thing, Alice ? "

" It seems to me a blessed mission," she replied.

" I would rather see you dead," said Mrs. Vale, forgetting, in her excitement, the caution her husband had given her the night before.

" There, there, wife, don't run to meet trouble: Alice has been separated from her uncle too many years to want to leave him in a hurry," said Mr. Vale, giving his wife a meaning look.

Alice laughed. " You flatter yourself, uncle," said she.

" I think not," was the reply. " I only feel tha᠎ you would be as unwilling to give me up as I would you. Why, puss, we haven't half lived over our childhood's days yet."

" Don't you two be saying too many sweet thirgs, or I shall be jealous," said Mrs. Vale merrily.

" Please don't be so cruel, and I will be good, aunt," said Alice, with a pretty pout upon her lip. " I couldn't bear that, indeed, I could not ; but I can't see as I am to blame after all, for it was not me that said the sweet things."

" Adam did it instead of Eve : eh, Alice ? " retorted Mr. Vale.

Little Alice came in at this moment for her share of attention, and there was nothing further said upon the subject.

The next day, Alice visited the medium again ; and, while she was absent, Mr. Shelton came. His daughter hastened to consult him in reference to the subject that was troubling her.

" It will never do to let this go on," said he, after listening to her story : " something must be done, and that is certain."

" Yes : but what ? it will be worse than useless to talk to her."

" Of course : insane people never listen to reason."

" And do you really think her insane, father ? "

" Certainly ; though not so as to be noticed, except by a close observer. Perhaps monomania would be the most proper term : all right except upon some particular subjects. But an asylum is the best place for her : indeed, it is the only thing that will save her."

" O father ! " exclaimed Mrs. Vale.

" I know it seems hard, my child ; but the end justifies the means. It can be done very quietly, — so quietly that the public will be none the wiser."

" But where can we take her, father ? "

" I have a friend who is a physician, and a man of deep piety, who has had some experience in these matters. He had a lovely daughter who came under the influence of these modern witches ; and he was obliged to shut her up to keep her from them. She proved incurable, and died in about six months. This almost broke his heart ; and, in the bitterness of his grief, he resolved to spend his life in trying to save others from this terrible delusion : so he fitted up his house and grounds as a private asylum."

" And has he been successful in curing those placed under his charge ? "

" Not as much so as he could wish : but you see, my child, that it prevents the poison from spreading ; and it saves the families with whom the unfortunate ones are connected from the disgrace of their going before the public, as they are sure to imagine that they must."

" I see," said Mrs. Vale thoughtfully ; " and this is where you would advise us to take Alice ? "

" It is, and the very best place I can think of."

" Well, I will talk with Mr. Vale about it ; but it seems hard."

" You ought to have learned before this, my daughter, that it is often hard to do right : duty and pleasure do not often walk the same paths in this life."

" It is not the doing of the right, but the knowing as to what is right, that troubles me," she replied.

" Ask God to help you : you do not pray enough, I fear."

" I suppose I am wicked, father : it must be so, though I am sure I don't wish to do wrong. Still, when I pray,

I sometimes find it so dark that I feel as if I can never make the attempt again."

> " 'The hosts of hell are pressing hard
> To draw you from the skies.'

" My child, I fear that you have an idol somewhere, —something that you think more of than you do of your God. He is a jealous God, and will permit nothing of the kind : be careful that he does not take your husband or your child from you."

" And do you think, Mr. Shelton, that such a loss would have a tendency to make her love him any better ? " asked Alice, who had come up just in time to hear the last sentence or two.

They both started, and looked so uneasily toward her, that Alice saw they had been talking of something that they did not wish her to hear ; so she said, —

" Indeed, I have not been eaves-dropping. I came up just in time to hear Mr. Shelton's last remarks ; and it seemed such a strange way for God to take to make us love him, that I could not well avoid speaking as I did."

" God's ways are past finding out; and we are presumptious to question," said Mr. Shelton solemnly.

That night, after Alice had retired, the subject was well canvassed in family conclave, and it was fully decided that Alice should be sent to Dr. Denning's.

" You will have to be very cautious," said Mr. Shelton, " or she will mistrust that something is going on, and refuse to go : these insane people seem sometimes to read one's very thoughts."

"And that," said Mrs. Vale, " is what makes me believe that it is their own peculiar sensitiveness, and not spirits, that makes them see and talk as they do. They become the mirror, as it were, to reflect the thoughts and feelings of the circle. If it was really as they pretend, — if it was really a spirit that Alice saw the other night, then it could warn her and defeat our plans in spite of our efforts to the contrary "

" If He be the King of the Jews, let him save himself," said Mr. Vale.

" Why do you quote these words?" asked his wife in astonishment.

" Because of the parallel in the mode of reasoning," he replied.

" James," said Mr. Shelton, in a tone of severity, " I very much fear that your spirit of reckless trifling will yet place you beyond the pale of hope and mercy."

" But I can not see the parallel," said Mrs. Vale.

" Neither is it best that you should," said her father : " this comparing sacred things with profane, Jesus with the claims of Spiritualists, is simply blasphemous."

" Are not the rules of logic and reason applicable in one case as well as in the other, father? " said Mr. Vale, with a look of perplexity upon his features.

" That, James, is the trouble with this age, — too much reason, and too little Bible. As though God's works, the laws of matter and mind, could be used to set aside his word."

" I stand rebuked," said Mr. Vale, " but I must confess that I can not see for what."

" God help you, my son, to find the true light."

" Amen," was the response; " but when shall our plans respecting Alice be put into execution?"

" As soon as possible : present duty should neve be neglected ; but perhaps you had better not move in the matter till after I am gone. She seems to have an instinctive aversion to me, and might object to going if she suspected that I had any thing to do with it."

" I was in hopes that you could go with us, father."

" No, child : it will not be best.   I can give you and James the necessary directions, and a letter of introduction ; but don't let her know but what you are old acquaintances."

" Then I must send the letter of introduction through the mail, explaining my reasons for doing so, and so describe our appearance and time of coming that he will recognize us upon sight ; for, if Alice should discover that there had been the least deception practiced, we should have trouble with her, and it will be hard enough to leave her there without any thing of that kind."

" Your suggestion is a good one, James.   Give me pen, ink, and paper, and I will write what is necessary now.   Nothing like doing a thing promptly."

About a week after this, while at the breakfast table one morning, Mr. Vale said to Alice, " I presume that you will be very lonely till Porter returns : what say you to a trip with us to visit some friends ? "

" To convince you, uncle, that I am not so dependent upon Mr. Porter for my happiness, as you may suppose, I move that I keep house, and let you and aunt go and enjoy yourselves at your leisure."

" Worse and worse : leave you here to dream of him from morning till night. No, no, that will never do : you must go with us, or we stay."

" Nonsense," she replied: " I will go of course, rather than keep you at home. I only said that to show you that I could live without Mr. Porter, and you, too, if necessary."

" Well, Miss Independence, be ready, then, early to-morrow morning: for it is a good day's drive, further than I ought to go in one day; and we can not possibly get through before dark."

" But you have not told me where you were going, uncle."

" To Clinton, or near there. 'It is some ten miles from —— River, and our road lies through the finest portion of the State."

" A relative ? " said Alice.

" Not exactly, or at least so distant that we claim nothing on that score. I believe his wife is a little related to Mother Shelton."

The next morning early, they were on their way, but did not reach the doctor's establishment till very late ; consequently Alice saw nothing to arouse her suspicions. She slept late the next morning; and, when she arose, Uncle James and his wife were gone.

I will not attempt to portray her feelings, for I have neither the power nor the disposition to do so : but, in the weary days and too often wakeful nights that followed, there was compensation ; for she had soul food of which they knew nothing, companionship tha their eyes were too dull to perceive.

CHAPTER XV.

AFTER MANY DAYS.

"Cast thy bread upon the waters, and after many days thou shalt find it again." — Bible.

E will now return to Ellsville, and inquire after our old friends, the Winchesters. Have they forgotten Alice Vale and the kindness that she showed them years before?

Addie could never forget, whoever else might; and, from the time that John Shepherd had been condemned to prison till now, her heart had gone out in one continued longing for the happiness of her stricken friend, in continued desire that in some way she might be able to pay a portion at least of the mighty debt of gratitude that swelled her soul.

"I wonder where Alice is to-night," said she to her husband one pleasant evening, as they sat around the family board.

"I am sure I can not tell: somewhere in the West though, as I am told that she went home with her father's brother a few months since," was Mr. Winchester's reply.

"From whom did you learn that?" she asked.

"I had a letter from a friend of Mr. Dare's, in which this fact was mentioned. I thought I had told you."

"This is the first that I have heard of it, Edward."

"Strange that I should have forgotten it; but I know now why I did, wife: it was on the morning that I went to the city, and I was so hurried that it put it entirely out of my mind."

"And I have thought so strange that she did not write to me. I wish I could hear from her; for I believe she is in trouble."

"Why do you think that, Addie?"

"I hardly know why, but I can not get rid of the feeling; and why does she not write to me?"

"You know that she was nearly insane after John's death; and she may not be in a condition to write."

"True; but I wish, oh! I wish that I could see her."

Winchester regarded his wife a moment in silence, and then said, "You are growing thin and pale, Addie. I think a journey would do you good: what say you to a trip West?"

"I should like it very much, if you could go with me; but where should we go?"

"I have an aunt, a sister of my mother's, living near Clinton ——; and we might go there. I want to see the country, and don't know but I can leave my business now as well as any time. How soon can we be ready?"

"As soon as you please, Edward."

"Well, then, say the first of the week. To-day is Thursday: I can be ready to start by Monday." And so it was settled that Addie Winchester and her husband should go West.

The next day, when Winchester came to dinner, he brought Addie a letter with a Western post-mark. "Here is something for you," said he, as he threw it into her lap; "and it looks like Alice's handwriting."

"It is hers," was the reply, as she broke it open, and glanced at the signature. "O Edward!" she exclaimed, when she had read it, "William Holten is dead. He confessed that John was innocent, and that he poisoned him. He was trying to carry Alice off when he received his death-wound; and what else do you think?" she asked, with a merry twinkle of the eye.

"I am sure I can not tell: she is not married again?"

"Fie, now! you know better than that, Mr. Winchester. No: she has been attending circles, and believes in spirits."

"I am glad of that; for she is an earnest soul, and what she believes she will advocate fearlessly. Alice Shepherd is no common woman."

"So I am glad; but I hardly thought you would speak out so boldly, Edward."

"I have concluded, wife, that it does not pay to be a coward; but where is she?"

"At ——, some forty miles from ——."

"That is not more than a day's drive from Clinton. We can go to Uncle Denning's first: then I will take you there, and you can visit with Alice while I look at the country."

"Don't you want to see Alice too?"

"Yes, Addie, and will, but can not spend as much time with her as you will wish to. Does she speak of any particular trouble?"

"No: she seems very happy, but says that Pete — you remember Pete, the boy that lived at Stiverton's?"

"Yes: he died when Alice wasn't more than fifteen."

"Well, he and Alice were great friends. She says

she has seen him, and that he tells her that there is trouble ahead, but that she is not going to worry about it, as there will be time enough to meet it when it comes."

" A wise conclusion, wife, and one that you would do well to heed."

" But my best of husbands has no occasion for the use of such a maxim, I suppose ? " said Mrs. W., with a quizzical glance at her monitor.

" Too much, altogether too-much, need for it, Addie," was his frank reply; and then the conversation turned upon other subjects.

Monday came, furnishing two passengers for the stage that ran daily to the nearest railroad station; and, the day following, Addie and Edward Winchester were whirling along at railway speed toward their place of destination, one of the broad prairies of the, to them, Far West. Day and night the iron horse sped on his tireless way. Thursday noon brings them to the terminus of their journey, so far as the cars are concerned; and the stage is again in requisition. Clinton is reached an hour after dark, and here they remain till morning.

" Finishing our journey on Friday, — rather an unlucky omen, is it not ? " asked Mr. Winchester.

" Nonsense, Edward: I hope you do not believe in such whims ? "

" Not exactly, Addie: still, early education will have its influence, and my mother would never commence a thing on Friday."

" Well, we didn't start on Friday; and, if there is bad luck to any one, it will be to those where we are going. I prophesy that we shall have a grand time. By the way,

13

I dreamed of Alice all night; and she looked so pleased,
and, at the same time, seemed pleading for help.
Strange, isn't it?"

"Ha, ha, wife! who believes in omens now? I am
sure I do not think it strange that you should dream of
Alice, considering the circumstances: rather strange if
you did not," replied Winchester.

"Did you dream of her?" asked Addie.

"I did not: but you women are so susceptible; and
then it would hardly do for me to be dreaming of other
women, with you by my side. I might talk in my sleep,
you know, and then you would be jealous."

Addie's reply to this sally was a hearty laugh; for the
idea that she could have such a feeling toward Alice
was simply amusing. The conveyance that was to carry
them to Dr. Denning's residence was now at the door;
and, taking their seats therein, they were soon speeding
their way toward the grove that was their point of destination. Twelve o'clock brought them to the doctor's
grounds. A servant opened the gate that gave them
entrance; and, sweeping down the graveled carriage-way,
they were soon in front of the almost palatial residence.
Making themselves known, they were cordially wel-
comed; but almost the first question that the doctor asked
was, —

"Are you sick, Mrs. Winchester? You are looking
very pale."

"Why, Addie, what ails you? you are as white as a
ghost!" exclaimed Mr. Winchester.

"Nothing serious," said she, trying to smile. "Doctor, have you friends stopping with you?"

"I have a few patients: there are none others here,
except my own family. But why do you ask?"

" I thought I saw a familiar face at an upper window, as we drove up; but I must have been mistaken," was the reply.

Winchester was looking directly at the doctor when Addie said this, and noticed his startled look, succeeded immediately by a bland smile, as he replied, —

" Resemblances often surprise us into the momentary belief, madam, that we have previously met individuals whom we have really never seen before. I have often wondered at the goodness of God in not permitting more of such resemblances; for they would be the source of a great amount of annoyance, to say the least."

Winchester turned again to his wife, and saw, from her look, that there was something more on her mind than her words indicated. She opened her lips as if to speak, closed them again, cast an appealing glance at her husband, rose partly to her feet, and then sunk back into her seat.

" Addie, you are certainly sick ! "

" I believe I will lie down a little," was her reply.

" Certainly, certainly," said the doctor: " wife, show Mrs. Winchester her room; is there nothing I can do for you first ? Will you not have something to take ? "

" Not any thing, thank you : I only need a little rest."

Mrs. Denning conducted Addie to a room off the parlor. " Now lie and rest as long as you please, my dear: there will be nothing to disturb you," said she kindly, as she was about closing the door.

" Will you please send my husband to me ? I wish to see him a moment," said Addie.

" Certainly," was the response.

" O Edward ! " exclaimed Addie, as soon as they

were alone, " Alice is in this house, for I have seen her. Just the same glad, pleading look that I saw in my sleep. What does it mean ? "

" You must be mistaken, Addie: it can not be possible ; " and then, as he recollected the doctor's startled look, he said to himself, " There is something strange here." .

" I am not mistaken, Edward," said she earnestly : " if I ever saw Alice, I saw her to-day ; and it was so exact a counterpart of my dream, that I nearly fainted."

The doctor's first expression, when his wife returned, was, " Wife, I shall have to dismiss Miss Wells, as valuable as her services are to me ; for she will never learn to obey orders."

Mrs. Denning looked up inquiringly.

" She has been permitting some of the patients to look from the front windows again," he continued ; " and I am certain that Mrs. Winchester recognized whoever it was."

" I believe, doctor," said Mrs. Denning, " that Miss Wells is in sympathy with the patients, and particularly with the last one who came. I doubt if she thinks her insane at all."

" Then the sooner we get rid of her the better," said the doctor.

" And would that be the wisest course ? " asked Mrs. Denning.

" I do not know what else we can do," he replied. " I wish I had never gone into this business : it is a source of constant anxiety, and I don't see as things are getting any better. For one that we shut up to prevent contagion, hundreds spring up in every corner of the land."

" That is true," said the lady, " and I wish that we were well out of it. But self-preservation is the first law of nature; and, if you permit Miss Wells to leave us now, the public mind is in such a state of ferment, that she will be able to turn the indignation of the community against us. The only safe course that I can see is to make a patient of her."

" It shall be done, wife," said the doctor; " and see to it, that she holds no communication with your nephew and his wife while they are here."

Mr. Winchester was just leaving his wife's room, and caught the doctor's last words. He listened for more; but a movement from within warned him that there was danger of being discovered, so he stole quietly back to his wife's room.

" I believe you are right, Addie. I recollect now that Uncle Denning keeps a sort of private asylum: can it be possible that Alice has gone wholly deranged ? "

" I can not believe it, Edward, for her letter was so hopeful; she seemed cheerful, — so reconciled to the past. ' Bitter as my experience has been, I believe that a loving Father has permitted it all in wisdom: ' these are her very words; and I can not believe, after all that she has passed through, that her mind has become unbalanced now."

" Some people really think that a medium is insane : perhaps that is why she is here."

" Perhaps it is," said Addie thoughtfully.

That evening, as they were conversing upon different subjects, Mr. Winchester turned to his aunt, and said, " I believe you have the unpleasant task of caring for

the insane : what induced you to undertake such a
task ? "

The quickly starting tear told how tender the chord
he had touched. " Excuse me, Edward," said she : " it
is a painful subject, — one upon which I can not speak
to-night."

" Pardon me, aunt; but I have a particular reason
for desiring to know something of your patients. We
have a dear friend, who has been sadly afflicted, — so
much so, that it was feared at one time that she would
lose her mind ; but, the last we heard from her, she was
well, and seemed to be reconciled to, yea, happy in, her
lot. Now, my wife insists that she saw her face at an
upper window to-day, as we drove up."

" What was your friend's name ? " asked the doctor.

" Mrs. Shepherd, — Alice Shepherd : her name was
Vale before marriage."

There was a momentary struggle in the doctor's mind,
which was noticed by no one but Winchester; and he
could not have done so, had he not been watching, for
its appearance upon the surface was scarcely perceptible.
But, when he spoke, his tones were as calm as a summer
morning. Turning to Addie he said, —

" Only a resemblance, Mrs. Winchester; only a resemblance. I trust that your friend is well and happy."

" Can I see your patients to-morrow, uncle ? " she
asked.

" I do not often permit them to see strangers ; but, as
a special favor to you, I will," was the smiling reply.

Addie arose, and walked to a picture hanging near
the front door. She felt a restlessness, a sense of being
wanted somewhere, that she could not account for ; and

yet she could not banish it. The doctor was beside her in a moment, talking to her in tones as smooth as oil, explaining the different points in the painting, and making himself obnoxious generally; for the pure, straightforward nature of Addie Winchester shrank from the atmosphere of dissimulation which surrounded him.

She bore it for a short time, and then, walking away, took a seat close by a side door. Dr. Denning cast upon her a keen glance, and then entered into conversation with her husband. Addie rested her head against a window-frame near her, and, as she did so, fancied that she heard her name called. Rising quickly, she stepped out into the open air, ere those within had divined her intention : as she did so, a paper was thrust into her hand, while a female form flitted around the corner of the building, and disappeared.

Addie had barely time to put the note into her pocket ere Mrs. Denning was by her side.

" Are you sick again, my dear ? " she asked.

" No, only a little restless : I presume I am nervous from riding so far," was the reply.

" I feared you were, you looked so pale ; but I guess a night's rest will restore you. Perhaps you would like to retire ? "

Now, this was just what Addie wanted ; for it would give her an opportunity to read her note.

" I think I will, aunt," she said : " I presume it will be the best thing I can do."

Her request was acceded to with alacrity ; for it was fondly thought that she was thus secured, for that time at least, from contact with those who might tell her that which they did not wish her to know.

On arriving at the room, another difficulty presented itself; for, instead of leaving Addie alone with the light, Mrs. Denning kept moving here and there, talking of this and that, till poor Addie was nearly desperate.

"Were you waiting for the light, aunt?" she at length asked.

Mrs. Denning colored. "No, not exactly : I thought I would wait and see if there was any thing you needed."

"Nothing, aunt,—nothing but quiet; and, as the wife of a physician, you certainly know how to apologize for nervous people : if you want the light, I will call when I am done with it," said Addie, with a smile as bland as any the doctor could assume.

Thus fairly dismissed, the lady could do no better than leave the room. "Alone at last," was Addie's mental comment.

"The impudent jade!" soliloquized Mrs. Denning. "I presume she thinks that I am not acquainted with her early history. I wonder where she would have been now if Edward had not married her."

As soon as Mrs. Denning disappeared, Addie closed the door, and produced the note from her pocket. With trembling hand, she unfolded it and read, —

"DEAR ADDIE, — Surely the angels must have sent you here for my deliverance. The trouble I wrote you of has come ; and I am here a close prisoner, charged with insanity.   ALICE SHEPHERD.

"P..S. — My keeper is my friend, and will give you this when she can do so without being observed.
                                        "A. S."

She had just time to read these few words when footsteps were again heard, and had hardly thrust the note into her pocket, when the door was opened without ceremony, and Mrs. Denning said, —

" Here, Mrs. Winchester, are some matches. You can extinguish the light when you are done with it, as we shall not need it."

Addie was now left alone till her husband came. She could not sleep; but the restlessness that had so tortured her was gone, and she quietly awaited his footstep.

" I will manage this," said he, when he had heard her story : " you keep quiet, and wait the development of events ; but, when we leave this place, Alice goes with us."

In the morning, Addie arose refreshed : she felt that the object desired would be accomplished, and had rested upon that assurance. She was complimented upon her improved looks, and replied with a smile. When breakfast was over, they all repaired to the sitting-room, where, after about half an hour's conversation, Mr. Winchester said, —

" Uncle, do you include me in the promise made to my wife last evening ? "

" What promise ? " asked the doctor, with a look of annoyance.

" That of seeing your patients, uncle."

" Oh ! I hoped you had forgotten that : I hardly think I ought to have made it. I should very much like to gratify you ; but my first duty is to them, and they always seem worse after seeing company."

" Then you do not intend keeping your promise ? " said Addie.

"If you insist upon it, I must, of course; but I was hoping that you would release me."

Mr. Winchester glanced at his wife with an expression that said "Wait;" and then, turning to the doctor, asked, "What seems to be the greatest inciting cause to insanity just now, uncle?"

"There are various causes, sir; but the principal one just at this time seems to be the monomania about spirits. I don't know where it will end; but I pray God that it may not be permitted to go much further, for it is bringing ruin and desolation to many a family."

"Are any of your present patients here from that cause?"

"I make that my specialty, — the work to which I am willing to devote my life; hoping thus, through my own affliction, to become a blessing to others."

"Your own affliction, uncle?"

"Yes: have you not learned the sad history of your Cousin Helen?"

"I have heard that she was married, — nothing since then."

The doctor sighed, and his wife turned away her head to hide the fast-gathering tears. "She was our only one, and the darling of our hearts," said he at length; "but we have been sorely punished for making an idol of any earthly object. She married, and married well. Her husband was not exactly the one we should have chosen for her, --- not that he was not good enough; but we could not bear to have our darling subjected to the trials that necessarily fall to the lot of a minister's wife. But they loved each other, were devotedly attached, and all went well while he lived.

" At his death, which was eighteen months after their marriage, — at his death, the work of retribution commenced ; for she had made an idol of him, and we of her."

" I think, uncle, that you and I might differ somewhat in our views upon this subject ; but please go on. If I understand you aright, Cousin Helen became insane."

" She did ; and the first symptom that we noticed came in the form of what thousands of poor deluded souls call spirit-manifestations."

" How ? " asked Addie.

" When she went to her room to pray, she would come out insisting that she had seen Albert ; and the more we tried to reason with her, to show her the fallacy of such an idea, the more positive she became in asserting that it was really true."

" How did this belief seem to affect her ? " asked Mr. Winchester.

" Very pleasantly at first ; but, when she found that she could not convince us of its truth, she began to droop, and to spend more time by herself, till one day she came to me with tears in her eyes, saying she believed that God had forsaken her.

" ' Why do you think that, my child ? ' I asked.

" ' Because, father, I was not content with making an idol of my husband when here : I have kept it up even beyond the tomb ; and now, when I go to my closet to pray, Jesus hides his face, and only Albert is present. I can see nothing else ; I can think of nothing else. Alas ! alas ! I fear that this idolatry has cost me my soul.'

"'God is very merciful,' I replied: 'only believe, and all will yet be well.'

"'But I can not believe, I can not pray. O father, pray for me!' she fairly shrieked: and, if ever earnest prayers ascended from mortal lips, they were those that went up from her mother and myself for the next hour; but, alas! we arose from our knees to clasp her in our arms a raving maniac."

There was silence for a few moments; and then Mr. Winchester asked, "Did your daughter know any thing of Spiritualism? had she read any of their works?"

"I did not know as she had at that time; but I learned afterward, that, while she was in school, some two or three of the girls used to steal away, and visit one of those modern witches called mediums, and Helen sometimes went with them. Here was the first step in the wrong, — disobedience to parents and teachers, in prying into that which was forbidden."

"And for which you both forgive her from the very depths of your parental hearts."

"Most certainly; but that did not prevent the consequences," was the prompt reply.

"And whence came those consequences, uncle?"

"From breaking God's just and holy laws, of course."

"Consequences which we must reap whether the law is broken ignorantly or willfully?"

"Why, yes, in some cases; that is, physically: but moral law is quite a different thing," was the hesitating reply.

"If I put two substances into a bottle, both of which are harmless in themselves, but by chemical action in their union they become poison, and I drink that poison, will my ignorance of the fact prevent its legitimate action ? "

" Certainly not : I conceded that."

" Never mind, uncle : I wish to ask you one or two more questions, and then to show you the why. If the chemical action of those two substances is too great for the strength of the bottle, will any amount of praying prevent its breaking ? "

" What a strange question ! " said Mrs. Denning.

" Not so strange as it may seem, madam. You believe in obedience to parents, of course ; but suppose you ignorantly command your child to take poison, will the fact of her obedience prevent the legitimate action of that poison ? "

" Certainly not," said the doctor.

" If there is a remedy at hand, that, if taken in time, will cure her, but you think it will make her worse, and forbid her taking it, — if she feels that she must have it, and takes it in spite of your prohibition, will the fact that she has disobeyed you prevent the action of that remedy in saving her life ? "

" Of course it would not ; but what are you aiming at, Mr. Winchester ? "

" I wish to show you, uncle, that your affliction is the result of the violation of physical, and not of moral law."

" That is not possible, sir, — not possible. There was no physical law violated, only moral and mental : she was perfectly healthy in body, even to the day of her death."

" How did she die, then ? "

" By violence : she managed to secrete a knife, and

destroyed herself with it. True, she did not die immediately ; but that was the cause of it. The loss of blood, however, seemed to cool the fever of her brain ; and she was very calm during the last hour of her life, and was perfectly reconciled to go, — said that she had sinned, but that God had forgiven her, and all was well. Were it not for this, I am certain that I should go mad with despair. But I regard Spiritualism as the cause of her ruin ; and, while I live, it shall be my sole effort to put it down."

" I told you, uncle, that I should not agree with you ; for I do not regard Spiritualism as in the least to blame for your daughter's death."

" To what, then, do you attribute it ? "

" To the result of her early teachings, combined with the ignorance of those who had the care of her."

The doctor flushed. " No disrespect, uncle : the best and wisest of people can not be otherwise than ignorant of that they refuse to investigate, or, if they make the attempt, do so from their own past standards, instead of applying the rules that belong to the new development. Now, this is just what our church people have done in reference to Spiritualism. They have utterly refused to investigate, or have done so from wrong stand-points ; consequently, are ignorant of its true significance."

" Does not the Bible tell us to let these things alore ? "

" The Bible tells us to ' prove *all* things, and hold fast that which is good.' "

" And I have proved it, and found it an upas-tree of bitterness, sir."

" And that is just where I wish to show you that you are mistaken, doctor. You have shown me by your own confession, that you believe God punishes sin, outside of the act itself: still, in your answers to questions that I have asked you, have proved an entirely different doctrine. For instance: you speak of disobedience to parents and teachers, as the first step toward your daughter's ruin, and yet have conceded conditions in which disobedience might prove a blessing, and its opposite a curse."

"And would you counsel disobedience to parents, then?" exclaimed Mrs. Denning.

"No; but I would show you that it is the relation which the act sustains to God's laws, and not the fact of a parent's command, that decides the result. God's laws are infallible, and can not be set aside; man's judgment fallible, liable to be in the wrong."

"And what has this to do with Helen's case?" asked the doctor.

"Simply this, uncle: just as long as you believe an affliction, that has no direct connection with a particular act, to have come in consequence of that act, you will never seek for the true cause."

"And what do you believe the true cause to have been in her case?"

"The violation of physical law, caused by false religious teaching."

"And do you, Mr. Winchester, ignore the religion of the Bible?"

"I know what you would say, uncle. I do ignore much that is called the religion of the Bible; for instance, the idea that God punishes us for loving our friends too well by taking them from us. I believe this idea to be dishonoring to God, and ruinous in its ten-

dency; and the belief that God punishes us outside
of the legitimate consequences of violated law is, to my
mind, equally so. Now, by your own confession, you
believe both of the above, and taught them to your
daughter."

"Does not the Bible say that God is a jealous God?"

"Suppose the Bible told me that God was a devil,
would I be under obligation to receive it? Certainly not,
you will say; and yet you regard jealousy, as exhibited
by men and women, as one of the most despicable traits
of character, — sufficient proof that God, the Infinite
Spirit of love and truth, could never stoop to being jealous of the love of his creatures."

"You are talking very strangely, sir."

"I presume it appears so to you; but hear me through.
Your child learns something of the philosophy and facts
of Spiritualism, — enough to induce the belief that the
return of the loved one is possible. She loves her husband intensely; and, in thus loving him whom she had
seen, she loved God, whom she had not seen. He dies;
and her heart goes out after him with an intensity of
yearning that is like taking the kingdom of heaven by
violence. Love responds to love; she feels his presence;
his spirit-magnetism, acting in conjunction with her in-
tense desire, stimulates the natural but hitherto dormant
faculty of clairvoyance, and she sees him.

"Now, what is the result? Does she love God less?
No: but more, much more; and she is happy, and would
have continued so, had she been let alone. But she has
confidence in you, her parents: your disbelief in the reality of that which gives her so much comfort makes
her doubt. Her love to God, and love to man in the

person of her husband, are so blended that she can not separate them; and thus these two loves, so naturally harmonious, become the source of a terrible conflict in her mind, through the false idea that one is sinful, and opposed to the other. In this conflict, the brain, like the bottle in the illustration I gave, unable to stand the pressure, gives way, and she is a maniac."

The doctor groaned aloud, and Mrs. Denning seemed about to faint. "This may seem cruel," said Mr. Winchester: "but I am not intentionally so; and I believe, that, when you have learned the true lesson contained in this bitter affliction, you will take an entirely different course from that which you are now taking."

There was silence for a few moments: then Mr. Winchester continued, "Now, uncle, I do not know just what your motive is for concealing the fact; but you have one patient here that we must see before we leave. I mean Mrs. Shepherd. She has been here but a short time, and, so far, has received no particular injury; but, if not permitted to leave, may become as insane as was your daughter."

Had a shell exploded in their midst, the doctor and his wife could not have been more astonished, more completely taken by surprise. "What do you propose doing with her?" was at length asked.

"Take her home with us," was the prompt reply.

"She was left in my care; and, if I let her go, her uncle will hold me responsible."

"Let him make trouble about it if he dare," was the response: "Alice Shepherd is no more insane than he is; and he knows it."

The doctor still hesitated. "Did he bring cert'fi-

14

cates from competent physicians to show that she was insane ? " continued Winchester.

" I will bring her down," was the reply ; for this last question awakened him to the fact that the proceedings had been illegal throughout.

In a few minutes, Alice and Addie were clasped in each other's arms ; and, on the following day, she went forth with her friends from what, to her, had so nearly proved a living tomb. The impression made by Edward Winchester upon the doctor and his wife did not pass away with the occasion. They commenced an earnest investigation of that which they had so unqualifiedly condemned ; and the result was, that they were soon numbered among its strongest advocates, and their house became the home of, instead of a prison for, mediums.

CHAPTER XVI.

MOST FEARED.

"That which I most feared came upon me." — *Bible.*

EVER was this text more fully exemplified than in the case of the Vales. Their principal object in sending Alice to Dr. Denning's establishment was to prevent the disgrace of having a relative of theirs go forth publicly to advocate an unpopular cause; and mark the result.

When Porter returned to N——, he, of course, called to see Alice, and was very much surprised to learn from her uncle that she was no longer with them. The doctor had written to Mr. Vale, stating the circumstances under which she had left there; and he had hardly recovered from the chagrin consequent upon her escape, when his equilibrium was again disturbed by this call of Porter's.

He could have wished the intruder anywhere else but there, but still was forced to treat him civilly.

" Gone back East!" said Porter wonderingly. " Was it not rather unexpected?"

" Rather," was Vale's hesitating reply. " She went with us to visit some friends, — old acquaintances of Father Shelton's, residing in Williams County, — and found, when she reached there, that the lady was a relative of some of her old friends in Ellsville; and, while there, these friends came out on a visit: so she concluded to return with them."

"Have you heard from her since she left there?" asked Porter.

"Not directly: she will probably not write till she reaches her old home; and, as they expect to stop at different points, they will be some time on the way."

"Do you recollect the name of the people she went with?"

"Of course I do, Mr. Porter," said Vale, with some asperity in his tones. "You are questioning me as closely, sir, as if you doubted the truthfulness of my statement. The name was Winchester, and the gentleman is a nephew of Mrs. Denning's." Mr. Vale could have bitten his own tongue with vexation when he saw the expression upon Porter's face at the mention of this last name.

"And there is where you went, was it?"

"It was," he replied, with as much self-possession as he could assume. "Are you acquainted with them?"

"Keeps a private insane asylum, I believe," continued Porter.

"He has sometimes taken such patients, at the particular request of friends."

"And may I inquire, Mr. Vale, if you met those friends of Mrs. Shepherd's, or did they come after you left?" asked Porter coolly.

"Sir," said Vale, rising to his feet, while his face flushed with anger, "your questions are becoming impertinent: what is it that you would insinuate?"

"Nothing, if there is nothing hidden," replied Porter, bowing himself out.

Now, Mr. Vale was not what would be called a bad man ; but he had something of the same stubborn nature as his brother, Alice's father, — was unyielding, even when proved in the wrong. He merely regretted taking the course that he had done in reference to Alice and her mediumship ; but, the wrong step taken, it required still another to keep it out of sight : and, as to being defeated, he had no idea of permitting it ; that is, the disgrace that he had sought to avoid.

Mrs. Vale was busy when Mr. Porter called, and did not see him, but wondered at her husband's troubled countenance when she came into the room soon after his visitor had left. " What is the matter, James ? " she asked : " are you sick ? or is something troubling you ? "

" My head is not feeling quite right this morning," said he, trying to smile. " I think I will go out into the air a while ; " and, taking his hat, he, without any definite object in view, started toward the post-office. " What shall I do ? " said he to himself, as he walked along. " It will never do to let this thing get out, and yet Porter will be sure to find out every thing. Alice will write and tell him, if he learns it in no other way."

Right here he came to a full stop, just as if some new thought had occurred to him, and he could not decide to act upon it without a moment's quiet. " I think I will try it," said he, after a moment's reflection. " Denning's daughter married a brother of the postmaster here ; and, if there is any thing on earth that he hates, it is a Spiritualist ; " and, walking briskly forward, he soon found himself in Uncle Sam's distributing office.

" Is there a letter here for J. N. Porter ? " said he in so low a tone as not to be overheard by those standing around.

The postmaster looked up as if a little surprised, but, seeing who it was, supposed it was all right, and quietly put one into his hands. Mr. Vale glanced at it, and knew, from the writing and post-mark, that it was from Alice. " Are you very busy, Mr. Rawson ? " he asked.

" Somewhat, though not so much so but that I can bear an interruption, if there is any thing of importance on hand," was the reply.

" I wish very much to have a few moments' conversation with you," said Vale.

" Very well, walk this way then."

" I want, in the first place, Mr. Rawson, that you should look at this letter : examine the post-mark, and especially the hand-writing, so closely that you will know it if another comes here from the same person ; and, when you have done so, I will tell you why."

" No harm, I hope, to you or yours, Mr. Vale," was that worthy's reply, as he took the letter, and commenced the required examination.

" Yes : there is a great deal of harm threatened. This Porter is a Spiritualist ; and I have reason to think that he is courting my niece. She went nearly crazy when she lost her husband : indeed, we feared that she would be quite so ; and, just as she began to be a little more cheerful, she made this fellow's acquaintance. He induced her to go to circles, and has so far psychologized her that she really believes herself a medium for spirit communication. She has gone East again, through the influence of some old friends : and what I want now is to break up all correspondence between them ; for, if this thing goes on, she will be as insane yet as your brother's wife was."

Mr. Rawson stood a moment as if irresolute. "What is it that you wish me to do, Mr. Vale?" he at length asked.

"That which I would not wish you to do under almost any other circumstance," was the reply; "but Alice is very dear to me, and I must save her if I can. I wish you to retain her letters, all of them, and give them to me; for, if she can not accomplish her object by writing directly to Porter, she will write to that medium, Ellen Bell."

"What, that young siren! indeed, I will do any thing in the bounds of reason to defeat the like of her. It is dangerous business, Mr. Vale, this tampering with letters; but, in fighting the Devil, I don't know as we should be choice of our weapons. If nothing else could influence me to act for you in this matter, the memory of my lost brother, and the fate of his unhappy wife, would decide the question."

"Thanks,—a thousand thanks; but had you not better keep the envelope to this?" asked Vale, as he tore it from the letter inclosed.

"I think it a good idea; for one can compare better than they can judge from memory," was the response.

Things being thus arranged to his satisfaction, Mr. Vale left the office; for he was anxious to read Alice's letter, but not there.

Porter, after his interview with Mr. Vale, went directly to Miss Bell's. She had company at the time of his arrival, and could not see him just then; and he waited at least half an hour before he was summoned to her presence.

" How do you do, Mr. Porter ?   Glad to see you;
but our friend has gone," was the greeting he received.

" So I perceive ; but can you tell me where ? "   He
said this, first for the purpose of testing her powers in
this direction, and, further, because he had his doubts in
reference to what was told him of her going East.

"I can," said she, "and that without using my
mediumship."

He looked up inquiringly, and she continued : " Henry
Pond, one of the members of our circle, was down at
Mr. Shelton's place last week on business, and one of
their preachers was there.   Pond says that he don't
know what made him do as he did ; but, when he went
into the room, almost the first question asked him, after
they learned that he was from this place, was, if he knew
any thing of the medium here ; and without a moment's
thought, or even an idea of what he was going to say,
he responded that he never inquired after such trash.

" He says that they looked very much pleased, and
asked if he was a member of any church.   Now, Pond
belonged to the Methodists before he came here, and has
never had his name taken from their books ; so he told
them that he was a Methodist, or had been, but, as he
was not settled as yet, had not joined anywhere since
he came West.

" ' Dangerous, dangerous, young man, to live without
the watch-care of the church,' said the preacher.
' You ought to take a letter, and hand it into the class,
if you don't stop in a place more than six weeks, or at
least to report yourself, and claim that brotherly watch-
care to which you are entitled.   I fear that you have
not done even this, my young friend ; for N—— is on

my circuit, and I do not recollect seeing your face in our meetings there.'

" ' Perhaps I have been a little careless, but will try to do better in future,' was Pond's response."

" The croaking hypocrites! " exclaimed Porter: " they wouldn't get me to make any such concessions."

" Wait, and hear the sequel," said Miss Bell. " Mr. Pond did not intend it as a concession: he can do better, much better, in the future, and so can we all. Progress is what we are aiming for; but it does not follow that we shall do what they think is better, or progress after their fashion."

" Strange kind of progress it would be, I am thinking; but what next ? "

Miss Bell looked at him fixedly for a moment, while her eyes assumed a far-off expression. " Joseph," said she at length, " will you never learn to separate that tinge of bitterness from your otherwise noble nature ? "

The young man made no reply to this appeal, but, dropping his head into his hands, sat silent for some minutes ; and a close observer would have seen the tears trickling through his fingers, while the medium, resuming her natural expression, said, —

" Oh! you wished to know what next. I believe I must have lost myself for a moment. Pond said that they then commenced talking of the evil tendency of Spiritualism, — said that it was setting people crazy all over the country ; and, in confirmation of that statement, Mr. Shelton spoke of Alice, — said she was losing her reason, and that he had advised her removal to a private asylum.

" 'And did her friends follow your advice ? ' asked

Pond. Mr. Shelton looked as if he thought he had said too much perhaps, and replied rather hesitatingly, ' I think not : they talked of doing so ; but I hear that she has gone back to her friends in New York ; ' and then the conversation turned upon my humble self."

" Ah ! and what did they have to say about you ? "

" They seemed very much troubled as to how they could put an end to my influence ; asked Mr. Pond various questions, and among other things what he thought had better be done."

" And what did he tell them ? " asked Porter.

" That 'most any means was justifiable in abating a nuisance ; and then the preacher proposed to burn me out."

" Ha, ha ! and what did Mr. Shelton say to that ? "

" That it would not do ; for, if found out, it would do their cause more harm than I could if left undisturbed."

" The old fellow has a little sense left, I really must acknowledge ; but did you learn nothing further of Alice ? "

" Nothing further, Mr. Porter ; but there are some here who think she is in a private asylum in Williams County, and they are going to take steps to ascertain ; would have done so immediately, but my controlling spirit told them to wait."

" I think it is just as well that you did ; for I hardly believe she is there now, though she may have been taken there in the first place," said Porter in reply, and then related what occurred at his interview with Mr. Vale.

" Have you been to the post-office ? " asked Miss Bell.

"I have not: I was not expecting let'ers here; but why do you ask?"

"If Alice is free, Mr. Porter, — if she is where she can control ·her own acts, — she will write to you or me."

"I never thought of that: I will go this minute," said Porter, starting to his feet.

"And inquire for me, if you please, though it may be no use, even if there is one there; for I have sometimes thought that I did not get all my letters."

"He would not dare retain them, Miss Bell," said Porter, with flashing eye.

"Don't get excited now," said she quietly: "it is a long road that has no turn to it. But please hurry; for they will not keep your letters, if they do mine; and I am anxious to know if there is any thing from Mrs. Shepherd."

Thus importuned, Porter was not long in making his way to the office, but with what result our readers already know.

On leaving the office, Porter passed down a different street from the one he came, and, without intending it, found himself going in the direction of Vale's. He had gone about three squares, when a letter, lying partly under the edge of a plank, caught his attention.

"Some one has lost a letter," said he to himself; but, not thinking that it could be of any interest to him, he had passed quite by, when a feeling that he could not account for prompted him to turn, and pick it up. The envelope was undirected; but, being open, he proceeded to look within: and judge of his astonishment to find that it was addressed to himself, and from Alice.

"More villainy!" was his involuntary thought; and, looking up the street, saw Vale coming around the next corner, glancing here and there with a quick, nervous movement, as though searching for something that it was important he should find. Porter held the letter quietly in his hand till Vale was close upon him, and then asked, —

"Have you lost any thing, Mr. Vale?"

That gentleman glared upon him as though he would say, "What is that to you?" but, on seeing the letter in Porter's hand, turned white to the very lips. Porter held up the letter with the utmost coolness, saying, —

"I just picked up this, which I find is addressed to me. I did not know but it might be what you were looking for."

Vale saw, that, so far as moral certainty was concerned, Porter knew that he had taken his letter; but there was no legal proof: so, putting on a show of indignation, he exclaimed, —

"What in God's name do you suppose I want with your letters?"

"Take care there, now: don't be calling upon strangers," said Porter, in his most provoking tones. Vale had too much self-respect, or, I should rather say, too much regard for his reputation, to fight; but his rage was so great, that the only way in which he could restrain himself was to turn and walk abruptly away.

"The wicked flee when no man pursueth," called Porter after him; but just then the words, "Will you never learn to separate that tinge of bitterness from your otherwise noble nature?" flashed through his mind; and, with all disposition to taunt or trifle gone, he walked on in sober silence. And now a word as to Vale's losing the letter.

He had left the office, as we have already seen, that he might be able to learn the contents of the letter without danger of interruption, fearing that, if he waited to read it there, a friend of Porter's, who was present, might, by some chance, catch a glimpse of some word it contained: so he hurried out, first slipping it into another envelope. He resolved not to look at it till safely seated in his own room and the door locked; but alas for human calculations, and especially when guilt takes part therein!

He had not gone more than half the distance to his home, when he met a friend, who said, " Glad to meet you, Vale: have you that note with you? I wish to pay it now."

" I believe I have," was the response; but in his absent state of mind, together with the tremulousness that conscious wrong gives to those who are not hardened, he thrust his hand into every pocket but the right one; and, in his search, the letter upon which so much depended, fell to the ground without either of them perceiving it. Judge, then, of his feelings, when, upon reaching his room, he found that it was gone.

He looked so perplexed when he met his wife at dinner, that she insisted upon knowing what troubled him. " If I never believed the Bible before, I should do so now," was his impatient response.

" Why, what new proof have you had of its truthfulness ? "

" There is a declaration therein which reads something like this: ' That which is done in secret, shall

be proclaimed upon the house-top ; ' and it is becoming
literally true as it regards our course toward Alice.
Every step that we have taken to keep her from making a fool of herself, and disgracing us, is being made
public as fast as possible."

" How can that be ? " she asked.

" Because the heart of modern infidelity is full of
eyes round about, — yes, and ears too ; and the birds
of the air whisper the secret thoughts of the heart."

" Can't you speak intelligibly ?   How bitter you are ! "

" I feel bitter," was his response ; and then, after a
moment's silence, he told her of his interview with Porter in the morning, the course he had taken to prevent a communication between him and Alice, finishing
up with the lost letter and the fact of its falling into
Porter's hands.   " That he, of all others, should find it,
is what provokes me," said he.

Mrs. Vale paled with fear.   " O husband ! how
could you take such a step ?   You have not only done
wrong, but have made yourself liable to imprisonment."

" As to the wrong, I can not see it ; for, if Alice needed treatment lest she should become insane, she is certainly unfit to be trusted with a correspondence that
will injure her best friends in the eyes of those who do
not know the true state of the case : and, as to the other,
he has no proof as to who took the letter from the office.
Still, the impression will be made upon the minds of the
people that I did it ; and the disgrace will be as great,
even greater, than if we had left Alice to pursue her
own course : for, in that case, it would have b1en indirect ; in this, it is direct."

" Do you mean to say that there is no wrong in

breaking open a letter addressed to another?" asked Mrs. Vale in astonishment.

"No: I did not say that. What I mean is this. If the first step was justifiable, the last was. If we had a right to confine Alice, we have a right to open her letters. I am satisfied that the whole thing was wrong from beginning to end; for, if the principle was carried out, there would be an end to personal safety. She has just as good a right to confine us if we are taking a course that does not please her, as we have to confine her."

"You do not pretend to say, Mr. Vale, that Christians have no right to prevent their friends from taking a course that will end in the ruin of both body and soul?"

"If people are determined to go to hell, God does not interfere to prevent it; and why should we? No, wife: Christians have no such rights. God never gave them such rights; for such is the weakness of man's judgment, that all safety of person would be at an end, even if the very best of them were permitted to assume such a prerogative."

"It seems to me that God's children — those who are striving to obey his laws — ought to have some rights over those who are constantly trampling these laws under foot."

"It may seem so to you; but, were it so, our free institutions would soon be no more. I tell you, wife, that the liberties of our country would be safer in the hands of any other class of people than that of the clergy."

"O James! how can you say that, when the very spirit of Christianity is that of liberty?"

"The liberty to do what they claim to be right."

" Not what they claim, but what God in his holy book has declared to be right."

" A book which one class of men declare means one thing, and another class that it teaches right the opposite. Why, even Spiritualists claim that the Bible would be but a shell if Spiritualism was taken out of it."

" Their claiming this does not make it so."

" True, wife ; but, when claims conflict, who is to decide ? It will never do for one class to have or hold pre-eminence over another: each must decide for himself, and each be fully persuaded in his own mind."

Mrs. Vale sighed, looked at her little one, and said, " You may be right, James ; but it seems hard that we can not be allowed to suppress that which may yet involve our own children in ruin. Could I have my choice between seeing my child a corpse and having her grow up a Spiritualist, I should say, Let her die."

" And the Jew would say the same thing in reference to his child's becoming a Christian."

" There is no use in talking with you, James," said she, with a touch of indignation in her tone ; " for such comparisons are simply ridiculous. We know that we are right, — know that the Christian religion is the only hope of the race. Such being the case, there is some difference between enforcing its claims and that of others."

" So thought the founders of the inquisition, or, to come nearer home, those who hung the Quakers."

" James ! James ! are you turning infidel ? "

" I am questioning ; and, the more I question, the more I am mystified."

" God help you, my husband ! " said she earnestly ;

to which he responded with a fervent " Amen ! " and then there was silence between them.

In the mean time, Porter had gone to Miss Bell's with the letter that had been so nearly lost to him. Finding several friends there, he gave them the history of the way in which it came into his hands, and then read to them Alice's account of the manner in which she had been deceived into visiting Dr. Denning's establishment, of her feelings when she found that they had left her there a close prisoner, the difficulty which she had in communicating with her friends after accidentally getting a glimpse of them from a forbidden window, to which she had access through the kindness of her keeper, and her joy at the recovery of her freedom.

This was read, re-read, and commented upon ; and twenty-four hours had not elapsed ere it was known all through the place that Mrs. Shepherd's uncle had taken her to an insane asylum because she was a Spiritualist, that she had been taken from there by friends from the East, and that he had tried to prevent her communicating with her friends by taking her letters from the office.

It was in vain that his friends urged that there was no evidence of the latter : the idea became fixed in the minds of the people, and could not be eradicated without proof to the contrary. The result of all this was, that those who sought to avoid disgrace by doing violence to the rights of another found themselves enveloped in such an atmosphere of distrust, that they actually sold their property at a sacrifice, in order to es ape its withering effect.

CHAPTER XVII.

FURTHER EXPERIENCES, SLANDER, ETC.

O foul-mouthed slander !
Myriads of souls are crying from the ground
Against thee, — souls filled with aspirations high,
But all too weak to draw thy poisonous fangs;
And woman more than all has suffered thus.

LICE found a warm welcome in the little village from which she had been absent less than two years; and yet the events that had been crowded therein made it seem an age to her. "I have lived a lifetime since I left you," she said; "and if —

'Where the share is deepest driven,
The best fruits grow,' —

my future life ought to be worth something to myself and to humanity."

Edward Winchester and his wife were interested in the new phenomena, and circles met weekly at their house for the purpose of investigation. It was found that Alice was to be both a test-medium and a speaker. She did not hesitate to walk in the path indicated, and was soon quite a favorite with the public in the latter capacity.

But this did not seem to be her permanent field of

labor ; for the pleadings of her woman's heart, in connection with the earnestly-pressed suit of another, induced
her, some eighteen months after, to take upon herself,
for the second time, the vows of marriage. She lost
none of her personal freedom as Mrs. Porter, consequently went before the public occasionally, that is,
when she chose to do so ; but feeling, as every true
woman does, that the domestic altar is the most sacred
of all fanes, she did not choose to be absent long enough
to let its fires grow dim. But, as a test-medium, her
home became the resort of many.

It was not to be expected, however, that she could
pursue an unpopular course, and escape unscathed.
There are foes for every one to face ; and every soul
must stem the flood of opposition if it would attain to
real excellence. The cross and the crown of thorns
belong not alone to Jesus. There is a principle in nature which makes it necessary that each should bear the
cross, and wear the crown of thorns, ere he can wear
the crown of glory.

Alice felt this ; and when scandal made itself busy with
her name, or foes watched for her feet to slide, she held
firmly on her way, realizing that "one self-approving
hour" outweighs whole years of condemnation from
those who do not understand us or our work. It is a
serious thing to trifle with the good name of another :
still, there were some incidents that occurred in this connection, in her experience, which were so laughable they
will bear repeating.

Alice had an engagement to fill some forty miles from
home ; and Mr. Porter had business that led him partly
in the same direction, and would occupy about the same

length of time : so they went together as far as tley could, and then agreed to meet at the same place on their return.   Alice reached the point designated some two hours in advance, bringing with her a lady lecturer, who had accepted an invitation to spend a few weeks at her home.

" Well, Alice," said Porter, as soon as they were comfortably seated, after the introductions were over, " I have some news for you."

" News is no new thing: what is it? " she replied quietly. .

" Only listen to her now, Miss Holstein," said Porter ; " so quietly indifferent, and still as anxious to hear as can be. I have a notion not to tell her any thing about it."

" Oh, do, please ! " said Alice, putting on a mock look of distress.

" Then, since you so desire to know, we have parted : you have run away with another man."

" Ah ! that is news indeed : when did it happen ? "

Just a moment before, the landlady had come into the room, and taken a seat by the window ; but her presence did not interfere with the conversation of our party.

" That is what I did not learn ; but it has surely happened, for the man who told me said that my brother told him.   I am certainly very much obliged to him for giving me a brother ; only I should like to see him soon, having never had the happiness of having one before."

" Please stop your nonsense, Joseph, and tell us just what you mean," said Alice.

" Getting anxious, are you ? Well, the night I left

you, I stopped with a farmer some two miles from the little village of S——: Deacon Barnes, they call him. I gave them my name; but it seems that they did not quite understand it. After supper, the conversation turned upon general subjects; and, among the rest, I mentioned Spiritualism."

" The deacon had been rather quiet before: but this loosened his tongue, and for at least half an hour I was regaled with an account of the follies and crimes of Spiritualists; and, among others, a Mrs. Porter was named, — a lecturer, he said, who had recently left her husband, and gone away with another man.

" ' Indeed ! ' said I ; ' and do you know any thing of this woman ? '

" ' Not personally ; but my information is as direct as this: her husband's brother told our minister.'

" ' Did he give any thing of her previous history ? ' I asked ; for I wished to ascertain if it was really my wife that was intended. ' It appears,' he continued, ' that she has been twice married. She went insane after the death of her first husband, and was just recovering when she fell in with some Spiritualists, who persuaded her that she was a medium, and ought to go into the field as a speaker. Soon after, she married this Porter; but it seems that she has found some one else that she likes better, and is practicing what she preaches by going off with him.'

" ' I think there must be a mistake somewhere,' said I. ' The history of two persons of the same name has evidently been mixed ; for it can not be the lecturer who has thus left her husband.'

" ' No mistake at all, sir ; no mistake at all. I guess his brother would know if any body did.'

· " ' You are sure, then, that there is no mistake ? ' I questioned, looking him full in the eye.

" ' Quite sure,' was the prompt reply.

" ' Well,' said I, ' this is the strangest thing that I ever heard. I parted with my wife this morning with perfect good feeling between us ; and I never had a brother.'

" ' You ! ' exclaimed the deacon, starting to his feet.

" ' Yes, sir : my name is Porter, and it is my wife of whom you have been talking.' Indeed, Alice, you would have laughed, could you have seen the consternation depicted upon the man's countenance."

The landlady now remarked that a Mrs. Porter, living near there, had recently left her husband, and that was probably the one intended.

" Was she a Spiritualist ? " asked Alice.

" She was not, or, if so, had never made it public."

" Why, then, do people couple it with Spiritualism ? why must I bear the blame of her acts ? "

" Because, madam, Spiritualism has that tendency. It is a part of their teachings, and the people know it," was the positive answer.

" Have you ever heard them teach such things ? " asked Miss Holstien.

" I never go after such teachers : we are commanded to ' go not after them,' " was her reply ; " but I can tell you of a case that occurred in the neighborhood where I lived before I came here, which shows plainly enough what the tendency is. Still, I do not mean to say that there are no good people among them," she added, seeming for the first time to remember that she was talking to Spiritualists.

" Please tell us of the facts in the case referred to," said Alice.

Thus interrogated, the lady said, " About two years since, a woman came into our neighborhood, and commenced lecturing on Spiritualism. She was quite popular with the people : no fault could be found with what she said, for she denounced evil in every form. Weeks passed ; and there was hardly a village within fifty miles, up and down the river, where she had not spoken one or more times ; and, at length, she came close to our place, and stopped with a family by the name of Stintson. She staid there about a week, I think it was, and then went to a little town some fifteen miles away, to give a course of lectures.

" And now comes the sequel to all her fine talk. Some ten days afterward, Stintson got angry about some trifle, and declared that he would not stay with his family any longer ; ordered his carriage, drove directly to where this woman was staying, and, taking her with him, went some forty miles up the river ; was gone three nights, and then returned, bringing with him another of their speakers to help make peace again at home."

" Was the last-named speaker a woman ? " asked Porter.

" No ; but his wife was with him, and report says that he had forsaken his own family for her."

" Never mind what report says," remarked Miss Holstien : " did they succeed in their mission of peace ? "

" It was thought that they had for a while : but it seems that he was not sincere ; for, after a few months, —

after a sufficient length of time to enable him to put his business into good shape, — then he left, and it is supposed that they are together somewhere."

"I think," said Miss Holstien, "that what report says, and 'it is supposed,' should be left out of the question entirely. It would certainly be more in accord with the sweet spirit of charity, as neither of the above statements is true."

Alice and Porter looked up in surprise; while the woman, who had been so positive in her assertions, asked, with an evident trepidation in her voice, "Are you acquainted with the parties?"

"With one of them intimately, and with the others slightly," was her reply. "I have known that speaker for years; and she would sooner sever her right arm from her body than to take another woman's husband from her."

"How, then, do you account for the facts in the case?"

"Madam, you have not given the facts, — only a very distorted version of them."

"Will you please give the correct version, miss?" said the lady with a sneer.

"I can," was the firm response; "but, first, let me say, that any man who would leave his family as you have represented this one's doing — that is, with no provocation but his own fancy — is just no man at all, is worth no woman's attention. Secondly, the woman of whom you say, 'It is supposed that she is with him,' knows no more of his whereabouts than if she had never seen him."

"Perhaps you will inform me how you know these things?" asked the lady.

"I will; for I am that woman, and ought to know the facts in the case."

Porter and his wife were somewhat surprised at this announcement, and so amused that they could hardly restrain their mirth; but the landlady's confusion was pitiable to behold. She tried to apologize, but was prevented by Miss Holstien's saying, "Only listen to my statements, and be as faithful in reporting them as you have those of the other side, and it is all I ask.

"When I was at Mr. Stintson's, I had not the most distant idea that there was the least trouble between him and his wife, or ever had been. True, there was one thing that annoyed me somewhat; and that was this: I had one appointment, some seven miles distant, to which he took me, neither his wife nor daughter accompanying us. But, as they had attended my other lectures, I accepted their reasons for not going as sufficient, and put my unpleasant feelings aside.

"When I left there, I did not know certainly that I should visit the place from whence he took me at the time you tell me that the public inferred so much; and as I had held no communication with him, if he knew that I was there, which he said he did not, he learned it from some other source. I had finished my engagement, and was to go that day to another point; the gentleman who was to take me being already in town.

"I was nearly ready to start when he came in, bringing Mr. Stintson with him. 'I have but a moment to stop,' said Stintson; 'for I must go to Elder Whitney's to-night; but, learning that you were here, I thought I would call.'

"'Going up to the elder's?' said I. 'If I had no appointment out, I would go with you, if you would take me ; for I have promised them that I will visit them before I leave this part of the country, and I can not get within six or seven miles of there by public conveyance.'

" 'I can take you just as well as not if you wish to go,' was his reply ; ' but you will not have much time to visit, as I am going on purpose to bring them back with me ; for their signatures are necessary to complete a business transaction that I have on hand.'

" ' But I can not go,' said I, ' as I have an appointment to fill to-night.'

" The other gentleman then said that he would withdraw that appointment for me, and I could fill it when I returned.

" 'I do not know as I shall return this way at all,' I replied ; 'for, when I go, I have business at M——, a hundred miles farther north, and I may wish to go east from there.'

" 'If that is the case,' said he, ' you had better go now : for speakers are not any too well paid ; and, if you go that far with Mr. Stintson, it will save you as much in stage-fare as you would get to-night.'

" ' How soon can you be ready ? ' asked Mr. Stintson.

" ' In ten minutes,' I replied ; ' for I was nearly ready to start for the Grove when you came in.'

" ' Well,' said he, ' I can wait that long ; for I must call at Wilson's store a moment before I can start.'

" And that is how I came to take that ride with Mr. Stintson. We had gone several miles, chatting as we went, upon various subjects, when he turned to me, and said, —

" ' You will be surprised when I tell you that I am arranging business to leave my family.'

" ' Leave your family ! ' said I.

" ' Yes : there has been no peace for me there for years ; but pride has kept the trouble hidden. I can bear it no longer, and will not. I shall leave the farm to them, take what ready money I have and my horses, and go where I shall not be found fault with all the time.'

" ' Mr. Stintson,' said I, ' had I had the most distant idea of this, I would not have come one step with you ; for do you know that I shall have to bear the blame of this ? '

" ' I did not think of that,' he replied, ' or I would have made some excuse for not bringing you ; but it is too late now. Still, I do not see how they can lay the blame upon you : you have had nothing to do in the matter.'

" ' True,' I replied : ' but the public can not know that ; and, if you persist in leaving your family now, you will do me an irreparable wrong. Were I a Methodist or a Presbyterian, it would be different ; but people are watching Spiritualists, expecting, hoping, to see them stumble, and, with the least excuse for believing evil of them, they are certain to do so.' When we reached the Elder's, the matter was talked over again ; and both he and his wife joined with me in entreating Stintson to stay with his family, but with what result I never knew. I have seen none of them since ; and, the Elder moving away shortly after, I lost their address, consequently could not write to them.

" I did not wish to write to others about it, as I did

not know but the trouble was so settled that other parties knew nothing of it. I hoped that it was."

"How happened it, Miss Holstien, that Mr. Stintson was gone three nights, when, according to your statement, there was no necessity for his being absent but one."

"I am not Mr. Stintson's keeper, madam, and can not, therefore, be held responsible for his acts; but I can tell you what I know upon the subject. I staid at the Elder's only one night. But I heard him tell Mr. Stintson that they could not possibly leave before Saturday; and Mr. Stintson replied, 'I shall not go home till you and your wife go with me, if I have to stay a week.' This was on Thursday; and, if he waited till Saturday, he would have to stay two nights longer."

"Strange, isn't it?" said Porter, "upon what a small foundation a four-story report can be raised."

"And stranger still," added Alice, "that each addition upward can increase in size, and still the structure remain firm."

"And do you intend to say that all the cases reported of Spiritualism's breaking up families can be explained as readily, have as little foundation in truth, as these have?" asked the landlady.

"I do not," replied Miss Holstien; "but I do say, that, as far as my observation goes, it can be said of at least two out of every three; and if you will take cases of this kind that occur in the church, and multiply them by three, I think the number thus attained would startle the most unthinking."

"You will acknowledge that divorces are more common now than formerly, I presume."

" That may be true. I think it is ; indeed, I know it, though I have not examined the statistics on this point : and there is a cause for it that surface thinkers do not perceive ; and, not knowing what else to say, they attribute it to the influence of Spiritualism."

" How do you account for it, Miss Holstien ? "

" In the same manner that I account for the swelling of the buds in spring-time. There is a new life, the vital tides of an increased growth, flowing through the veins of humanity ; and the old channels are too circumscribed for its expression. The old conservative condition, like the bark upon the tree, resists this tendency to expansion, until it becomes so strong that it forces itself through the very walls of its prison to reach the light.

" It is true of the human, as of the vegetable, that many a promising bud, many a beautiful blossom, will blast, will come to naught, under the influence of wind, storm, or unseasonable frosts. And it is equally true that the tree of humanity will never give us the leaves that are for the healing of the nations till woman holds a place in society where she is not subject to man, till she stands before the law as his equal, with equal rights as a citizen. Man may continue to be the bark, the inclosing rind, protecting the body of the tree from destruction ; but when he asserts the same power over the buds and blossoms in the time of their appearance, will not give them an equal right with himself to sunlight and air, his claims are certain to be disputed, and not only disputed, but set aside."

" Woman's rights, I perceive."

" Not woman's rights, madam, but human rights ; for the rights of one portion of the race can not be violated without wrong to each and all."

"You believe, then,—you Spiritualists,—that man and wife have the right to separate if they can not agree."

"Can not agree and will not agree are two different things entirely: and, if it was only among Spiritualists that this state of things existed, there might be some show of justice in your accusations; but you have only to look at society to find this spirit pervading all its ranks. A friend of mine once examined the records of his county to learn how many of the divorces granted were to parties known to be Spiritualists; and, of eighty, there were only four of this class."

"Well," said Porter, taking out his watch, "it's my honest opinion that there is not so much difference between Jew and Gentile, after all; and I see that it is nearly train-time. Miss Holstien, if you will go home with us, I will try and not run away with you."

"No need for that, Mr. Porter," was her playful reply; "for, as your wife has left you for another, you are entitled to a divorce."

"True, true: I did not think of that. Come, then, we will go; and Mrs. Porter can follow on, repentant, or go and find her other man;" and, catching Miss Holstien by the arm, he hurried her out of the house. But Alice was too quick for him; and, before he could close the door between them, she was hanging upon his other arm.

"Oh, these old wives! it is impossible to get clear of them," said he, looking at her with an expression of tenderness that belied the light raillery of his words.

"Free lovers," said the landlady, looking after them with a sneering expression upon her otherwise fine features. But her distrust could not penetrate the

armor of their conscious rectitude. It stung only herself; for while they, seated in the cars that were
bearing them swiftly to their destination, chatted away
the hour that intervened, with joy in the present and
high hopes for the future, she went about sighing, as
she dwelt upon the dark shades of the picture formed
by her own imagination.

CHAPTER XVIII.

INQUIRIES, LIFE'S PROBLEMS, ETC.

"Other foundation can no man lay than that is laid."—Bible.

 FEW days after the occurrence above related, Alice was surprised by a visit from her uncle. He was evidently much embarrassed; for they had not met till now, since the time that he had so cruelly deceived and betrayed her into the hands of Dr. Denning. The doctor and his wife, as I have already stated, had investigated the facts and philosophy of Spiritualism, till, like Paul of old, they were now the zealous advocates of that which they had once so strenuously opposed.

James Vale and his wife had learned this, the indirect result of the course they had taken in incarcerating Alice; and this, together with other influences brought to bear upon them from time to time, had set them to questioning also. But, though losing faith in the old forms of thought, they were not prepared, as yet, to accept the new. They longed to recognize therein all that was claimed by its advocates, but found many things to stagger them, even at the very threshold.

There was a recklessness of speech and manner, a carelessness as to life-conduct, in many of its warmest defenders, which, it seemed to them, illy comported with the claim of holding communion with the angels. And there were many other things which made them, and especially Mrs. Vale, fear to walk in what might prove to be a forbidden path.   While talking this matter over one evening Mr. Vale said, —

"I am going to see Alice, wife.   She can explain these things if any one can ; and, as to the wrong, you will never find her doing or advocating that which she believes to be such."

"But belief, my dear, can not change the character of an act, as you well know," replied Mrs. Vale.

"That may be, so far as the act itself is concerned ; that is, the results of the act as it regards physical well-being, or otherwise : but the moral character of any and every act is certainly determined by the motive. In reference to Alice, her experience in this matter is certainly greater than my own, and she ought to be able to give me some light on the subject.   Still, though I may think it wise to question her, she must convince my judgment before I shall accept her conclusions.   So, little wife, never fear for me ; for I certainly shall not go it blind."

"No, husband : I think you would be more likely to shut your eyes against the light, than to consent to walk where there was none, judging from past experience. However, if you wish to visit Alice, I have no objection ; but how do you suppose she will receive you after what has passed ? "

"Like her own self.   If she holds hardness toward me, I shall know that her new theories have made her worse, instead of better, and shall, of course, have nothing further to do in that direction."

16

Alice was very much surprised; but she met him cordially, never once showing, by either look or manner, that she felt a shade of unkind feeling toward him on account of the past. Indeed, she did not feel any, — neither against him nor those who had acted in concert with him; for she realized most fully that they knew not what they did.

Porter was differently constituted, and could not *feel* just as Alice did. There was a little bitterness in his heart, as he thought of the past; but for her sake he did not show it: consequently, the proud spirit of James Vale was even more chafed by the reception he met, than if a portion of that which he felt he deserved had been meted out to him. Nevertheless, he had come for a purpose, and he intended to accomplish it: so, when the evening meal was over, he turned to Alice, and said, —

" I have come here, Alice, to question you about your Spiritualism ? "

" Very well, uncle," she replied : " proceed with your questioning, and I will answer to the best of my ability."

" Well, then, in the first place, I wish to know why so many d——d fools and d——d knaves are attracted to it ? "

Alice smiled : " Why do patients whose diseases are the most virulent, or whose lungs are the nearest consumed, — why do such always go to the most noted physicians, uncle ? "

" Sharp as ever, you little Yankee : we are not talking of hospitals."

" Not of hospitals, but of one great moral hospital,

such as society is, and will be till thoroughly renovated. And it is to this end that the true physician directs his attention, — to the removing of the causes of disease more than to dealing with effects. Wherever the best physician is, there will the sick congregate in the greatest numbers. This is as true morally as it is physically."

" So you think that Spiritualism is a better physician than the religion of Jesus ? "

" I believe that Spiritualism proper is the religion of Jesus ; and not only his, but of all the lovers of the race who have had a zeal according to knowledge." ·

" Spiritualism proper ? "

" Yes : when accumulated snows have been melted by the warmth of the sun in spring-time, or when heavy rains have fallen, thus swelling the body of a stream to treble its size, you certainly would not call the driftwood, or the soil that is thus dislodged and carried forward, making the crystal waters turbid with the mixture, — you would not call this, these foreign ingredients, a portion of the stream proper, would you ? "

" Certainly not ; and the same can be said of the Christian religion."

" True, most true, uncle : therefore I say that Spiritualism proper and the religion of Jesus are the same. But what is called the religion of Jesus is a far different thing. The idea of three Gods in one, vicarious atonement, an eternal hell, &c., did not originate with him, are no part of his religion. These were all taken from heathen mythology, — were extant long before his advent upon earth, therefore can not be called his in any especial sense."

" What, then, do you recognize as the distinguishing feature of his teachings ? "

" The pre-eminent value of man ; God pledged to the welfare of man, and not man sacrificed to God ; the sabbath for man, and not man for the sabbath ; and, carrying out the same principle, the Bible for man, and not man for the Bible : in a word, that man is the lord and master, and all things his servants, his tools with which he is to work out his own salvation."

" But suppose he cuts his fingers with these tools : what then ? "

" Which he is pretty sure to do till he learns to use them skillfully : he must bear the smart, and learn the lesson intended."

" All this is very well, Alice ; but somehow you have led me from the track, — have so covered up the kna-very and folly of professed Spiritualists under the mantle of general principles, that I had forgotten the main question."

" I have not intended this, uncle : let us come back to the point, then."

" Well, to state my first question more definitely, why do so many Spiritualists swear, lie, break the sabbath, &c. ? Why are they so reckless of sacred things ? "

" To be reckless of sacred things, and to disregard what some one else considers as such, are two things entirely ; and, as to swearing, lying, and the like, I suppose those who do such things, do them because they like to."

" Because they like to ! "

" Yes : if a person really desires to do an act, he is in the moral condition indicated by the status of that act, whether he performs it or not."

" Then you would have people do just what they want to ? "

" I would have people do right from a love of the right."

" But suppose they do not love the right ? "

" Then they can not do the right, in any true sense of that term ; but they will love the right if properly instructed."

" How do you show that, Alice ? "

" From an axiom that is as true of morals as are the axioms of mathematics. Do not men and women, if left unrestrained, always take the course that seemeth to them best ? "

" Well, I really don't know but they do ; but they make some awful mistakes."

" Yes ; and so do children in following out their own inclinations. Sometimes it is best to restrain them, and sometimes it is better to let them have their own way for the sake of the lesson. Still, in each case, the principle is the same : both desire happiness ; both are ignorant of the mode of obtaining it."

" I don't see what that has to do with the love of right."

" Do you believe it possible for human beings to desire their own misery ? "

" Certainly not, — that is, misery for its own sake : though they may desire it for the sake of the happiness that may accrue from the results."

" True ; but it is the happiness that is *desired*, while the misery is only *endured*. This proves that self-love is the broad foundation upon which the structure of universal love must be reared. This is the foundation that is already laid in the very nature of things, and man has no power to remove it, no power to put another in its place. Thus, you see, my dear uncle, that, as it is impossible for a man to desire his own misery, so must he naturally love that which will secure his happiness, just as fast as he realizes what it is. But he must realize this for himself, and not another for him."

" You mean to say, then, that he will love the right just as soon as he truly learns that only through the right can such happiness as the soul seeks be his ? "

" I do, uncle; and not only this: he can no more help loving it than two and two can help being four when placed together."

" Why, then, if man's sins are the result of ignorance, does God punish him for committing them ? "

" He does not: man punishes; God teaches."

" Very emphatic teaching, I should think, — some of it at least."

" True; but if the burning of a finger so teaches us the nature of fire, that we, by that means, are able to save the whole hand, is not the lesson a cheap one ? "

" That may be true; but I tell you, Alice, I believe that Spiritualism makes people worse instead of better. I have known good church-members, men who had the confidence of all who knew them, — I have known such become Spiritualists, and then become reckless; families broken up, wives forsaken, and home ruined generally. Now, if these things are not the result of Spiritualism, why did they not occur before such individuals came under the influence of its teachings ? "

" Because of fear. People often desire to do things that they dare not perform."

" Is it not better that we should be restrained by fear than not at all ? "

" For our external interest, yes ; for our spiritual good, no."

" How do you show that ? "

" From the fact, that, so long as one desires to do a thing, he believes that it is good for him, that it will conduce to his happiness ; and, till he learns the reverse, he can not cease to desire it. This being true, it is better for him to learn it from experience than not at all."

" And what is the harm if he never learns it ? "

" No harm, only that there is a bar across the pathway of progress which he will never get over."

" I should call that doing evil that good may come."

" And I should call it rooting out the evil that good may take its place. Is not the latter the most reasonable version of the point at issue, uncle ? "

" You may be right, Alice ; but it seems to me that this would be a strange world if everybody did just what they wanted to."

" And how much worse would you be, uncle ? "

" A good way, that, to find out just what your uncle would like to do, puss."

" Isn't it, though ? Would you like to steal, uncle ? "

" No, Alice : I never felt the least desire to steal."

" Then you have no occasion to learn better. Would you like to break the marriage covenant by sleeping with your neighbor's wife ? "

" No, indeed : I should scorn to do such an act."

" Do you think you would like to do these things if you should become a Spiritualist ? "

" Not I : if becoming a Spiritualist involved the love of these things, I should never be one "

" But suppose, uncle, that you did desire to do these things, and believed that Spiritualism sanctioned them: what then ? "

" I should be very likely to advocate its teachings."

" Advocate what you supposed to be its teachings, you mean."

" Well, what I supposed to be its teachings."

" Can you not see, then, how others who do desire to do the things that you repudiate, — can you not see how they might mistake the freedom to burn their fingers if they wished — or, in other words, the privilege of learning the evil of these things for themselves, — as a sanction of the wrong ? "

" Certainly I can, Alice ; but I never looked at it in that light before."

" And do you not know that those who expect to receive the greatest benefit from any given thing will, in accordance with the law of self-love, be its most earnest advocates ? "

" You do not mean to say that the most earnest advocates of Spiritualism are all of this class ? "

" No, uncle ; for there are those who so understand the real principles thereof, that they can not help but advocate it with earnestness. But there are those who are loud in its advocacy, only because they believe that it gives them license. When such learn, through experience, that every indulgence has its price, — a price that must be paid in suffering, even to the utmost farthing, — then they will either forsake the ranks of Spiritualism, or they will advocate it from far different motives. In a word, Spiritualism is the religion of manhood, — a religion that teaches to walk in one's own strength, instead of being carried like babes in the arms of a nurse : and, if babies rush into its ranks, they must necessarily stumble ; but, in doing so, they will eventually learn to walk, even if they should have to go back to the arms of the nurse for a while."

" But all this refers to the philosophy, to the moral bearings, of Spiritualism : what of its mediums, of the law of communication ?"

" Did you ever see an individual acting as interpreter between two persons of different nationalities, uncle ?"

" I never happened to witness such a thing, as I recollect ; but then I know that it is often done."

" In order to do this, the one interpreting must understand both languages."

" Certainly, certainly."

" Do you not know that no one is able, till they have learned, to understand even one language, much less two ?"

" Why, of course I do: what is the use of all these foolish questions, Alice ?"

" Wait and see.   Do you not know that some persons are, from birth, more disposed to the acquisition of one kind of knowledge, and some to another ; for instance, some learn to sing and play with the utmost ease, and others take as naturally to mathematics ?"

" It is too evident to be questioned."

" Then those whose natural forte was language would make the best interpreters, the best mediums of communication between two individuals of different languages : would they not ?"

" Self-evident truth, that even a child could understand."

" Well, uncle, mediumship, the *law* of communication between two worlds, two states of existence, *is* just as natural as are the laws which govern the above self-evident truths, as you call them. This law must be learned, and the conditions complied with in one case as well as in the other ; and there are individuals whose particular forte, power, gift, or whatever you may choose to call it, lies in this direction, as well as those who are natural musicians, mechanics, &c. Such persons are called mediums."

" This may be true. If so, it seems to me that mediums should be very good, much better than other people ; and yet the evidence is right the reverse."

" How ? worse than others ? "

" It seems to me so, Alice."

" Have you been personally acquainted with many ? "

" No : I have never talked with any but yourself and one other."

" Have judged from common report, then. Fie, fie, uncle ! I thought you had better sense than that."

" But has common report no foundation ? "

" I suppose that it has two strong pillars : the first is the claim which you have already made, that they should be better than others ; and the other rests on the fact that they do many things which do not properly belong to them as individuals, they being simply the channels through which others act."

" But why should they not be better than others ? It seems to me, that, if I could talk with angels, I would never do any thing wrong."

" Why, then, do wrong now ? You talk with angels every day."

" I ! "

" Yes, uncle : what is it that leaves the body at death ? "

" The spirit, I suppose."

" Could a spirit leave the body if it were not in the body ? "

" Of course not ; but I see what you are aiming at : you mean to say that it is spirits who have left the body that mediums talk with, and spirits who are still in the body that we talk with ; and, if we call one class angels, the other class must be angels too."

" Well, is not the claim a just one ? "

" I do not know but it is ; still, we have not been accustomed to looking at things in this light, and it is hard to realize that it is so."

" True, uncle : we have been in the habit of using a mental magnifying glass when thinking of those who have left this state of existence ; consequently they have appeared to us much more than they really are. But, even if our estimate of them was correct, it would not follow that those who could communicate with them, or be controlled by them, would necessarily be better than others. If a beggar should bear a message from a far-mer to a judge, it would not have the least tendency to make him either one or the other ; neither would it tend to make a truthful man of a liar, should one who was truthful employ him to carry a letter to another of the same character."

" I see, I see, Alice ; but does not mediumship itself tend to degrade the individual, from the very fact of their negative condition ? You yourself have admitted that they do many things that do not properly belong to them as individuals."

" If conditions are not right, it may have that tendency ; but what shall we do in the case ? — ignore the fact of mediumship, turn our back upon those who are such, and leave them to sink in the mire if they will ? "

" I think, if I were a medium, Alice, I would give it up, — would have nothing to do with it whatever."

" And if you were a sponge, uncle, you would not be a sponge, lest you might sometime fall into muddy water, and thus absorb its filth."

" Nonsense : what becomes of our free agency in that case ; that is, if your illustration is a good one ? "

" What becomes of your free agency in the color of your eyes or hair, in your height, sex, or the color of your skin ? You may dye your hair ; but it will grow out again, the same color as before. You may dress in woman's clothes, but you will be a man still. And so on through the list : nature will assert herself in spite of you. It is the same of mediumship : it is a physiological condition, over which you may have a partial, a temporary control ; but, in spite of it all, you are a medium still."

" Have mediums, then, no individuality ? "

" They have. Place a sponge in milk, and it will absorb milk ; but it is a sponge still, and the milk absorbed is no part of it : and thus of every substance, capable of being absorbed, in which you may place it. A sponge is one of the connecting links between the vegetable and the animal kingdom. If you place it in connection with a liquid vegetable substance, it absorbs it ; if in connection with a liquid animal substance, it will do the same. Mediums are the connecting links between those who live in the material world and those who live in the spirit world; and they also have their distinct individuality."

"Who, then, shall judge them?"

"The God within their own souls: none other need attempt it, and expect to judge righteous judgment. And this is as true of others as of mediums. Still, it is a hard lesson for humanity to learn; for, measuring others by ourselves, we are too apt to blame if they dare to differ from us, and especially if it is upon points that we deem of vital importance. The words of Pope, —

> "Let not this weak, this erring hand
> Presume thy bolts to throw," —

And those other words spoken by Jesus so long before, 'Judge not, that ye be not judged,' — these need to take deep root in every heart, and must, before we can exercise that 'charity' which 'suffereth long, and is kind.'"

"Well, Alice, I do not see as there is much use in talking with you, as one can not get the advantage of you: you will make your side smooth all the time," said Mr. Vale, laughing.

"And did you wish to get the advantage of me, uncle?"

"No: I don't know as I did; still, I did not think you would always have so ready an answer. But you have not satisfied me upon every point: I think I will go to bed, and study the matter over a little."

"Better go to sleep, uncle, for I know that you are tired; and, if you expect me or any one else to satisfy you on every point, you will find yourself mistaken. The soul must answer its own questioning."

"Must answer its own questioning! what do you mean by that?"

"Simply this: another may throw light upon our path; but we must travel it for ourselves, if we would know to a certainty what lies at the end of it."

"What a puss you are! you are as ready at comparisons as a cat is at catching mice; but do you ever doubt and question, Alice?"

"Often, often, uncle. The problems of life call me out in this direction continually; so much so that I sometimes agonize for the solution."

"And you expect to find the solution at last?"

"Sooner or later, I shall."

"What do you intend to do then?"

"Use them as a torch to light the pathway of others, these that I solve while here; and those that I can not solve till I leave the body, I hope to find some medium to use them for me."

"I hope you will if there is any truth in this matter; but I shall need a somewhat different torch to light me to bed, — material light for material persons like myself."

"Will this lamp answer your purpose, uncle?"

"Capitally, puss."

"What! just as it is?" said Alice, looking up with a merry twinkle in her eye.

"No, you rogue: it must be lighted, of course."

"How?"

"With a match, I presume: that is what I generally use."

"And they must be ignited by friction?"

"That is the rule, I believe; that is, when there is no fire within reach to touch them to."

" And even then the brimstone must be burned off before they are of any use."

" Yes, yes ; but what sage application do you intend to make of that fact ? "

" Simply this, uncle : when the friction of life has taken you beyond the brimstone of past teachings, the lamp of your soul will burn so clearly that you will not need to say ' if there is any truth in this matter ; ' for you will know for yourself that there is."

" God speed the time, and good-night," said he, as he disappeared up the stairway, and Alice was left to her own reflections.   Porter had been busy with some writing, and had taken no part in the conversation, though he had heard a portion of it.   Putting aside his work soon after Mr. Vale retired, he said, " Come Alice, is it not most bedtime ? "

Alice was sitting with her face buried in her hands, and replied, " Don't wait for me : I am thinking."

" Solving problems ? "

" Yes : trying to."

" I will leave you, then, to your own thoughts," said he, as he retired ; and, with your permission, kind reader, we will do the same, for, rest assured, she is not thinking for herself alone.

THE END.

CATALOGUE

OF

SPIRITUAL AND REFORM BOOKS,

ALSO

LIBERAL AND PHILOSOPHICAL WORKS,

ETC., ETC., ETC.,

PUBLISHED AND FOR SALE BY

WILLIAM WHITE & COMPANY,

No. 158 WASHINGTON STREET,

BOSTON, MASS.

COMPLETE WORKS OF A. J. DAVIS,

Comprising Twenty-Three Volumes, all neatly bound in cloth.

Arabula ; or, The Divine Guest. Containing a New Collection of Gospels. $1,50, postage 20 cents.

A Stellar Key to the Summer-Land. Illustrated with Diagrams and Engravings of Celestial Scenery. $1,00, postage 16 cents.

Approaching Crisis. Being a Review of Dr. Bushnell's Lectures on Supernaturalism. $1,00, postage 16 cents.

Answers to Ever-Recurring Questions from the People. A Sequel to the "Penetralia." $1,50, postage 20 cents.

Children's Progressive Lyceum. A New Manual, with full directions for the Organization and Management of Sunday Schools. 70 cents, postage 8 cents ; 12 copies, $8,00 ; 50 copies, $30,00 ; 100 copies, $50,00. Abridged Edition, 40 cents, postage 4 cents ; 12 copies, $4,00 ; 50 copies, $16,00 ; 100 copies, $28,00.

Death and the After-Life. Eight Lectures, and a Voice from the Summer-Land. Cloth 75 cents, postage 12 cents ; paper 50 cents, postage 8 cents.

Great Harmonia : Being a Philosophical Revelation of the Natural, Spiritual and Celestial Universe, in Five Volumes. Vol. 1—The Physician ; Vol. 2—The Teacher ; Vol. 3—The Seer ; Vol. 4—The Reformer ; Vol. 5—The Thinker. $1,50 each, postage 20 cents each.

History and Philosophy of Evil. Paper 50 cents, cloth 75 cents, postage 12 cents.

Harbinger of Health. Containing Medical Prescriptions for the Human Body and Mind. $1,50, postage 20 cents.

Harmonial Man ; or, Thoughts for the Age. Paper 50 cents cloth $1,00, postage 16 cents.

Magic Staff : An Autobiography of Andrew Jackson Davis. $1,75, postage 24 cents.

Memoranda of Persons, Places and Events : Embracing Authentic Facts, Visions, Impressions, Discoveries in Magnetism, Clairvoyance, Spiritualism. Also Quotations from the Opposition. $1,50, postage 20 cents.

Morning Lectures. Twenty Discourses delivered before the Friends of Progress in New York. $1,50, postage 20 cents.

Philosophy of Special Providences, and Free Thoughts Concerning Religion. Neatly bound together. 60 cents, postage 12 cents; also in paper, 20 cents each.

Philosophy of Spiritual Intercourse. $1,00 postage 16 cents.

Principles of Nature : Her Divine Revelations, and A Voice to Mankind. In Three Parts. Thirty-First Edition. With a likeness of the author, and containing a family record for marriages, births and deaths. $3,50, postage 48 cents.

Penetralia : Being Harmonial Answers to Important Questions. $1,75, postage 24 cents.

Spirit Mysteries Explained. The Inner Life; a Sequel to Spiritual Intercourse. $1,50, postage 20 cents.

Tale of a Physician; or, The Seeds and Fruits of Crime. In Three Parts—complete in one volume. Part I—Planting the Seeds of Crime; Part II—Trees of Crime in Full Bloom; Part III—Reaping the Fruits of Crime. $1,00, postage 16 cents.

☞ Price of Complete Works of A. J. Davis, $26,00.

SPIRITUAL AND PROGRESSIVE WORKS.

Arcana of Nature ; or, The History and Laws of Creation. By Hudson Tuttle. 1st Vol. $1,25, postage 18 cents.

Arcana of Nature ; or, The Philosophy of Spiritual Existence and of the Spirit-World. By Hudson Tuttle. 2d Vol. $1,25, postage 18 cents.

After Death ; or, Disembodied Man. The Location, Topography and Scenery of the Supernal Universe; Its Inhabitants, their Customs, Habits, Modes of Existence; Sex after Death; Marriage in the World of Souls; The Sin against the Holy Ghost; Its fearful Penalties, etc. Being the Sequel to "Dealings with the Dead." $1,50. postage 20 cents.

A B C of Life. By A. B. Child, M. D. 25 cents, postage 2 cents.

A Letter to the Chestnut-street Congregational Church, Chelsea, Mass., in Reply to its Charges of having become a Reproach to the Cause of Truth, in consequence of a Change of Religious Belief. By John S. Adams. 15 cents, postage 2 cents.

Apostles. By Ernest Renan, author of "The Life of Jesus," being part second of "The Origin of Christianity." Translated from the French. $1,75, postage free.

Blossoms of Our Spring. A Poetic Work. By Hudson and Emma Tuttle. $1,00, postage 20 cents.

Brittan and Richmond's Discussion. 400 pages, octavo. This work contains twenty-four letters from each of the parties above-named, embodying a great number of facts and arguments, pro and con., designed to illustrate the spiritual phenomena of all ages, but especially the modern manifestations. $2,50, postage 28 cents.

Brittan's Review of Beecher's Report of Spiritualism ; wherein the conclusions of the latter are carefully examined and tested by a comparison with his premises, with reason and with the facts. Cloth bound, 75 cents, postage 8 cents.

Brittan's Review of Rev. C. M. Butler, D. D. This is a brief refutation of the principal objections urged by the clergy against Spiritualism, and is, therefore, a good thing for general circulation. 50 cents, postage 4 cents.

Be Thyself. A Discourse by Prof. William Denton. 10 cents, postage 2 cents.

Bible Convention at Hartford. $1,50, postage 16 cents.

Bouquet of Spiritual Flowers. By Mrs. J. S. Adams. $1,00 ; gilt $1,50, postage 16 cents.

Branches of Palm. By Mrs. J. S. Adams. A book for every Spiritualist and Friend of Truth and Progress. $1.25, postage 16 cents.

Celestial Telegraph. $1,50, postage 20 cents.

Christ and the People. By A. B. Child. $1,25, postage 16 cents.

Courtney's Review of Dod's Involuntary Theory of the Spiritual Manifestations. A most triumphant refutation of the only material theory that deserves a respectful notice. 50 cents, postage 8 cents.

Christ and the Pharisees upon the Sabbath. By a Student of Divinity. 25 cents, postage 2 cents.

Deluge. By Prof. William Denton. 10 cents, postage 2 cents.

Dissertation on the Evidences of Divine Inspiration. By Datus Kelley. 25 cents, postage 4 cents.

Dealings with the Dead: The Human Soul—its Migrations and its Transmigrations. By P. B. Randolph. 75 cents, postage 12 cents.

Day of Doom; or, A Poetical Description of the Great and Last Judgment, with other Poems. By Rev. Michael Wigglesworth, A. M. From the sixth edition of 1715. $1,00, postage 12 cents.

Future Life: As Described and Portrayed by Spirits. Through Mrs. Elizabeth Sweet. With an Introduction by Judge Edmonds. $1,50, postage 20 cents.

False and True Revival of Religion. 10 cents, postage 2 cents.

Faith, Hope and Love. A Discourse by Cora L. V. Daniels. 20 cents, postage 2 cents.

Further Communications from the World of Spirits, on subjects highly important to the Human Family. By Joshua, Solomon, and others. Paper 50 cents, postage 8 cents.

Footfalls on the Boundary of Another World, with Narrative Illustrations. By Robert Dale Owen. $1,75, postage 25 cents.

Fugitive Wife. By Warren Chase. Paper 35 cents, postage 4 cents; cloth 60 cents, postage 8 cents.

Free Love and Affinity. A Discourse. By Miss Lizzie Doten. 10 cents, postage 2 cents.

Geology: The Past and Future of our Planet. By Prof. William Denton. $1,50, postage 20 cents.

Gospel of Good and Evil. By Joseph S. Silver. Printed on fine tinted paper, beveled boards, &c. $1,50, postage 20 cents.

Gist of Spiritualism: Being a Course of Five Lectures delivered by Warren Chase in Washington. 50 cents, postage 4 cents.

Gates Ajar. By Elizabeth Stuart Phelps. $1,50, postage 16 cents.

Gates Wide Open; or, Scenes in Another World. By George Wood. $1,50, postage 20 cents.

Healing of the Nations. Second Series. By Charles Linton. 363 pp. $2,50, postage 30 cents.

Hierophant; or, Gleanings from the Past. By G. C. Stewart. $1,00, postage 12 cents.

History of the Supernatural. By William Howitt. Two Volumes. $3,00, postage 40 cents.

History of the Chicago Artesian Well. By George A. Shufeldt, Jr. Fifth Edition. 25 cents, postage 2 cents.

Hymns of Progress: Being a Compilation, original and selected, of Hymns, Songs and Readings, designed to meet a part of the progressive wants of the age, in Church, Grove, Hall, Lyceum and School. By L. K. Coonley. 75 cents, postage 12 cents.

How and Why I became a Spiritualist. By Wash. A. Danskin. 75 cents, postage 8 cents.

Improvisations from the Spirit. By J. J. Garth Wilkinson. $1,00, postage 12 cents.

Intellectual Freedom; or, Emancipation from Mental and Physical Bondage. By Charles S. Woodruff, M. D., author of "Legalized Prostitution," etc. 50 cents, postage 4 cents.

Instructive Communications from Spirit-Land. Written through the mediumship of Mrs. S. E. Park, by the instrumentality of her spirit husband, who departed this life in 1863. $1,25, postage 16 cents.

Incidents in My Life. By D. D. Home, with an Introduction by Judge Edmonds. $1,25, postage 16 cents.

Jesus of Nazareth; or, A True History of the Man called Jesus Christ: Embracing his Parentage, his Youth, his Original Doctrines and Works, his career as a Public Teacher and Physician of the People, &c. New Edition. $1,75, postage 24 cents.

Joan D'Arc. A Biography. Translated from the French, by Sarah M. Grimké. With Portrait. $1,00, postage 12 cents.

Kingdom of Heaven; or, The Golden Age. By E. W. Loveland. $1,00, postage 12 cents.

Lily Wreath of Spiritual Communications. Received chiefly through the mediumship of Mrs. J. S. Adams. $1,25, postage 16 cents.

Life-Line of the Lone One. By Warren Chase. New Edition. $1,00, postage 16 cents.

Lyric of the Golden Age. By Thomas L. Harris. $2,00, postage 20 cents.

Light from the Spirit-World. By Rev. Charles Hammond. $1,25, postage 12 cents.

Legalized Prostitution; or, Marriage as it Is, and Marriage as it Should Be, Philosophically Considered. By Charles S. Woodruff, M. D. $1,00, postage 16 cents.

Modern American Spiritualism: A Twenty Years' Record of the Communion between Earth and the World of Spirits. By Emma Hardinge. $3,75, postage 40 cents.

Man and His Relations. Illustrating the Influence of the Mind on the Body, the Relations of the Faculties to the Organs, and to the Elements, Objects and Phenomena of the External World. By Prof. S. B. Brittan. M. D. Although treating of the profoundest of subjects, it is written in an elegant and attractive style, clear and logical. Printed on fine tinted paper. One volume, 8vo. $4,00, postage 40 cents.

My Affinity, and Other Stories. By Lizzie Doten. A book for Lyceums, Libraries, Associations, &c. $1,50, postage 20 cents.

Man of Faith. By Henry Lacroix. 25 cents, postage 2 cents.

Night-Side of Nature; or, Ghosts and Ghost-Seers. By Catherine Crowe. New edition, substantially bound in cloth. $1,25, postage 20 cents.

Natty, a Spirit; His Portrait and Life. By Allen Putnam. Cloth 75 cents, postage 8 cents; paper 50 cents, postage 4 cents.

Plain Guide to Spiritualism. A Spiritual Handbook. By Uriah Clark. $1,25, postage 16 cents.

Poems from the Inner Life. By Lizzie Doten. Sixth Edition. Full gilt $1,75, postage free; plain $1,25, postage 16 cents.

Peep Into Sacred Tradition. By Rev. Orrin Abbott. 50 cents, postage 4 cents.

Poems. By Achsa W. Sprague. $1,50, postage 20 cents.

Principles of Nature, as discovered in the Development and Structure of the Universe. Given inspirationally, through Mrs. J. King. 327 pages. $2,00, postage 24 cents.

Physics, Ethics, Religion and Spiritualism. By Amicus Anonymous, A. M. 25 cents, postage 4 cents.

Progress of Religious Ideas Through Successive Ages. By L. Maria Child. Three Volumes. $6,75, postage 72 cents.

Physical Man, Scientifically Considered. By Hudson Tuttle. $1,50, postage free.

Philosophy of Mesmerism and Clairvoyance. Six Lectures, with instructions. 50 cents, postage 4 cents

Philosophy of Electrical Psychology. In Twelve Lectures. By Dr. Dods. $1,50, postage 16 cents.

Physical Perfection: Showing how to acquire and retain bodily symmetry, health and vigor, secure long life, and avoid the infirmities and deformities of age. By D. H. Jacques. Beautifully Illustrated. $1,75, postage 16 cents.

Planchette's Diary. By Kate Field. 50 cents, postage 4 cents.

Rules to be Observed for the Spiritual Circle. By Emma Jardinge. 10 cents, postage free.

Report of an Extraordinary Church Trial: Conservatives *versus* Progressives. By Philo Hermes. 25 cents, postage 4 cents.

Road to Spiritualism. By Dr. R. T. Hallock. 50 cents, postage 4 cents.

Rose and Lily, the Twin Sisters, and their Testimony to the Truth of the Spiritual Philosophy. 15 cents, postage 2 cents.

Reply to the Rev. Dr W. P. Lunt's Discourse against the Spiritual Philosophy. By Miss E. R. Torrey. 25 cents, postage 2 cents.

Seers of the Ages: Ancient, Mediæval and Modern Spiritualism. By J. M. Peebles. Second Edition. $2,00, postage 32 cents.

Spiritual Harp: A collection of Vocal Music for the Choir, Congregation, and Social Circles. By J. M. Peebles and J. O. Barrett. E. H. Bailey, Musical Editor. Third Edition. $2,00 single copy; 6 copies, $10,00; 12 copies, $19,00; 25 copies, $38,00; 50 copies, $72,50; when sent by mail, postage 24 cents per copy.

Spirituelle; or, Directions in Development. By Abby M. Laflin Ferree. 30 cents, postage 2 cents.

Soul Affinity. By A. B. Child, M. D. 20 cents, postage 2 cents.

Spiritual Invention; or, Autobiographic Scenes and Sketches. 20 cents, postage 2 cents.

Soul of Things; or, Psychometric Researches and Discoveries. By Prof. William and Elizabeth M. F. Denton. $1,50, postage 20 cents.

Spirit Minstrel. A Collection of Hymns and Music for the use of Spiritualists in their Circles and Public Meetings. Sixth Edition, enlarged. By J. B. Packard and J. S. Loveland. Boards 50 cents, paper 35 cents, postage free.

Self-Contradictions of the Bible. 144 Propositions, without comment, embodying most of the palpable and striking self-contradictions of the Bible. 25 cents, postage 2 cents.

Spiritualism. Vol. 1. By Judge Edmonds and Dr. Dexter. $2,50, postage 32 cents.

Spiritualism. Vol. 2. By Judge Edmonds and Dr. Dexter. $2,50, postage 32 cents.

Six Lectures on Theology and Nature. By Emma Hardinge. Steel plate Portrait of Author. Cloth $1,00, postage 12 cents; paper 75 cents, postage 8 cents.

Spirit Works, Real but not Miraculous. A Lecture, read at the City Hall, in Roxbury, Mass., by Allen Putnam. 35 cents, postage 4 cents.

Sabbath of Life. By R. D. Addington. $1,50, postage 20 cents.

Shekinah. Vols. I, II and III. By S. B. Brittan. $2,50 per volume; gilt $3,50 per volume; postage 30 cents per volume.

Seeress of Prevorst. By Justinus Kerner. A book of facts and revelations concerning the inner life of man, and a world of spirits. New Edition. 75 cents, postage 4 cents.

Spiritual Songs. A Collection of Original Music for Spiritual Gatherings and Lyceums. By S. W. Tucker. 15 cents, postage 2 cents.

The Davenport Brothers, the World-Renowned Spiritual Mediums: their Biography, and Adventures in Europe and America. Just published. Illustrated with numerous engravings. $1,50, postage 20 cents.

The Question Settled: A Careful Comparison of Biblical and Modern Spiritualism. By Rev. Moses Hull. $1,50, postage 20 cents.

Triumph of Criticism: A Critical and Paradox Work on the Bible and our Theological Idea of Deity, as received from its authors. By M. B. Craven. 40 cents, postage 4 cents.

The Living Present and Dead Past; or, God made Manifest and Useful in Living Men and Women as he was in Jesus. By Henry C. Wright. New and Revised Edition. Cloth 75 cents, postage 8 cents; paper 50 cents, postage 4 cents.

The Harvester: For Gathering the Ripened Crops on every Homestead, leaving the Unripe to Mature. By a Merchant. $1,00, postage 12 cents.

Theodore Parker in Spirit-Life: A Narration of Personal Experiences. Inspirationally given to Fred. L. H. Willis, M. D. 25 cents single copy; 50 copies $8,00; 100 copies $15,00.

Thirty-Two Wonders; or, The Skill Displayed in the Miracles of Jesus. By Prof. M. Durais. Paper 35 cents, postage 2 cents; cloth 60 cents, postage 8 cents.

The Voices: A Poem in Three Parts. By Warren S. Barlow. $1,25, postage 16 cents.

Truth for the Times, gathered at a Spiritual Thought Concert. 15 cents, postage 2 cents.

The Worker and His Work: A Discourse. By Dr. R. T. Hallock. 15 cents, postage 2 cents.

Twelve Messages from the Spirit of John Quincy Adams, through Joseph D. Stiles, medium, to Josiah Brigham. $2,00, postage 32 cents.

The Bible: Is it of Divine Origin, Authority and Influence? By S. J. Finney. Cloth 60 cents, postage 8 cents; paper 35 cents, postage 4 cents.

Tracts. By Judge Edmonds. No. 1 to No. 10 inclusive, in neat cover, 30 cents, postage 4 cents; No. 10, Letters to the New York Tribune, 20 cents, postage 4 cents; No 11, Instances of Spirit Communion, 10 cents, postage 2 cents.

Tracts. By Lois Waisbrooker. Subjects: No. 1, What is Spiritualism? No. 2, God's Image; No. 3, The True Second Birth; No. 4, The Laws of Inspiration; No. 5, The Manifestations Undignified; No. 6, Do n't Want to Know; No. 7, Is there not a Cause? No. 8, Hell; No. 9, Their Fruits; No. 10, The Laws of Mediumship. These ten numbers are stitched together. 10 cents per set, postage 2 cents.

Voices from Spirit-Land. By Nathan Francis White, medium. 75 cents, postage 12 cents.

What is Spiritualism? An Address delivered by Thomas Gales Forster, in Music Hall, Boston, Mass., Sunday afternoon, Oct. 27, 1867. 25 cents single copy; 50 copies $8,00; 100 copies $15,00.

Whatever Is, is Right. By A. B. Child, M. D. $1,00, postage 16 cents.

Whatever Is, is Right Vindicated: Being a Letter to Cynthia Temple, briefly reviewing her Theory of "It is n't all Right." By A. P. McCombs. 10 cents, postage 2 cents.

ENGLISH WORKS.

"Primeval Man." The Origin, Declension and Restoration of the Race. Spiritual Revealings. $2,50, postage 20 cents.

Supramundane Facts in the Life of Rev. Jesse Babcock Ferguson, A. M., L.L. D., including Twenty Years' Observation of Preternatural Phenomena. Edited by T. L. Nichols, M. D. $1,75, postage free.

MISCELLANEOUS AND REFORM WORKS.

American Crisis; or, The Trial and Triumph of Democracy. By Warren Chase. 25 cents, postage 2 cents.

Apocryphal New Testament. $1.25, postage 16 cents.

Age of Reason: Being an Investigation of True and Fabulous Theology. Cloth. 50 cents, postage 8 cents.

Astro-Theological Lectures. By Rev. Robert Taylor. $2,00, postage 24 cents.

Art of Amusing: A Collection of Graceful Arts, Merry Games, Odd Tricks, Curious Puzzles and New Charades; with suggestions for private theatricals, tableaux, all sorts of parlor and family amusements, etc. By Frank Bellew. $1.50, postage 20 cents.

Alice Vale: A Story for the Times. By Lois Waisbrooker. $1.25, postage 16 cents.

A Trip to the Azores, or Western Islands. By M. Borges D. F. Henriques. $1.50.

Adventures of Elder Tubb. 65 cents, postage 8 cents.

Arnold, and Other Poems. By J. R. Orton. $1,00 postage 12 cents.

Atlantis, and Other Poems. By Amanda T. Jones. $1.25, postage free.

Biography of Satan; or, A Historical Exposition of the Devil and his Fiery Dominions, disclosing the Oriental origin of the belief in a Devil and future endless punishment. By K. Graves. 50 cents, postage 2 cents.

Better Views of Living; or, Life according to the doctrine "Whatever Is, is Right." By A. B. Child, M. D. $1.00, postage 12 cents.

Basic Principles of Organization; With a brief synopsis of the Coöperation Universal, or Divine Mutuality. Part No 1. 25 cents, postage 2 cents.

Book of Religions: Comprising the Views, Creeds, Sentiments or Opinions of all the principal Religious Sects in the World. By John Hayward. $1.75, postage free.

Book of Notions. By John Hayward. 75 cents, postage 12 cents.

Chester Family: A New Temperance Story. By Julia M. Friend. $1.00, postage 12 cents.

Common Sense Thoughts on the Bible. For Common Sense People By William Denton. 10 cents, postage 2 cents.

Cosmology. By George M. Ramsey. $1.50, postage 20 cents.

Combe's Constitution of Man. Twenty-Eighth American Edition. One Volume, 16mo. $1.50, postage 16 cents.

Companion Poets for the People. Illustrated. Vol. 1—Household Poems, by H. W. Longfellow; Vol. 2—Songs for all Seasons, by Alfred Tennyson; Vol. 3—National Lyrics, by John G. Whittier; Vol. 4—Lyrics of Life, by Robert Browning. Each volume complete in itself. 50 cents each, postage 2 cents each.

Complete Works of Thomas Paine, Secretary to the Committee of Foreign Affairs in the American Revolution. Three Volumes. Consisting of his Political, Theological and Miscellaneous Writings. To which is added a brief sketch of his Life. $6,00, postage 90 cents.

Clairvoyant Family Physician. By Mrs. L. Tuttle. $1.25, postage. 12 cents.

Diegesis: Being a Discovery of the Origin, Evidences and Early History of Christianity, never yet before or elsewhere so fully and faithfully set forth. By Rev. Robert Taylor. $2,00, postage 24 cents.

Dawn. A New Work of Exciting Interest. $1,75, postage 24 cents.

Dissertations and Discussions. By John Stuart Mill. Three Volumes, 12mo., cloth. $6,75.

Eliza Woodson; or, The Early Days of One of the World's Workers. A Story of American Life. $1,50, postage free.

Uni
S

S'

www.ingramcontent.com/pod-product-compliance
Lightning Source LLC
Chambersburg PA
CBHW060615030726
47498CB00005B/1690